Threads of Fate

An Olandris Legacies Title

Lyn Gilleland

Thank you for entering my giveaway!
Best wishes!
Lyn Gilleland

Dedicated to my friend Audrey. Thank you for your enthusiastic support of my work and for helping me find joy in writing again. Thank you also for entrusting me with your character concept of Weiss. It has been so much fun exploring these stories together!

CONTENTS

Preface   VII

Auroran Calendar   IX

Map of Aurora   XI

1. A Light in Winter   1

2. A Moment Worth Treasuring   15

3. What Friends Are For   31

4. When the Tree Falls   40

5. A Shield for Xanom   53

6. Ruin   67

7. The Black Cat   84

8. The Kid   101

9. Trials of Khul   113

10. Reforged   134

11. Cavalier Romance   152

12. The Apprentice   167

In the works...   181

Also By   195

PREFACE

Writing, like all artistic pursuits, is a journey. My journey started early in life, on a little family farm outside the sprawling metropolis of Austin, Texas. Sticks became just about anything—deer antlers, swords, Wild West muskets—and little red wagons became covered wagons on an imaginary Oregon Trail. My brother, cousins, and I all spent hours walking circles around our grandparents' house, working together to tell stories of adventure and family on our make-believe travels.

My first real exposure to cultures outside my own was my introduction to Japanese anime, followed by my mother marrying my Ecuadorian stepfather. Though our family over the years has experienced its fair share of ups and downs, one thing I must say: my world became a lot bigger that day, a lot bigger than country music and imaginary covered wagons.

My world expanded further when I entered college as an English major and joined the honors program offered there. I was blessed to attend a smaller university, filled with professors who genuinely cared about their students. And it was those professors who made it possible for me to take part in the honors tour that landed me in Spain in the summer of 2013. I will never forget walking along the streets of Toledo or through the courtyards of the Mezquita in Cordoba and reading placards declaring that the paths on which I stood had been built over a thousand years before. All I could think of was, "How many others have stood in this very spot? Who were they? Where did they come from? What were they like? Who did they love?"

I looked around at the people coming and going beside me, some tourists, some native Spaniards. They were all people, just like me, with hopes and ambitions, loves and joys, beautiful in their diversity and yet still so much like me.

So why the preface? Well, I wanted to clarify something.

I am someone born into a small, rural, culturally limited community. There is nothing wrong with that. I have so many precious memories of my childhood. But it also means that as I create and explore the world and cultures of Olandris, I am creating and exploring through the lens of someone who is still learning: through what I read, where I go, and who I choose to spend my time with. The setting of Olandris is inspired by those experiences, but is in no way meant to represent real-world cultures. At most, it is meant to be a nod of appreciation toward the beauty that is diversity in the real world.

Along with my love of studying human history and culture, I also have always been fascinated by the inner workings of the mind, the psychology behind what drives people to be who they are. This means that many of my characters come with their own psychological quirks and struggles. I am no psychologist, but I do love to explore what makes characters tick. It has also been refreshing for me, personally, to explore the possibility of heroes who aren't perfect, heroes who hurt and struggle but in the end are able to dust themselves off and rise again. To me, that's the mark of a real hero.

My hope for this collection of short stories, and for any books that follow after, is that it provides a window into the beauty of the world around us, and that it emphasizes a belief I hold very dear: more connects us than divides us.

Auroran Calendar

In order to understand the progression of this collection of short stories, it may be helpful to first understand how the passage of time is recorded in the world of Olandris.

Most of the tales in this collection center around Aurora, the "Isle of the Gods" that sits at the center of the world at large. Surrounded by a vast, foggy expanse known as the Clouded Sea, Aurora separates its history into three different eras: the Lost Era (LE), the Era of Discovery (ED), and the Arcane Era (AE).

The **Lost Era** refers to the time prior to Aurora's discovery. It was the era of the Rahani elves of Taj and the Alimazi Titans in the region west of the Dragonspine Mountains. How much time that designation truly covers is unknown, as records and accounts of that history have only recently begun to surface.

The **Era of Discovery** refers to the 1,042 years that encompassed the discovery, exploration, and settlement of Aurora. It is the era in which the vast majority of cities and kingdoms on Aurora were properly established, from the city-states that would become the Free Cities of Nor, to the Xanomes Kingdom in the Rahan Wilds, to the Thal Sultanate in the Wailing Desert.

The **Arcane Era** was marked by the beginning of an alliance between the city-states in the southeastern corner of Aurora. Led by elvish explorer Nor Velkin and starting with the city-states of Arcanum and Avannon, this movement unified a diverse collection of settlements, providing the trade agreements and broad scope of skills and experiences needed to usher in an era of increased understanding and use of magic.

The Auroran calendar is separated into ten months of 35 days each, all named after and paying homage to one of the ten gods of the Desayat Pantheon, the major religion of Aurora and many of the continents across Olandris at large.

1. Giyus (The Month of Beginning) – named after the mother goddess, Giya

2. Zhivis (The Month of Growth) – named after Zhi, goddess of knowledge and wisdom

3. Mirial (The Month of Prosperity) – named after Miri, goddess of peace

4. Molnar (The Month of Stormfall) – named after Moln, god of sea and storm

5. Kuzal (The Month of the Forge) – named after Kuz, god of craftsmen

6. Oynis (The Month of Struggle) – named after Oyn, god of war and justice

7. Zhayan (The Month of Harvest) – named after Zhaya, goddess of field and harvest

8. Novis (The Month of Festivals) – named after Nova, goddess of festivals

9. Sumeris (The Month of Twilight) – named after Sumer, god of travelers

10. Gilium (The Month of Endings) – named after Gil, god of death and memory

The most celebrated time of the year is on the last night of Gilium, the Spring Equinox, when the aurora borealis from which the island got its name emerges. It is believed that on this very special night, the connection between gods and mortals is especially strong, the one time of the year in which they may walk the mortal plane together.

< To Parras

To Xanaris >

Nisyo

Medens

Cszaki

Titan's
Necropolis

Dragonspine
Mountains

Temple of
the Memory Tree

Rahan Wilds

Isle of
Brigrit

Ghul
Tribes

The
Crystal
City

Meshiri

The Blooming
Grove

Wailing
Desert

Nightwind
Vale

Ruins of
Taj

Iron Vault

Tokula
Tribes

Cair
Cathair

Xanom

Krasi

Al-bar

Liakos

Nesiri
Tribes

Greyhaven

Bay of
Arcanum

Alimazi
Oasis

Eiseli

Port City of
Arcanum

Amesa
Tribes

Ridan

Valis

Saffir
Sarth

Soleis

Avannon

Burning
Crags

Gazar

Free Cities of Nor

Epilos

Beseria

Obsidian
Halls

Labyrinth

Zeqra

Dulin

Seneschal

Aurora
AE 50

N

W   E

S

1

─ ◦ ─

A Light in Winter

21st day of Gilium, AE 4

Snowflakes. They were delicate...fragile...possessing an ephemeral beauty that was best appreciated in the moment. Together with others of their kind, they could be built into beautiful works of art or thunder down the mountainside with the fury of an army, but alone, their existence was fleeting.

Noelani, a girl of seventeen with warm copper skin and raven black hair pulled into braids on either side of her face, reached out a gloved hand, watching as a snowflake landed lightly on her open palm. Nearby, an ember in the campfire snapped as though in warning to the fragile form in Noelani's hand, and quietly the girl watched as the snowflake melted into a small water stain on the soft leather of her glove.

A whimper caught her ear then, and she glanced down at the tiny bundle cradled in her arms.

"Oh, *wakisa*, my strong, brave little son," Noelani called softly to the swaddled infant, drawing him closer to her chest and placing him firmly between her own body heat and the warmth the campfire in front of her offered. "It is a cold day, isn't it?"

She leaned down, kissing the baby's swaddled head, and the child snuggled against her, his body relaxing in the safety of his mother's arms.

A movement caught the corner of Noelani's vision then, and she glanced up as a middle-aged woman stepped out of one of the wagons that encircled the small camp. It was her mother, Enola, and the girl watched as the older woman circled over toward her, squatting down and giving her a sympathetic look.

"Noelani, *inyela*, you should come inside. It is too cold for your little one out here."

Noelani sighed, casting her gaze past the wagons and out into the snow-laden forest beyond. It had been days since her husband, Bidziil, had left the camp with a couple other members of the clan to go hunting. She was starting to worry, but she knew her mother was right. She had to think of her child first. She couldn't wait forever and risk detriment to herself or the baby in her arms.

Ignoring the snow that had settled on her head and shoulders, Noelani followed Enola into one of the ornate wagons that surrounded the small camp, pausing to survey the faces of the others gathered around. Her aunts, her grandmother, a few cousins...all huddled together and chatting as they worked on various crafting projects. Noelani knew that the men who remained in camp would be in one of the other wagons. Keeping close to each other was the best way to stay warm amidst the cold of winter.

The other women glanced up when Noelani entered, Enola at her heels, and called out greetings to her as she took a seat next to her grandmother on one of the benches.

"Still no word from the others?" one of Noelani's aunts questioned.

The girl shook her head, pulling her infant son closer to her heart, more to comfort herself than to comfort him.

"I'm sure they're fine," her grandmother soothed, wrapping an arm around Noelani's shoulder in a hug. "Perhaps they simply had to take shelter from the snow. Bidziil is a strong man, you know. It will take more than a little cold to defeat *him*. And his son is strong, too! Little Akoni hardly made a sound the whole time you were out in that miserable weather."

As though recognizing his name, the baby in Noelani's arms stirred, and she lowered him slightly to look into his face. At just shy of a month old, Akoni's movements were uncoordinated, but his reflexes were strong. As the young mother lowered him toward her lap, cradling him between her forearms with his small head in her hands, Akoni's dark eyes wandered this way and that before focusing in on his mother's face. Tightly swaddled to combat the cold, he couldn't move much, but Noelani felt her heart leap with joy as the hint of a smile appeared on his tiny lips. She leaned down, kissing Akoni's forehead before happily beginning to hum a lullaby.

Noelani was a member of the Sinti, a diverse and nomadic people group and one of the few descended from the original inhabitants of the isle of Aurora. Her home was in the Rahan Wilds, a dangerous landscape both in terms of nature and of magic. Winters were hard, but that didn't mean that the rest of the year was any easier. When severe weather and poor hunting weren't a concern, there was still always the threat of something far worse: the morgrim, the dark monsters that haunted the Rahan Wilds.

It had been a long time since the clan had crossed paths with the morgrim, which tended to stay closer to the ruins of the ancient city of Taj, but that did not mean they were no longer a threat. And though Noelani felt joy staring into her child's face, she couldn't deny the lingering worry at the back of her mind. Her grandmother was right. Bidziil was a strong man. But the snow had not been so heavy as to overcome his talent in tracking and navigation. He should have been home by now.

The chatter between the other women was distant and incomprehensible to Noelani as she comforted herself and her son with a quiet song. The song she sang was one passed down through her tribe—the Wiyota, followers of the naiad-like Droma spirit, Nashtera—and featured a story of a baby rocked to sleep by waves in Nashtera's embrace. As she sang, Noelani rocked her own baby, and slowly Akoni drifted off into slumber.

Her child now fast asleep, Noelani drew him back against her chest and leaned her own weight into the cushions behind her. Her free hand reached up, clutching at the small, carved naiad figure she wore around her neck, and she closed her eyes, breathing a soft prayer for wisdom and safety, both for herself and for her husband, wherever he might be. And slowly, she drifted off into a light sleep.

It was the shout of unfamiliar voices that broke Noelani from her rest, and quickly she sat up. The abrupt movement startled Akoni, who began to cry. Noelani lifted her child to her shoulder, patting his back comfortingly as she and the other women hurried out of the wagon to see what all the fuss was about. Already, other members of the clan had left the wagons they had been taking shelter in.

Always a shorter woman, Noelani couldn't see above the heads of those gathered around, but somehow she could sense that something wasn't right. With Akoni held firmly against her, the girl began to push her way toward the front. When she arrived, however, Noelani froze in place.

There were four people standing in front of the crowd. She recognized one, her younger brother Wakpa. He was badly wounded and hurriedly bandaged, crimson stains oozing through the crude strips of woven dog wool covering his body. Next to him stood three strangers, all in varying states of injury and disarray. One was a red-scaled drakonite, a dragon-like humanoid, whose right arm was cut off at the elbow and covered by a bloody bandage. Next to him, probably a third of his height, was a male halfling, not missing any limbs but equally as bloody. The last of the strangers was a pale-skinned human man of roughly Noelani and Bidziil's age who seemed the least injured of the three strangers. And there, on a makeshift stretcher at their feet, was the torn, bloody form of Bidziil.

Noelani felt a cry of horror escape her lips before she could stop it. All eyes turned toward her as she rushed to her husband's side and dropped to her knees in the blood-stained snow. Enola joined her, checking Bidziil's wrist for a pulse. Noelani watched as her mother's countenance fell. The older woman closed her eyes, then turned a sympathetic gaze on her daughter. She shook her head faintly.

Tears burned at the corners of Noelani's eyes, freezing to her cheeks as they fell. Akoni, seeming to sense his mother's distress, began to cry even louder than before, and the young woman pulled her child more firmly against her chest as she bent down, pressing her forehead to Bidziil's and allowing her tears to join with her child's cries.

*No...please, no...*antakiya, *I am not ready to say goodbye...*

"Explain again what happened," she heard her grandfather's voice say in trade speech.

"We became lost while exploring nearby, and then the morgrim attacked," one of the strangers explained, his voice hoarse. "Your clan members rescued us, but it was all we could do to drive the morgrim off. And in the process..."

"Morgrim," Wakpa's voice cut in. "All the way up here. Bidziil sacrificed himself to help us escape, but those *things* are still out there."

A murmur rippled out through the gathered crowd.

"We're not but a day's journey from the Blooming Grove, nowhere near Taj," Noelani heard one of her aunts say worriedly. "If they've come this far..."

Quietly, Noelani shifted, pressing her lips to Bidziil's. She wished desperately for the warmth those lips had offered her in the year they had been together, but this time she was met with nothing but cold emptiness. She had to accept the reality before her. Her husband was gone. And now, the things that had killed her husband might be coming for the rest of her family, too.

Tucking her grief back for a more appropriate time, Noelani stood to her feet, turning to comfort her crying child. As she stood, she felt all eyes turn toward her, and she glanced up as the three strangers bowed in front of her.

"Madam, I am so sorry," the pale-skinned human said, voice filled with audible remorse. "If we hadn't been so foolish and placed your people in danger..."

"No," Noelani said, interrupting the man's apology and shaking her head. "Do not apologize. It will only cheapen the choice that my husband made. Tell me, what kind of morgrim attacked you, and how far out do you think they might be?"

The strangers exchanged glances before the drakonite spoke.

"I don't know what the creatures are called, but they are almost insect-like, something between a centipede and a spider in the torso, but with four sharp appendages for arms. They also have a shadowy aura about them, though from what I hear, that is true of most morgrim."

Noelani stood silent for a moment, then glanced up at the others.

"That sounds like an arachne," she said. "Their corrupted aes aura can paralyze you with fear if you are not strong enough to withstand it. However, they are sensitive to bright light. We should prepare the camp. They will most likely make their move after dark. We should heal the wounded and prepare for combat."

Still cuddling Akoni's tiny form against herself, shielding him from the bitter cold, Noelani started explaining what each member of the clan would benefit from doing. It was hard to know if the arachne were the only morgrim prowling the forest, but they were at least one thing the clan could prepare for.

Noelani's mother, the clan's shaman, was in charge of leading the healing and support. She and some of the other members of the clan removed Bidziil's body to one of the wagons to be prepared for burial as they waited for the others to have need of their services. Noelani's father and grandfather were talented fighters with many years of experience between them. With Noelani's advice, the pair began coordinating watches, making sure there was an even balance of skills available on each watch. A few among their number were druids, and with Noelani's instruction, they began to magically prepare the surrounding environment to provide them with whatever strategic advantages they could manage. In the dead of winter, there were few plants available to work with, but the land itself still offered some measure of resources.

Magic talent among them was limited, resources even more so, but soon the clan was moving about and performing their assigned tasks as though they were a trained military unit. And all the while, the three strangers stood off to the side with eyes wide and mouths agape, watching in wonder as the young widow with the baby in her arms seemed to take command even of her elders, and no one paused to question her.

It was close to an hour before at last the camp's activity began to settle into an uneasy rhythm, and with her adrenaline starting to fade, Noelani suddenly realized she felt incredibly dizzy. Her knees buckled beneath her, and she was prepared to sink into the snow until she felt a pair of strong hands catch her by the elbow, steadying her. She glanced up to see the pale stranger, who offered her a half-smile that was more grimace than anything.

"Can I help you to a place to sit, at least?" the man questioned.

Noelani nodded blankly.

"I want to see Bidziil. I want to see my husband," she said.

It took a moment of silence before Noelani realized she had naturally answered in the Sinti language instead of trade speech, and she shook her head, as though that would somehow clear the fog that was gathering there.

"I'm sorry," she said, this time in a language the stranger could understand. "That wagon."

She nodded in the direction Bidziil's body had been taken, and the stranger nodded solemnly in reply. Noelani was glad for the support as she walked. Her feet felt heavy, and she knew it wasn't just because of the snow now caked to her fur-lined boots.

At the wagon, the stranger knocked lightly on the door. It opened immediately, Noelani's mother appearing in the aperture. As soon as Enola saw her daughter, she called to one of Noelani's aunts, and soon, the young woman felt herself hoisted into the relative warmth that the wagon provided. It wasn't until that moment that she realized just how numb she felt, both inside and out.

The pale-skinned stranger who had walked her to the door turned to leave, but Enola called out to him.

"Come," she said, "your wounds need tending to, and I'm sure you would appreciate some reprieve from the cold."

"I'm alright," the stranger began to protest, but Enola wagged a finger at him.

"No sense arguing," she replied, her tone commanding. "I'll not hear it. Come in."

Noelani watched for a moment as the man cautiously entered the wagon, his gaze shifting to Bidziil's inert form on the bed at the far end before shifting uncomfortably away again. At the same moment, Noelani felt one of her cousins reach for Akoni.

"I'll take care of him," she soothed, motioning with her head toward Bidziil. "Go say your goodbyes. Take all the time you need."

The snow on Noelani's boots was already beginning to melt into puddles, but she ignored the tracks she left as she squeezed past the wagon's other occupants and over to her husband's side. The blood and grime had been cleaned away, no doubt thanks to Enola's magic, and to the untrained eye, it might have only looked like Bidziil was sleeping. Noelani wished that were the truth. She wished he was only sleeping, and that he would soon open his eyes and offer her the shy smile she had fallen in love with. Softly, she traced her fingers over the man's rugged jawline and down his sinewy arms. Then, she buried her face in his chest, clenching his shredded coat in her fists as she at last let the grief run its course.

Activity in the wagon stilled, the other occupants listening solemnly to the young woman's cries. A familiar arm wrapped around her shoulders, followed by Enola's gentle voice, "We are here for you, *inyela*."

When at last Noelani's sobs had faded to soft whimpers, the voice of the pale-skinned man broke the stillness, his words cracked and faltering as he muttered softly, "Is there anything I can do to make it up to you? I know you told me not to apologize, but..."

Noelani opened her eyes, wiping the tears from her face as she sat up and turned to the stranger. He was a tall young man, dirty and unkempt, with unruly brown hair and sharp blue eyes. His thin lips were partially obscured by his facial hair and a wool scarf wrapped securely around his neck, and he wore a long, tattered coat over threadbare traveler's clothes. A pair of wire-rimmed spectacles rested atop an angled nose, and a light crossbow hung from the belt at his hip.

"What is your name?" Noelani questioned.

The stranger turned toward her, looking confused.

"Ezra," he replied. "Ezra Stowe."

"And your companions?"

Ezra tipped his head curiously.

"The halfling is Elry Mistfellow, and the drakonite is Veldras Sulrakas. May I...ask why?"

"I merely wanted to know the names of the people my husband gave his life to protect," Noelani replied evenly, choking back the tremor in her voice. "You must understand. This is the way of our people. We protect who we wish to protect. We love whom we wish to love. We aid those we wish to aid. We make our choices, and we expect no favors in return."

She watched as Ezra bowed his head. He still looked remorseful, as though it would be easier for him to continue to apologize than to merely accept that it was the choice his rescuer made, but he didn't argue. And so Noelani continued.

"Ezra, tell me. What are your skills? And those of your companions? If you wish to help us now, I will not stop you. And if you would tell me what you are best at, I may be able to help you find your place among my people."

The man's eyes brightened slightly.

"Well," he began, rubbing his chin in thought, "I'm best at alchemy, but I have some knowledge of arcane items as well."

He reached down to the light crossbow at his hip, patting it lightly.

"And I can shoot marginally well with this, too."

One of Noelani's aunts sat down nearby, looking the young man up and down curiously.

"I don't see any ammunition," she noted. "Are you in need of more after your earlier fight?"

"Oh, no," Ezra chuckled sheepishly. "I've enchanted the crossbow. It creates magical ammunition on its own whenever I use it."

The others in the wagon exchanged wondering glances.

"That would be incredibly convenient," Enola mused. "Is that something you could recreate and trade for?"

Ezra pursed his lips, then shook his head.

"Not right now, unfortunately. But when I get back to Arcanum, I'll try to create another one. If I do, I'll be sure to send it to you. As for my companions' skills, though..."

He paused to think before continuing.

"Veldras and Elry are both skilled at up close and personal combat. The problem is that those creatures that attacked us earlier..." He shivered. "Those creatures are horrid. Get too close and they will tear you to pieces..."

He paused, glancing over at Bidziil's inert body, then lowered his head and looked away as though regretting that he had said as much out loud.

Noelani turned back to her husband, gently, lovingly running her hand along his familiar form. She paused when she noticed something unusual in the pouch at his hip, and she reached in, withdrawing an ornate beaded necklace.

"What is this?" she murmured, mostly to herself, but her words caught the attention of those still in the wagon.

"That isn't of Sinti make," Enola mused, coming to sit next to Noelani and eyeing the necklace curiously.

"That looks like a relic from Taj," came Ezra's voice, and the others turned to look at him.

He glanced up from the necklace to Noelani, intrigued.

"Would you mind if I examined it?"

The young woman nodded, holding the item out for Ezra to take and watching with interest as he began to ritually cast a spell. A few minutes later, the man glanced up wonderingly.

"The beads on this necklace are made out of aes crystals," he explained. "You said those creatures are weak to bright light, didn't you? That is something you could cast from this necklace if you were able to tap into its power."

"The rest of us can hide in the wagons when the morgrim arrive," one of Noelani's aunts suggested. "If you want, you can use that necklace to keep the creatures at bay."

Noelani pursed her lips, considering the suggestion before at last shaking her head.

"If and when they come, we should all be outside," she said. "I have heard the stories of the arachne. They would tear through the wagons anyway, and then you would all be trapped inside. Make sure that everyone is ready to run at a moment's notice, and stay in the groups that I have suggested to you. If you need to run, run with your group. Each group should have a combination of skills necessary to survive if we end up separated."

She turned to Ezra then.

"If you want, I can arrange you and your companions into a group as well. My hope is that no one will have to be separated, but with the morgrim, one never knows."

Noelani turned back to Bidziil as she finished speaking. She pressed the necklace close to her chest, squeezing her eyes tightly shut as she breathed a silent prayer.

Nashtera, keeper of river and rain, avalanche and snowfall, lend me the wisdom and strength to guide my people.

And then with that, she opened her eyes and placed the beaded necklace around her neck, turning her gaze toward the door leading out of the wagon. Even in death, Bidziil would protect her. And through the strength and the legacy he had left her, she would defend their family.

It was the shortest day of the year; fitting, Noelani thought, for the day she became a widow. The light of day faded quickly, and the heavy cloud cover only made a dark night darker. The temperature dropped further, and the snowfall became heavier. It wasn't a blizzard, but it was enough to obscure vision. Those in the camp took turns resting, Noelani most of all. Akoni, sensitive to his mother's distress and the general air of tension among the clan members, had become fitful. Noelani dozed in between the moments that her baby cried himself to sleep, and even then, it was little more than a light slumber. The waiting...the not knowing...that was the hardest.

Some time in the dead of night, however, a shout echoed out from the watch set up around the camp.

"Morgrim!"

The shout was a trigger. Noelani sat bolt upright, reaching out for Akoni and gathering him up in her arms. Her mother and several of the other women who were also sleeping in the wagon, sharing each other's warmth, bounded to their feet along with her. Some grabbed for weapons and shields; others, staffs or religious icons. And in a moment, Noelani found herself at the center of the camp, the campfire's light seemingly darkened by an eerie, shadowed aura as the sound of combat rang past the circle of wagons providing a barrier between the camp and the dangers beyond.

Ezra, who was perched atop one of the wagons and firing off into the night, yelled back to Noelani, "We need light!"

It was time.

Clutching Akoni tightly to her chest, Noelani closed her eyes, focusing on the necklace that she had found in Bidziil's pouch.

One last time, my love, let us defend our people together.

A pulse of magic energy rippled out from the necklace's central medallion, and when Noelani opened her eyes again, the camp was engulfed in a light so bright that, if she hadn't known better, she would have thought it were noon. Those fighting beyond the wagons fell back toward the light. The non-combatants crouched low at Noelani's feet while the casters encircled them, and as the warriors fell back, they formed a wall around the casters. The ranged combatants remained atop the wagons, peppering the enemy with projectiles as they advanced. The resistance didn't last long, and soon Ezra and the others jumped toward the center of camp, landing in the snow as a couple of the wagons were shattered.

Jagged, locust-like appendages pierced through solid wood, wagons snapping and splintering beneath the weight of their huge, insectoid bodies. They easily stood to the height of two or three men and, as the creatures came into the light, Noelani realized that the stories she had heard could not do them justice. To say the morgrim known as arachne were horrifying may have been too generous. No word in any tongue could describe what now crashed through the snow and wood debris toward her.

As the arachne came into the light, they skittered to a stop, letting out blood-curdling screeches as they attempted to back away from the arcane radiance.

"Flank!" Noelani's father shouted.

Half of the fighters in the group broke rank, surrounding the half-dozen arachne that had torn their way into camp, while the other half maintained their guard positions around the casters. To one side, Ezra and several of the archers swung back up onto wagons that remained intact, and from where she stood, Noelani could see the pale-skinned man level his crossbow at a nearby monster. Arcane runes lit up along the flight groove, an ethereal bolt comprised of pure, arcane force forming in the space only a breath of a moment before arching forward, striking into the arachne's carapace and vanishing.

Nearby, the red drakonite named Veldras rushed to flank one of the arachne, and in the light streaming from Noelani's necklace, she could see the glint of a metallic arm replacing the one that had earlier been missing. It didn't look like an item of recent make, but there was no time to ask questions. Veldras brought his metallic arm back before punching forward. A crack of something akin to thunder echoed out through the camp, and the arachne staggered before turning its attention to the drakonite. The distraction was all Noelani's brother, Wakpa, needed as he dove forward, burying a dagger into the monster's thick hide. The attack was followed closely by Elry, small though he was, pouncing on the arachne's back like an angry cat, driving his short sword hilt-deep into the monster below him.

As the warriors fought and the casters formed their sigils, Noelani turned a brief glance toward her mother. Enola caught her glance, giving the briefest of nods before her strong alto voice began to break through the din. Noelani joined her voice with her mother's, and soon other voices around the campfire began to sing as well. It was an ancient song, a song of entreaty to their guardian spirit, Nashtera. And then, just when it looked like the morgrim might be on the verge of gaining the advantage over the Sinti warriors, the snow at their feet began to stir.

At first, it was a gentle swirl, loose snowflakes kicked up in a light breeze. But as the song swelled, so did the vortex. Noelani watched in amazement as the snow roared around them, tearing at the arachne's thick hides but licking harmlessly around the clan members and the three strangers. For a moment, the arachne turned toward Noelani, the narrow cluster of eyes at the center of their heads flashing a dark amethyst. The young woman felt shadows creep into her mind, attempting to paralyze her with fear, but she willed the shadows away, focusing on the light from Bidziil's necklace. Almost on reflex, she shifted Akoni's weight into one arm, holding him ever tighter, trying to comfort his terrified cries as she lifted her other hand.

"*Kirae'a!*"

Noelani had heard her mother utter that short incantation countless times as she defended the clan from the unholy things that wandered the Rahan Wilds. But now, for the first time, it somehow meant something to her, too. She felt a surge of power and, like a star falling from the sky, a column of radiant flames descended on one of the morgrim. The creature let out a screech only a moment before the flames consumed it, leaving behind nothing but a pile of ashes.

For a moment, those who had been fighting the creature paused. Then they glanced back, saw Noelani with her arm outstretched, nodded with respect, and turned to help their companions. In what seemed like only moments, the last of the arachne fell, dissipating into shadow, and silence descended on the camp.

One of Noelani's aunts knelt to the ground, pressing her hand to the frozen earth and closing her eyes. A moment later, she looked up and smiled back at the others.

"There are no more morgrim nearby. We are safe now."

Relief flooded Noelani's body, and she collapsed to her knees in the muddy snow below her, clutching at the crying Akoni as tears of gratitude poured down her face. One by one, her gaze met those of her companions: Enola, Wakpa, Ezra, Elry, Veldras, and so many others. They were wounded. They were exhausted. But they were still alive. Though the darkness had surrounded them, a celestial light still burned both in the necklace that Noelani wore and in her heart.

Not even the darkest winter could snuff them out.

2

A Moment Worth Treasuring

3RD DAY OF ZHAYAN, AE 18

"Julia! Welcome home!"

Julia had to steady herself with the impact of the incoming hug. She laughed lightly, blue eyes dancing with amusement as she looked down at her assailant, an eight-year-old girl with bright brown eyes and silky brown hair pulled into a loose braid.

"Thank you, Kitty," Julia said laughingly, returning the little girl's hug as loose strands of her own rich brown hair tumbled out from beneath the handkerchief tying it back. "Did you have a good day?"

"Mhm!" the child replied energetically. "Some nice people paid me to do errands for them today, so I was able to get something for you. Sit down, okay?"

The child took both of Julia's hands in hers, pulling her toward a lumpy mattress nestled on the floor, close to a small hearth where a golden fire flickered, warm and inviting.

"Kitty, you didn't need to get me anything," Julia protested lightly as she allowed the younger girl to pull her over to the mattress.

"You're my sister, and you work really hard," Kitty argued, unfazed. "I want to do something nice for you since you always come home tired."

Julia sighed, giving her little sister a chagrined half-smile as the child gently tugged her down to sit on the mattress. Seeing that the older girl was making no further protest, Kitty began to busy herself with a dented and tarnished tin tea set. A moment later, Julia found one of the old tea cups being pressed into her hands.

"There," Kitty said, smiling triumphantly. "See what you think."

Julia offered her little sister another smile, then brought the cup to her lips. Already she could smell the rich aroma of herbs. Lavender, chamomile, perhaps a hint of licorice. She tasted the amber concoction and let out a contented sigh.

"It's lovely, Kitty. Thank you so much. I already feel better."

She smiled softly as the little girl's eyes brightened, a look of triumph crossing her face.

"I promise I'll work hard tomorrow so that I can do this for you again!" the child declared.

"Kitty, that's what I'm here for. You don't need to worry about those things."

The child pointed a determined finger at her older sister.

"You can't be the only one working hard, Julia. And you won't change my mind!"

Julia laughed.

"You are a stubborn one, aren't you?"

She was met with a bold grin before Kitty plopped down on the mattress next to her. Her grin faded, and quietly the child smoothed out the skirt of her dress which had been patched so many times it was hardly more than a shadow of its former self.

"Anyway," Kitty said at length, "I don't want to have to live in this basement forever, and I hate seeing you so tired and sick all the time. Maybe if I help, we can someday have a nice place to live again, the way things were when Mama and Papa were still alive."

Another sigh escaped Julia's lips and, wordlessly, she reached out one arm, pulling her sister into a hug. The little girl snuggled up to her, the pair falling into silence as they stared into the flickering embers of the fire in the hearth.

Quietly, Julia pressed her cheek against the top of Kitty's head, her mind wandering back to the past, to the days when life felt...normal. It had been four years since her parents' deaths, four years since the morgrim invasion that had taken her father's life. Her mother hadn't been able to handle the grief. The priests said she had died of a broken heart. It was all that Julia could do to keep from following in her path.

Julia had inherited from her mother a weak heart, so doing anything strenuous was a challenge. For a time, she and her sister had lived with her father's family, but they were farmers, and everyone in residence was expected to pull their weight. Sensing their censure and lack of welcome, Julia had taken a gamble and begged for a job up in the Commercial District. It was rare for someone like her, a resident of Xanom's Lower Ward, to find welcome in the world of the higher class citizens, but a florist had taken pity on her, at least providing her with a job she could not only do well but enjoy in the process. It didn't pay much but, coupled with her father's small penchant from his time as a knight, it at least afforded the little basement room with the cozy hearth where she and her sister now lived. She had her sister who loved her deeply, food to eat, clothes to wear, and a roof over her head. As far as Julia was concerned, she was blessed; she already had more than enough to be satisfied.

The girl gave her sister's shoulders a squeeze.

"Maybe someday we will live somewhere nicer," she said, pulling away so that she could look Kitty in the eyes. "But for now, I feel like a queen with this lovely tea and such a sweet little girl for a sister. So let's not worry about the what-ifs. Shall we make something to eat?"

Kitty smiled brightly at the suggestion.

"Yes! I'm starving!"

And with that, the child bounded up, trotting off to the containers of food goods and examining it all like an alchemist preparing to assemble an elaborate concoction. Ignoring her own fatigue and the ache in her feet, Julia stood to join her. It was in the simple moments that she found the most joy and, as such, there was so much joy to be had.

"Hurry and get your apron on. We've already got a dozen orders waiting."

"Yes, ma'am."

Julia had hardly stepped through the door of the florist's shop before her employer was barking orders at her. Hurriedly tying her hair back with a handkerchief, the girl set to work collecting the various flowers for the designated arrangements. For each, the girl wondered what their intended purpose might be. This arrangement contained flowers focused on friendship, that one would be good for a confession of love, and still another Julia could only guess was a last-minute gift with no thought placed into it for all the random selections that comprised it.

Men and women, boys and girls, each with their own temperaments, came and went from the shop. Many appeared to be servants of the noble houses. Several were of a more well-off common class, perhaps residents of the Commercial District themselves. Few looked to be from the Lower Ward. Julia wasn't surprised. It was a rare occasion indeed for a resident of the Lower Ward to spend money on something as frivolous as a bouquet. The girl wondered what it might be like to live a life so luxurious.

Slowly the sun began to trace its way across the sky. Other workers came and went, taking their afternoon lunch breaks. All the while, Julia fetched the flowers and fronds required for the arrangements she had been tasked to work on. Money was scarce, and lunch was a luxury she simply couldn't justify. Lost in her reverie, Julia hadn't even realized she was alone until a sudden bout of dizziness struck.

The girl paused, bracing one hand against her workbench and blinking rapidly. Her chest constricted slightly, and she drew in a deep breath, letting it out slowly as she attempted to still her heart. The feeling would pass. It always did. And yet the longer she waited, the more fatigued she felt. Her feet hurt. Her head hurt. Everything hurt. And then, she felt her knees buckle underneath her as her vision went black.

"Hey!"

A stranger's voice caught Julia's ear, followed by a pair of strong arms wrapping around her, slowing her fall. She felt the cool cobblestone of the shop's floor touch her back, and lying prone seemed to clear her head, as a moment later her vision began to return. The next thing the girl knew, she was staring into the face of a city guard.

The girl blinked. The guard was a young man, hardly older than herself, with short-cropped, dark brown hair and a chiseled jaw over which he had grown a short, trimmed beard. His mouth was drawn into a fine line and there was something stern about his features, but he gazed down at her with the most beautiful pair of honey-brown eyes the girl had ever seen.

Noticing that the girl had regained consciousness, the guard narrowed his already furrowed brow.

"You alright?" he questioned.

"Yes, thank you," Julia replied, slowly pushing herself to sit up.

Despite the severe expression on his face, the young man kept one broad hand positioned behind her shoulders to catch her if she fell again.

Julia glanced around. The shop was still quiet. She sighed. She hated to be a bother, but she was glad for the help. It was hard to know when any of the others would return from their afternoon break. She turned to look at the guard who was still watching her closely.

"I am sorry for the trouble, sir," she said, bowing her head. "I should be alright now."

She glanced up at him pensively. The man's expression remained dubious.

"Are you ill?" he inquired. "If you are, you should probably go home and rest. You would have been in a lot of trouble if I hadn't happened by when you fell."

The girl gave him a chagrined smile.

"I was born with a weak heart. This is normal. It just happens sometimes. I promise I will be more careful, though."

The mention of her heart seemed to only further the young man's concern.

"Where do you live? I can walk you home or call for one of your relatives if you would like."

Again Julia shook her head.

"It's quite alright." She stood shakily to her feet. "See? I'm just fine now."

The guard seemed hesitant but at last sighed and stood to his feet as well.

"If you're sure. I suppose if you no longer need my assistance, I'll return to my duties."

"Of course," Julia nodded, giving him a light curtsy. "Again, please accept my apologies for the inconvenience. If I may ask, however...what is your name? So that I can thank you properly."

The guard seemed to hesitate before shoving one hand into a pocket and turning his back to her.

"Nereus," he replied at length. "You?"

"Me? Oh, I'm Julia. It's a pleasure to meet you, Nereus. Sincerely, thank you for your help just now."

The young man grunted in reply, paused a moment longer, then continued off down the road. Julia watched his retreating form, wondering at the difference between his cold demeanor and the care he had shown her only moments before. She laughed at herself then. For as silly as it sounded, she hoped to see him again, that stern young guard with the honey-brown eyes.

"Alright, Julia. We're heading out for lunch now."

"Enjoy!"

The girl returned her coworkers' declaration with a smile, giving them all a friendly wave as they prepared to depart. The others waved back, only paying her half a mind as they chatted about where they might want to go for their afternoon meal. Perhaps Lily's Garden or the Lantern. Julia had heard them mention the places often, even walked by Tavern Row where the two establishments were located. Lily's Garden, a restaurant inside a solarium with outdoor seating in the prettiest little garden, looked especially nice. Of course, it was unlikely that she would ever have the money to visit such a place, Julia thought. It was still nice to dream, though.

With a smile, the girl focused back on her work. She had learned her lesson from the previous day, seating herself on a stool to prevent any future falls.

"Good afternoon, Miss Julia."

The girl paused in her work, turning curiously at the sound of a vaguely familiar voice. She was surprised to see the guard from the previous day, Nereus, standing in the doorway of the shop. The other girls, who had paused to argue about their intended destination, grew suddenly silent and wide-eyed as they looked between Julia and Nereus.

Feeling very self-conscious with all the attention, Julia stood quickly to her feet, giving the young man a polite curtsy.

"Good afternoon, sir. To what do I owe the pleasure of this visit?"

Julia bit back a laugh at the face Nereus made at the address, his nose twitching slightly into a wrinkle before he resumed his otherwise taciturn demeanor.

"Just Nereus is fine. My father is a sir."

The young man cast his gaze sideways, in the direction of a plain brown pot as though it had suddenly become the most interesting thing in the room. Julia blinked at him before biting back a smile, chewing lightly on her lower lip. Was he...embarrassed?

"Alright then, Nereus," the girl said, offering him a friendly smile. "Is there something I can help you with?"

He glanced back over at her, then shook his head faintly.

"Just thought I'd check on you on my way past."

Nearby, the other girls reacted with hushed gasps and giggles. Julia blushed.

"Oh, well, thank you. I'm alright. I've made sure I won't fall again. You needn't worry. I very much appreciate your kindness."

She patted the seat of the stool behind her for emphasis.

The young man nodded in acknowledgment before his gaze trailed over to the group of girls standing and staring between the two of them in wide-eyed wonder. He shifted uneasily in place and cleared his throat.

"Well, I best be off then. Good day."

With a crisp about-face, the young man turned and marched off. He had hardly disappeared out the door before Julia found herself swarmed by her coworkers.

"Julia! Nereus Lex! Really?! When did this happen?! You've been holding out on us!" one of the other girls exclaimed.

Julia stared blankly back at her companions as they bombarded her with questions, her mind attempting to process the words being spoken to her.

Nereus...Lex?

Her head suddenly felt light, and Julia scrambled for her stool, sitting down heavily on it and letting her face fall into her hands.

"Lex?" she questioned. "That guard...is a nobleman?"

The other girls quieted for just a moment, seeming stunned by her response.

"Wait, you didn't know?" one questioned in disbelief.

"Nereus Lex isn't just a nobleman, either," a second of the girls added. "He's the heir to House Lex. He's only recently been knighted. I heard someone say he was meant to work patrols outside the city but volunteered to serve a stint as a city guard because their forces here were lower than they would like."

Julia could feel her heart beating wildly in her chest at the thought. So...not only had she embarrassed herself fainting the day before...but it had been in front of the heir of one of the noble houses? If a person could die from mortification, Julia thought she might have done so then.

"I can't believe you didn't know!" one of the girls declared, sighing dramatically. "He wears the signet ring and everything!"

"I...didn't notice..." Julia replied weakly.

Truly, now that she thought about it, all she had noticed the day before was a pair of strong arms wrapped around her and the look of warm, honey-brown eyes regarding her with kindness. Who would have thought they would have all belonged to the heir of a noble house, a man so far beyond her reach she might as well have been touched by the sun itself.

It took a moment for Julia to realize that the other girls had long since lost interest in her, wandering out of the shop while chattering loudly about Nereus Lex. She sighed. Well, it had been kind of him to check on her if nothing else. She couldn't imagine that it was routine for a nobleman, especially the heir of a noble house, to show interest in a commoner's well-being. She wondered if he would have shown the same concern if he had known she was from the Lower Ward.

Julia was startled out of her reverie at the sound of a knock behind her. Thinking it was a customer, she bolted out of her seat, turning quickly to greet them.

"Welcome to Flower Fairy Florist, how may I..."

Her voice caught in her throat when she spotted a now-familiar figure standing in the doorway.

"Ner...um...Master Lex...I..."

The more she attempted to speak, the more embarrassed Julia felt. Nereus sighed audibly.

"I figured they'd tell you," he grumbled. "Seriously, just Nereus. Please. All those honorifics make me feel old. That's my father's job."

Julia paused, taking up handfuls of her skirt and casting her gaze to the ground.

"I'm sorry. I've never met a nobleman before. I'm just a poor girl from the Lower Ward. This isn't...I apologize, but I don't have anything to offer you but my thanks."

"I'm not here for any of that," Nereus replied.

Julia glanced up at him quizzically. If the man wasn't there for payment, she could hardly think of a good reason why he would continue to stop by the flower shop. Rather than offer a direct answer, however, Nereus glanced around the room filled with a wide assortment of plants and pottery.

"Do you always work the afternoon by yourself?" he questioned, wandering idly through the room and examining the flowers there.

Julia shifted uneasily where she stood.

"Why...do you ask?"

Nereus paused, seeming to consider something. All of a sudden, Julia watched as his face turned bright red.

"Gods, that's not what I meant," he grumbled, rubbing the back of his neck nervously and turning his face away, most likely to hide the obvious blush that had risen to his ears. "You should eat lunch, take a break. You could end up fainting again otherwise, and what happens if there's no one around to help you? I don't know much about medicine and heart conditions and whatnot, but working yourself to death can't be making it any better and I can't in good conscience just go about my business without saying something."

Julia blinked back at him disbelievingly.

"So...you just keep coming back...because you're worried about me, a stranger, a simple girl from the Lower Ward? And you truly don't want anything in return?"

Nereus glanced over at her quizzically.

"No?"

The look of utter confusion that crossed the young man's face was enough to make Julia forget herself, and she laughed. There was no deceit in that face. Though his persistence could easily have been interpreted as predatory, it was clear that his mind was so far from those thoughts that he looked more like an innocent little boy than a grown man and soldier.

Julia's laughter seemed to leave Nereus even more perplexed, and she was just about to venture an apology when a familiar voice caught her ear.

"Julia!"

The girl turned to see Kitty come bounding through the door, a tiny box in hand. The child ground to a halt when she spotted Nereus, covering her mouth and looking up at her older sister apologetically.

"Sorry. I didn't realize you had a customer," she whispered, though in truth her voice was loud enough to be heard across the shop.

"It's alright, Kitty. We were just talking. What brings you here now?"

Julia crouched to place herself on eye level with her sister and the child lifted the little box for her to see.

"I earned a lot of money this morning from my errands and got you a *lokma*! That way you're not hungry all day!"

Julia blushed at her sister's words, casting a pensive glance in the direction of Nereus. It appeared that the young man was putting forth a valiant effort to not eavesdrop on the pair's conversation, but the flexing of his jaw muscles told Julia he had probably heard anyway. It was hard not to with how loud Kitty was.

"Thank you, Kitty," Julia said, offering her sister a smile as she accepted the little box with the fried pastry inside. "How about we split it after I finish my visit with the gentleman there? I'm sure you'd like to try it, too."

The child looked conflicted at her sister's offer, but a rumble from her own stomach enticed her to nod sheepishly. Julia then turned back to Nereus. She was just about to offer him some reassurance that she would take better care of herself when the young man cleared his throat.

"I...um...I was about to head to lunch myself. Would the two of you like to join me today?"

Julia hesitated. How could she politely say she had no money to go anywhere?

Nereus seemed to notice her hesitation, because he added quickly, "It's on me. If...you're interested. No strings attached, I promise. I would...enjoy the company."

Nearby, Kitty drew in an excited breath.

"Like...a whole lunch?" she breathed.

Nereus turned to look at the child and nodded.

"A whole lunch. Anywhere you like."

Julia glanced between her plain work clothes and the patched dress her sister wore.

"That is very generous of you, but...are you sure you want to be seen with people like us?"

Nereus sighed.

"I wouldn't have offered if I wasn't."

Feeling that it would be rude to argue further, Julia nodded hesitantly.

"Alright. Well...thank you."

The young man nodded in return, then headed for the door, waiting patiently as Julia locked up the shop. Meanwhile, Kitty regarded him with wide-eyed wonder.

"You're really nice," the child noted. "By the way, I'm Katrina. My sister calls me Kitty. What's your name?"

"Nereus," the young man replied.

"That's an interesting name," Kitty mused. "How did you meet my sister?"

Julia froze at the question, casting a pleading look in Nereus' direction. She really didn't want Kitty to worry more than she already did. Nereus caught her look out of the corner of his eye before turning his attention back to Kitty.

"Just by chance," the young man answered vaguely. "Where would you like to eat lunch?"

Julia sighed softly. Crisis averted.

Kitty considered Nereus' question for several serious moments before looking back up at him.

"Julia has always wanted to visit Lily's Garden. Can we go there?"

Julia blushed profusely at the suggestion, locking the door to the shop hurriedly before rushing to intercept her sister.

"Lily's Garden is for special occasions, Kitty," the older girl chided lightly. "How about choosing somewhere less formal?"

"Lily's Garden is fine," Nereus replied, shrugging.

He turned, flagging down a coach. Neither Julia nor Kitty could stop their jaws from dropping as Nereus opened the cab door for them. He hesitated as they gawked.

"What?"

Julia was the first to recover, offering the young man before her a helpless smile. Of course a carriage ride would be nothing of note to a nobleman, though to her, one simple trip was the equivalent of a day's wages.

With a squeal, Kitty bounded into the horse-drawn vehicle, Julia gently calling out for her to be careful and polite. As the older girl approached, Nereus held out his hand. Julia blushed profusely, accepting the gesture and allowing the young man to help her inside. She felt dirty as she settled down on the polished leather cushion.

"Lily's Garden, please," Nereus called to the driver.

With a lurch, the carriage started forward, beginning its descent to the bridge leading to the Entertainment District. And all the while, Julia wondered if she was dreaming.

Julia had never felt so out of place as the moment she stepped into the restaurant called Lily's Garden. The establishment was every bit as charming as she had imagined it to be, with stained glass windows and gilded trim. Statues, fountains, and exotic plants decorated the solarium in which most of the dining took place, with ornate, wrought-iron tables strategically interspersed between it all. Stately gentlemen and elegant ladies occupied many of the tables—some in groups, many in couples—and more than one quizzical glance was cast in the direction of Julia and Kitty as they entered alongside Nereus.

Nereus at least looked like he belonged here, dressed to perfection in the crisp red and black uniform denoting a member of the city guard, a sword at his hip and the now very obvious signet ring glinting from his right hand. Next to him, clad in a stained and patched dress, Julia felt wretched. She was only thankful that Kitty remained oblivious to it all, looking about the space with the kind of wonder only a child was truly capable of. Meanwhile, Julia kept her head down, trying to ignore the prying stares of the other patrons.

"May we...sit outside?" Julia questioned nervously, her voice hardly more than a whisper.

Nereus shrugged.

"Sure."

The girl watched as the young man spoke with one of the workers and, a moment later, she found herself being seated at a table out in the garden attached to the solarium. Here amidst the foliage, shielded from the view of any moderately curious passers-by, Julia at last allowed herself to relax, taking in the atmosphere of her surroundings. From inside, she could hear a string quartet playing a light, swaying melody, and she closed her eyes, enjoying the pleasant sound and the sweet smell of the wisteria growing on a trellis nearby.

"This really is a place for rich people," Kitty said suddenly, breaking Julia from her reverie.

"Kitty!"

"What? Am I wrong?"

Nereus was silent for several moments, watching the two sisters interact, and Julia froze when she saw his usually stoic face pull into a frown. She bowed her head quickly.

"I am so sorry. I promise to work on her manners."

She peered back up at the young man pensively, but his frown had quickly turned into a look of surprise at her words.

"That's not...I apologize if my reaction alarmed you."

Nereus leaned back in his seat, crossing his arms over his chest.

"I guess I never gave it much thought, but...you work through the afternoon because you can't afford to eat. Am I correct?"

Julia blushed, hanging her head and turning her gaze to her hands in her lap. She fiddled idly with the threadbare fabric.

"Ever since our parents passed, it has been...difficult." Julia glanced up at Kitty who had fallen silent, seeming to sense how serious the conversation had just become. The older girl reached out, smoothing down the wilder strands of hair on her sister's head. "But we're alright, aren't we, Kitty?"

She offered her sister a smile, relaxing slightly as the little girl beamed back. When they turned back to Nereus, the faintest hint of a smile had also crept onto his face. His expression was softer than Julia had so far seen it, and his honey-brown eyes seemed to glimmer. She caught her breath, biting her lower lip as she felt a blush begin to creep onto her face again.

"You two really are close, aren't you?" Nereus mused.

Julia returned the question with an even broader smile than before.

"Well, we're all we have now, so that helps. And besides, I couldn't ask for a better little sister."

She looked at her sister affectionately, and Kitty grinned.

"I couldn't ask for a better *older* sister!" the younger girl responded brightly. The little girl turned back to Nereus, eyes dancing. "Julia's really pretty, too, don't you think, Mr. Nereus?"

Julia let out an exasperated sigh, finally accepting that her face was bound to be red the rest of the day.

"Kitty..."

Across the table, Nereus let out a chuckle of amusement.

"I can't argue," he replied softly.

Julia turned to look at the young man across the table from her, searching his face. He looked genuine and, when she made eye contact with him, he turned to examine a nearby plant, a hint of red creeping up to the tips of his ears. She watched as a play of emotions rippled across his features, like a war between that taciturn demeanor he had started with and the shyness he now displayed.

Julia giggled, a sound that turned Nereus' attention back to the present situation.

"I don't mean any offense," the girl mused, tipping her head curiously at the young man seated across from her, "but...I never thought a noble would take any interest in people like us. Is this something you do regularly or are we special somehow?"

Nereus shrugged, making as though to reply until a waiter arrived with their food. The young man remained quiet and stoic until the waiter had exited back into the main establishment. Then he turned to look at Julia.

"As a knight, I work side-by-side with people from all walks of life. You just seemed like someone who needed a hand. Even as a noble, I can't save the world, but I can make a difference in the part of the world that I touch."

Julia glanced down at the exquisite array of food laid out before her, holding her hands out next to it all and staring at the stains and callouses there. How strange it all felt, this moment in which the fates had deemed that two very different worlds should collide.

"All of Xanom would be a different place if there were more nobles like you...if there were more who were actually...noble," she mused, letting out a sigh.

Nereus leaned back in his seat, casting his gaze up to the sky.

"There are some, but...yes. The world would look very different." He snorted then, casting a somewhat playful glance in Julia's direction. "As long as they didn't all look like me." He took a bite of his food and glanced away again, muttering, "Scare off all the pigeons."

As if to emphasize his otherwise random comment, he tossed a crumb in the direction of a bird hopping about the garden nearby. Kitty giggled, and Julia couldn't help but laugh along with her. She still wasn't sure how she had gotten to this point or what it all meant. It was hard to know if she would ever see Nereus again after this. But still...for this moment, she was happy. Whether he meant it or not, this stranger had made her feel like a princess, and that was a moment worth treasuring.

3

WHAT FRIENDS ARE FOR

31ST DAY OF NOVIS, AE 36

D appled sunlight filtered in through polished windows, highlighting cherry-stained furniture and glossy marble floors, as eighteen-year-old Evanthe Vanko pushed open the heavy double doors leading into the Ivan Barlo Memorial Library. Clad in a crisp black and red uniform, it was clear to anyone who looked at her that she was one of the students associated with the Barlo Research Academy, one of the most prestigious learning institutions on Aurora and the only formal educational facility in the Xanomes Kingdom.

The library sat on the western edge of the campus, flanked by the class building to the north and the dormitory to the south, and was positioned in such a way that sunlight was nearly always filtering in through the windows on one side or another. It made for a cozy place to study, especially in the cooler months as the winter season crept ever closer.

Outside, a stiff wind buffeted the window panes, and Evanthe patted down the loose strands of brown hair that had been pulled out of the twin braids that fell over her shoulders. Then, satisfied with the correction to her appearance, the girl turned her gaze back to the large, open room lined with study tables in the center and balconies of bookshelves along the sides. Her bright brown eyes landed on a lone figure standing at one of the corner bookshelves and, with as much silence as she could manage for someone with so much energy in an echoing hall, the girl headed off in the figure's direction.

Her target, a young male half-elf with long, silvery white hair pulled into a simple ponytail and bright blue eyes, was thankfully fully absorbed in the book he held, and quickly Evanthe bounded up behind him, standing on tiptoe and reaching up to place her hands over his eyes.

"Guess who," she said, giggling as her companion gave a visible start of surprise.

His shoulders relaxed a moment later, and the half-elf let out a longsuffering sigh.

"Hello, Evanthe."

With another laugh, the girl removed her hands and skipped backward ever so slightly as her companion turned to face her.

"Are you finished with classes for the day then?" the half-elf questioned, the book still open in his hands.

Evanthe reached up, pulling the book down so that it was harder for her companion to become distracted by it.

"I am. And you know what that means?"

The half-elf made a face, clearly unsure what the girl was getting at.

"It means...you're free the rest of the day?"

Evanthe let out a dramatic sigh.

"It *means* it's time to celebrate Novistis, Egan! There are already festival stalls set up across campus and the Entertainment District! We should *go*!"

The half-elf, Egan, looked perplexed at the suggestion.

"Right now? The stalls will still be there on the 35th."

Evanthe placed her hands on her hips.

"What, am I interrupting something you can't *possibly* put on hold for the afternoon? Besides, I know you don't like crowds. There are comparatively fewer people out right now than there will be at the end of the month when everyone officially celebrates. And how long have you been in the library anyway? You need to get out and get some fresh air!"

Egan stood listening to the girl's tirade blinking and dazed. Then, when at last she had paused for a breath, the young man glanced down at the book in his hands, sighing helplessly.

"You're relentless. Alright. Let me stop by the dormitory and then I will be ready to go."

Evanthe shook a finger at him.

"You better not be thinking of hiding in your room. Don't think I won't come find you."

At this, the half-elf laughed lightly.

"I take your threats very seriously."

The girl narrowed her eyes at her companion, searching for signs of sarcasm. If he was being sarcastic, however, he was concealing his true intent quite well, offering her a friendly smile before placing the book back on the shelf and turning to head out of the library.

Evanthe scrambled to match Egan's stride, having to double her efforts just to keep up with the tall half-elf.

"Say, you know that Winter's Crest is just around the corner. Do you have any plans for that holiday?"

Egan responded with a faint shake of his head.

"No, I'll just be here studying," he replied.

His tone was clearly meant to just be a statement, but Evanthe could see a pained expression cross his face as he spoke. There was no way she could miss it, and so she quickly continued before her companion could ruminate on his thoughts further.

"Well, my family and I are going to Arcanum for the Winter's Crest Festival there. Would you like to come with me?"

At about the same time she finished her question, Egan pressed the library doors open, a gust of brisk autumn wind sending his long silver hair spiraling in all directions. For a moment, the half-elf blinked, seeming stunned by the combination of the wind and Evanthe's question, and he shielded his eyes from the late afternoon sun as he peered down at the smaller human girl.

"You want me to go to Arcanum with you?" he questioned incredulously.

"Of course! Well, I want you to know you're welcome, at least. Think on it?"

Egan paused a moment before nodding slightly.

"I'll think on it."

A complex play of emotions had surfaced on the half-elf's face, and Evanthe elected to not push further, trotting along at his side as she launched into an explanation of that year's Novistis events. Seeming relieved by the diversion, Egan's shoulders relaxed, and he offered nods and brief, quiet remarks to each of Evanthe's suggestions.

In truth, Evanthe already knew the reason behind Egan's reaction to her offer. She had hoped a friendly invitation would have eased the blow, but as she prattled off energetically about Novistis, internally she was reanalyzing her approach, wondering if there would have been a better way to invite Egan to join her and her family in Arcanum for the Winter's Crest holiday.

Evanthe had heard all the rumors and, over time, Egan had confirmed the vast majority of them. The young half-elf was the illegitimate son of Eustis Barlo, one of the research academy professors. Egan's mother, an elvin consort from the city-state of Avannon in the Free Cities of Nor, could not have cared less about her accidental offspring, and being illegitimate, Egan wasn't entitled to any inheritance from his father's side of the family, either.

The Barlos were a powerful noble family, one of the founding families of the Xanomes Kingdom, and the affair between Egan's father and mother had been a sore embarrassment for them. Professor Eustis had been gracious in providing Egan the same education the other Barlos enjoyed, studying at the Crystal Archives in the Thal Sultanate from the age of twelve until the age of eighteen, at which point his father had provided him with a place at the academy in Xanom. For an illegitimate child of a Xanomite noble, Egan wasn't at all bad off, but it was clear to Evanthe that the topic of holidays and belonging were both sore spots for her companion. They had only known each other for a few months, but already Evanthe had learned that much about him.

The pair soon found themselves in the lobby of the dormitory where those not from Xanom typically boarded. It was quiet here, most of the students scattered off across the city for the end-month festivities. Only a lone receptionist reading a book at the desk nearby was present, and she paid little mind to the pair as they stepped through the doors.

The silence had a melancholy effect on the place. Enchanted lights flickered in ornately wrought lanterns, casting a muted golden glow across plush lounge chairs and intricately carved statues. A bay window at the back of the room looked out onto a manicured garden and artificial pond with a fountain in its center. Egan scanned his surroundings briefly, and Evanthe bit back a frown at the lonely look that temporarily crossed her companion's face.

Determined to lighten the mood, the girl reached up, placing her hands on Egan's shoulders and turning him in the direction of the men's wing of the dormitory.

"You. Go do your thing so we can *go* already," Evanthe commanded playfully.

At first, the half-elf looked startled, but then he offered her a light laugh.

"I'm going, I'm going."

As Evanthe watched Egan disappear through the doors leading into the men's wing, she sighed lightly. There was nothing about that half-elf she didn't like except his complete inability to see the simple truths right in front of him. She liked him. A lot. But that seemed to be an incomprehensible concept for him.

The girl clenched one fist, pumping it once in front of herself as a determined look crossed her face. Alright. It was settled. She would confess her feelings for him today when they went out for the Novistis festivities.

Nearby, a light laugh caught Evanthe's ears, and she turned to see Io Ouranos, one of the older students, looking at her curiously from the direction of the women's wing. Evanthe only knew a little about her, mostly from attending some of the arcane archery classes, the area in which the older woman specialized.

Standing at well over six feet, black hair cut short and slicked back to one side, Io cut an intimidating figure to the vast majority of the first-year students. It didn't help that she was the granddaughter of Arseni Barlo, headmaster of the school and the country's chief arcanist. Still, in this moment, with the look of amusement in Io's warm brown eyes, Evanthe found herself relaxing in the presence of the older woman.

"You look quite determined," Io mused as she walked forward. "Evanthe, am I right?"

The smaller girl blinked back up at her wonderingly.

"You know who I am?" she questioned.

Io inclined her head slightly.

"You're Egan's friend, if I remember correctly."

Evanthe's eyes brightened at the older woman's words.

"You know Egan? I mean, I know you were a Barlo before you got married, but..."

The girl glanced back in the direction Egan had disappeared. How could she say, in an inoffensive way, that she knew the Barlos had all but forgotten about the illegitimate son?

Io followed Evanthe's gaze before sighing slightly, placing her hand over her stomach which was slightly rounded.

"Well," the older woman said, turning toward the door leading out of the dormitory, "most of the Barlos know about Egan. Even someone like me who is only distantly related." She patted Evanthe lightly on the shoulder. "Thanks for being there for him."

The younger girl stared back in surprise as Io headed for the exit. The older woman was halfway out the door before Evanthe found herself running after her.

"Io!" she called, darting through the door and allowing it to thud closed unceremoniously behind her.

The older woman paused, turning to look at the girl clamoring after her.

"Hm?"

For a moment, Evanthe opened and closed her mouth, debating how to say what she meant to say. Then, finally, she blurted, "Why can't Egan celebrate Winter's Crest with the rest of the Barlos?"

Io looked surprised at the younger girl's bluntness, but Evanthe stood her ground, hands clenched at her sides, and eventually the older of the two offered her a sympathetic half-smile.

"The life of a noble comes with a lot of complications, Evanthe," Io replied. "Trust me, Egan is better off not getting swept up in this life."

"But he wants his family!" Evanthe argued back. She swallowed hard when she heard her own voice crack, tears threatening to fall. "He wants...to be wanted...by his family. He won't say it, but I know it. I can see it in his face every time it comes up."

Io shook her head slightly.

"It isn't that easy. If you know what happened, you know why he can't be included. But that's why he needs friends like you."

Evanthe bit her lower lip, working her jaw as she fought the tumultuous emotions inside her.

"It isn't fair," she muttered.

Io inclined her head slightly in acknowledgment.

"Life rarely is."

Seeing that Evanthe offered no further protest, Io patted her once more on the shoulder, then turned and headed off toward the festivities. A few other students milled about, but no one paid any particular mind to Evanthe, and she used her sleeves to wipe away the few teardrops that had escaped down her pale cheeks. Then she turned, pushing the door open and slipping back into the dormitory lobby. She stumbled to a stop, however, when her gaze crossed to the bay window overlooking the garden and fish pond located behind the building.

There, standing in the bay window, was one of the female second-year students. She seemed to have cornered a very perplexed Egan, who leaned against the window panes with every indication that he would like, at that moment, to be able to sink right through them.

"Come on, Egan," the girl was saying. "What do you think? Just you and me? Even if you're not exactly legitimate, you're still a Barlo. We'd make a good pair."

Oh gods, no...

Evanthe was just about to rush to Egan's rescue when she heard him stammer out an apology and an attempt at an incantation, forcing Evanthe to watch helplessly as the half-elf forgot how to aim his spell and accidentally teleported outside, landing squarely in the fish pond just beyond the window. His feet slipped out from under him, and he collapsed with a splash in the opaque water.

The girl who had been trying to woo Egan stood staring in the direction the half-elf had rematerialized, mouth agape, as Evanthe rushed past, throwing open the door leading out to the garden and bounding into the pond. Egan sat stunned and unmoving, chest-deep in the cold water, and he barely blinked as Evanthe came splashing up beside him.

Nearby, several young couples who had been passing their time in the garden laughed loudly.

"Decided to sleep with the fishes, did you, Egan?" one of the boys called, eliciting another fit of giggles from his companions.

"Go hug a morgrim!" Evanthe shouted back, glaring at the group of onlookers.

She wasn't sure how seriously they took her. Certainly, at less than five and a half feet tall, Evanthe didn't look terribly intimidating. Still, she stood rigid and glaring until the other students acquiesced and moved along. Then she turned to Egan, kneeling down in the water in front of him.

"Well..." she said at length, "that was...exciting."

A crimson hue crept into Egan's face and he bowed his head, allowing the loose strands of his long, silvery hair to obscure his cheeks and eyes.

"I'm sorry..." he said at length. "You shouldn't have come in after me."

Evanthe watched as the half-elf struggled to his feet, trying not to slide again on the slick tiles that comprised the bottom of the artificial pond. Quietly, the girl stood up, looping her arm in Egan's and grinning up at him.

"Too late. Now come on. Let's get out of here."

Egan kept his head down as Evanthe helped him out of the pond and back to his room in the dormitory. The moment the door shut behind them, the half-elf dropped to the floor, a small puddle forming around him. He only looked up when Evanthe dropped a towel on his head.

"You had better dry off or you'll get sick," the girl said, placing her hands on her hips and offering her companion a playful smile.

Egan pulled the towel off his head, staring down at it forlornly.

"I'm really such an idiot," he said at length.

Evanthe made a face at his statement.

"No, the idiot is that girl who has no sense of tact or personal space. Who does she think she is, anyway? I've met horseflies with more respect!"

Despite his general mood, Egan couldn't hold back a snort of amusement. The reaction was encouraging to Evanthe, who squatted down in front of him.

"You know what? Festivals are overrated. I'll run home and change clothes, then maybe grab some food and come back here. Wasn't there a book you were wanting to tell me about, anyway?"

A perplexed expression crossed the half-elf's face.

"Are you sure? You seemed to really want to go."

Evanthe shrugged.

"There's always next year. And in any case, what I wanted to do was spend time with *you*." She poked his shoulder for emphasis. "I can do that anywhere. So, I'm going to leave, and you're going to get out of those soaked clothes, and we'll just relax and visit when I get back. Deal?"

She watched as her companion's expression softened, and he nodded.

"Alright. Deal."

With that, the girl stood up and headed for the door leading out of the room. Halfway out, she heard Egan call her name.

"Evanthe...thank you...for being there for me."

She leaned back, offering him a broad smile.

"That's what friends are for."

4

WHEN THE TREE FALLS

15TH DAY OF ZHAYAN, AE 40

Shadows swirled in a twilit valley, wisps of crimson and burnt amethyst that roiled across a barren landscape. Amidst the shadowed terrain was the form of a dark iron doorway set into a jagged hillside. The shape of a gnarled tree had been cast into the metallic barrier, some form of ancient script encircling the outer edges.

For a moment, Typhon Landelius stood in the midst of the shadows, staring blankly as he struggled to discern where he was and why he was there. Stormy blue eyes scanned the rippling darkness, but everything was a disorienting blur. He wasn't aware of the sweat forming at the back of his neck, the dread that burned in the pit of his stomach, or the frantic drum of his own heartbeat in his ears. He was only aware that he didn't want to be here...and that he was dreadfully alone.

"Ty!" a familiar voice cried in the distance.

It was a pained, frantic call, and the man attempted to whirl about in the direction of the sound. His movement was sluggish, like swimming through tar, and he stumbled.

"Dion!" he tried to yell back.

His voice sounded muffled, as though he were a thousand feet below water. And the more he tried to yell, the harder it became to breathe.

"Help!" another familiar voice called out.

"Cetus! Acastus! Elek! Where are you?!"

With each name Ty called out, it seemed that the shadows grew darker and more corporeal, clawing their way up the man's form.

By now, the shadows had taken hold of Ty's arms, and he fought against their grasp as they tried to pull him toward the ground. Or...to what had once been ground.

Ty glanced down, attempting to focus in on the entity that was trying to overtake him, and he froze. The surface below his feet was a dark crimson that rippled with each step. And in the distance, a disembodied chant began to emerge from the shadows.

"Why you? Why not us? Why you?"

Ty felt his body begin to tremble, and his heart hammered violently in his chest. He sank to his knees, down toward the crimson pool and clawing shadows. He gripped either side of his head, squeezing his eyes tightly shut as he fought the tears that threatened to fall. The strength in his body left him, and he bowed forward, curling as much into himself as possible.

I'm sorry. I'm sorry I couldn't do more. I'm so sorry.

Fingers of cold dread incarnate engulfed him, making his heart lurch. It was physically painful, but there was something deeper there, too. Something he couldn't quite place his finger on.

Ty awoke with a start, gasping for the breath he hadn't even realized he was holding as beads of cold sweat slid down his angular jaw, soaking the unruly, dark brown hair that framed his face. Even without moving, he could feel that his clothes and bedding were drenched in sweat, clinging fiercely to his trembling body.

Above him, late morning light streamed through an open window, a mild and pleasant breeze filtering into the room and carrying with it the sounds and smells of early autumn. In the distance, Ty could hear children laughing and birds chirping. Somewhere outside, a dog barked, and two men greeted each other like brothers. It was the sound of life, and joy, but to Ty it all seemed impossibly far away.

Slowly, stiffly, the man rolled onto his side before pushing himself to sit up. His gaze landed on a set of plate armor piled in the nearby corner, and quickly he averted his eyes. The sight haunted him, but somehow he couldn't bring himself to get rid of it. And so his armor sat there like a ghost, mocking his weakness.

Eager to escape his memories and the cold, sticky sensation of a night's worth of sweat, Ty grabbed a fresh set of clothes and headed outside. He paused and flinched as the bright sunlight hit his face, and for a moment he stood blinking as the sights and sounds around him began to take form.

It had been just over two months since that fateful day, the day that almost all of Ty's friends and comrades had been slaughtered by morgrim just outside of the Iron Vault. It was supposed to have just been a short survey mission. Instead, monsters born of pure evil and corruption had descended on them in a cascade of nightmarish horror. Just keeping himself alive had been a feat. And now, he was all but alone.

Where once he had considered himself a career man, married to the idea of being a knight, Ty now found himself unable to even lift a blade, and the night-mares that haunted him made sleep practically impossible. Living in his home city of Xanom had become unbearable. There was always that question, spoken or otherwise, that pervaded every conversation: "When will you just get over it?"

Ty had quickly come to realize that there was no "getting over it." His experience had become a part of him, somehow changed him, and though he didn't fully understand what was happening or why he felt the way he did, the reality remained that he would never be the same person he was before that moment.

It was for this reason that Ty had set out on a journey deep into the Rahan Wilds. He would rather continue to face the morgrim—the creatures that slaughtered his brigade—than face the incessant questions and prying eyes that existed in the Xanomes Kingdom. His travels had led him here, to the citadel of Veshiri, to live among the Sinti. Though the change of scenery had done nothing to soothe the nightmares, the relaxed atmosphere of Veshiri and the Sinti people had been a welcome relief for Ty. There was no prying, no questions of why he couldn't just get over the tragedy and move on. The Sinti were a free people, unmoved by the hardships of living in the Rahan Wilds not because they felt no fear or sadness but because they embraced it in a way that Ty could only admire. He hoped that in time he would learn to do the same.

As he walked toward the nearby spring, Ty's gaze swept across his surroundings. The citadel of Veshiri was nestled into a secluded hollow, framed by the Dragonspine Mountains to the west and the forests of the Rahan Wilds to the east. Fresh spring water cascaded down the mountainside into the citadel below, and the Sinti who had built the settlement had expertly diverted the water into a series of pools, irrigation channels, and even motes outside their multiple layers of hewn-log walls. All around, Ty could hear the soft gurgle of water, and somehow it was soothing amidst the fog that lingered inside his mind.

It was late morning and the beginning of the month of harvest, Zhayan, so by the time Ty wandered his way to the pool used for bathing and washing clothes, there was no one present. This was a relief for the knight, who had yet to become accustomed to the more...communal...culture of the Sinti.

Taking one more glance around to make sure he was alone, the man stripped off his clothes and stepped into the crystalline spring water. The chill bit at his skin, but it was a welcome relief after a night of fitful sleep, if sleep was even what such an experience could be called.

The memory of the previous night's terrible visions made Ty instinctively reach for his sweat-soaked bed clothes, dunking them in the water and scrubbing them against one of the smooth stones nearby, evidence of generations of Sinti who had done their daily cleaning at this spot for well over a thousand years. He watched as his own arms and hands worked the clothes against the stone, in and out of the water, scrubbing mercilessly. He knew they were his arms and hands, but they didn't feel like they were a part of him. Sinti tattoos had been traced in intricate patterns along his sun-tanned skin, rust-red marks hiding—but only barely—the scars that riddled his body. It was a weak attempt at forgetting the events of that fateful day. He knew that. But anything was worth trying at this point. Anything to ease the nightmares and the guilt, that pain in his heart that would never let him find peace.

Ty hadn't even realized how vigorous his washing had become until a feminine voice nearby caught his ear.

"I think it's sufficiently dead," the voice giggled.

Ty's head snapped up at the sound as he instinctively sank deeper into the water, trying to hide himself. He blinked up into the fair face of a young woman with short, raven black hair and doe-like eyes. She was holding an empty basket and watching him with amused curiosity.

The cold spring water suddenly felt very warm, and Ty's vision swam as he sank further into the water.

"Abey, could you please...just..."

He hadn't heard his own voice crack like that since he was a young boy, and Ty very much considered diving under the water and not ever coming back up. Unable to speak further, he made a circular motion with one hand, indicating his request for the woman to turn around so as not to see him completely naked. And no matter what, there was no way he could look her in the eye.

By now, the icy spring water was at Ty's chin as he curled up into a corner among the natural rock formations at the water's edge. Somewhere nearby, he heard Abey giggle.

"If I must. At the very least, don't drown yourself at my expense."

Ty listened to the light shift of the young woman's feet, and he glanced up to see that she had indeed turned her back toward him, one arm cradling the empty basket, the other braced against the curve of her hip. The moment Ty was certain that Abey wasn't going to see anything she shouldn't, he made a dive for his clean clothes, hurriedly dressing despite having no chance to towel off.

As he tugged his shirt over his torso, Ty cast a furtive glance back at the young Sinti woman waiting nearby. She had politely kept her back turned to him, gaze cast up to the trees that swayed back and forth in the gentle breeze, but the amused smile from before had yet to leave her lips. It wasn't the first time Ty had seen that look. All of the Sinti seemed amused by how private he was.

"You should see the *pahin* at the bathing pool," he had overheard one of the Sinti say once. "You'll never see someone bristle up and hide so fast! If I ran that fast, I could catch anything I hunted with my bare hands!"

Pahin, Ty had learned, was the Sinti word for "porcupine," and it had since become his nickname in Veshiri. It wasn't an insult though. Not among these people. Ty had quickly come to realize it was common for the Sinti to playfully call each other by nicknames associated with animals and their characteristics. And he could hardly deny how much he panicked and ran for cover every time someone saw him exposed. While the Sinti treated the body as just another part of nature, Ty's Xanomite upbringing could not seem to grasp the concept, and less still around Abey.

Abey wasn't a citizen of Veshiri, having only arrived at the beginning of the harvest month. Only members of the Natsiyi tribe kept dwellings here, and Abey was a member of the Soyala. But that was one of the interesting things about the Sinti. Though they carried their tribal names proudly, in the end, they all still treated each other like family. There was no vying for power or wealth in their culture. Not on the whole, at least. And Abey was by far one of the friendliest people Ty had met in his time here in the Sinti citadel. She seemed to have taken a particular interest in him, and despite his best efforts, Ty found himself at a loss for words in the young woman's presence. And now here he had been, completely naked right in front of her. He would have rather faced down a morgrim.

"Are you just enjoying the view or should I call a healer to revive you?"

Abey's teasing voice broke Ty from his thoughts, and he felt his face begin to burn with the suggestion.

"Sorry, you can turn around now."

The young woman spun lightly to face him, quirking an eyebrow as she eyed him up and down.

"If you're trying to hide anything, maybe wet clothes aren't the best way to go about it," she said, giggling as she motioned up and down with one index finger.

Cautiously, Ty glanced down at himself. Indeed, though his clothes had been dry before, his rush to put them on without toweling off had left them about as soaked as the clothes he had been washing. The light cotton fabric clung to every rise and fall in his body, which had for over a decade been trained in the athletic pursuits as a member of the Xanomes military. The man felt his face grow even hotter, and he slumped down onto a nearby rock, covering his burning cheeks with his hands.

"Kill me now," he muttered.

His embarrassment was short-lived as he felt a wicker basket land lightly over his head. He glanced up quickly, peering at Abey through the gaps in the weave. She was now standing with both hands on her hips, that same gentle, laughing smile lighting up her cherubic face. The warm, late-morning sun glowed against her copper skin. To Ty, she looked radiant. Too radiant, actually, and he quickly diverted his gaze.

"Why are you even here?" the knight muttered, pulling the upside-down basket further down to hide his face.

He flinched as Abey reached for the basket, lifting it so she could look him in the eyes.

"I went looking for you to ask for help in the rice fields and someone said you came this direction. I thought I might catch you before you undressed, but I can't say I'm disappointed in being wrong."

Between Abey's playful ribbing and proximity, Ty felt dizzy, and quickly he stood up to put some distance between himself and the young woman.

"Quit teasing me," he grumbled. "I'll help in the field."

Half blind with embarrassment, the knight took off at a hurried pace toward the steps leading up the cliffside to the terraces where the rice fields grew. Somewhere amidst the haze, he could hear Abey trotting along lightly behind him.

"Can I at least have my basket back?" he heard her say laughingly.

Ty paused, only now realizing he had taken off with the basket still perched like a hat. Now more embarrassed than before, he lifted the object off his head and held it out, adamantly avoiding eye contact.

He felt the basket's weight lift away from his hand and waited until he heard Abey's footsteps move off again. Then he followed. Quietly, Ty trudged along behind the Sinti woman as they climbed the carved stone steps leading up to the rice terraces overlooking the citadel, but he paused in surprise as Abey fell back into step with him at the top.

"We'll work on that section over there today," the young woman said, pointing to a spot where the mountain springs from the crags above cascaded into a crystal clear waterfall that tumbled across the rice terraces and into the large hollow that housed Veshiri below.

Ty followed the woman's gaze. He could see the citadel better from this vantage point. A thousand years lay between Veshiri's founding and now, and the knight couldn't help but wonder at the sight of it all. All of the permanent dwellings were built along the trunks of the enormous trees that grew in the hollow, rising up into the sturdy branches and laced together here and there with bridges of rough-hewn plank and hempen rope.

The falls that wound their way down the mountainside eventually found their way to the floor of the hollow, shaped into the channels and motes he had passed by earlier on his way to the bathing pool. The rice terraces had been cut into a series of natural ledges above the village, the water from the falls expertly channeled to provide irrigation to these upper fields as well.

Both above and below, Ty could see the people of Veshiri going about their daily lives: the villagers hard at work tending their crops and livestock, the children playing in and jumping across the myriad of streams, the friends and comrades who laughed together and the lovers who embraced each other in the mild, late-harvest sun. It all felt a world away, but it was a world that Ty desperately longed for.

"Ty?"

Abey's gentle voice broke the knight out of his thoughts, his gaze snapping up quickly to meet hers.

"Sorry. Don't mind me."

Ty rolled up the legs of his pants. Abey watched him silently for a moment before turning and stepping into one of the pools where the rice grew. Ty moved to mimic her, gathering the ripe grain as his bare feet sank into the muddy soil beneath. Here and there, fish darted away from his movement, startling him back to reality whenever his mind began to wander.

It never ceased to amaze Ty, the way in which the Sinti lived. They were the most harmonious people he had ever met, in tune with man and beast alike. Little was wasted in Veshiri, and there was always a symbiotic pattern to the Sinti methods of living.

The rice fields were a good example. Rice, Abey had explained once, grew well in wet environments, so the terraces in which the Sinti cultivated it were kept flooded to keep the weeds away. Fish were added to these pools to eat the bugs that would harm the plants, fertilizing the water in the process. The fish also served as a source of food when the time for harvest came. Once the harvest had passed, the ducks that were kept in the village below would be moved to these pools, to fertilize and clean in preparation for next year's planting. It was all so different from the rigid, organized methods of farming back in Xanom.

A frown crossed Ty's face at the thought. Thinking of Xanom made him think of his old brigade, and thinking of that...

Ty yanked up a nearby plant by the roots, a desperate and feeble attempt to conceal how his hands had begun to shake. Little was lost on Abey, though. The young woman paused in her work, glancing up at Ty and watching him carefully. The man turned his back to her. He didn't want her to see him that way: weak...pathetic...unable to face *himself*, much less his kingdom or the beautiful woman who had sacrificed so much of her time to help him feel at home in this foreign place.

He froze when a soft hand came to rest on his arm.

"Would you come sit with me for a moment?" Abey's voice echoed in his ears. "I would like the company."

Still avoiding eye contact, Ty gave a faint nod, and Abey led the way to a large stone at the edge of a waterfall that cascaded down into the village below. Seemingly without a care in the world, Abey breathed in deeply and stretched.

"At the rate we're going, we'll have everything harvested before the end of the week!" the young woman mused, looking pleased. "You've really been a great help."

Ty grunted in reply, only half present and waging an internal war against his own anxious thoughts. He glanced up sharply, however, when Abey plopped down on the stone next to him, so close he could feel her body heat. All thought of Xanom and the Iron Vault faded, replaced with a different variety of overwhelming panic. Ty startled so quickly at Abey's movement that it was all he could do to keep from falling backward into the nearby stream. Still, Abey's expression remained solemn as she studied him closely.

"You've looked troubled all morning," the woman said, leaning forward to get a better look at Ty's face. "Did you have another nightmare?"

The knight blinked back at her with visible surprise.

"How...?"

Abey pursed her lips, eyebrows narrowing in concern.

"You mentioned shortly after we met that you had experienced a nightmare. You tried to pass it off as nothing, but you get this haunted look in your eyes whenever you've had one. Or did you think I wouldn't notice?"

Ty buried his face in his hands, half in an attempt to keep Abey from assessing his soul further, half in an attempt to hide the growing pain in his heart.

"Pathetic, aren't I?" the knight muttered at length. "I know. I should be thankful that I survived, should just get over it and move on, but..."

His voice caught in his throat, his spoken thoughts crashing down the cliffside and out of reach with the rush of the waterfall. There was the briefest pause before Abey's gentle voice broke the quiet.

"No," she replied softly, turning her gaze east in the direction of the forest and the dangerous, forbidding landscape that made up the Rahan Wilds. "You cannot chastise the tree that falls in the storm and say, 'You should have been stronger,' hoping it will find a way to go back to growing tall and strong, nor can you tell the river, 'You must return to your previous course,' when the flood has battered its banks. Life's sorrows inevitably shape us. We can become something new if we choose, but we can never go back to what we were before the storm. And there is no shame in that. That is the natural course of life on the mortal plane."

Ty lifted his head, feeling his heart skip as his gaze met Abey's. The sensation made him feel ashamed, and he quickly turned away, focusing on the distant horizon.

"Those are pretty words," Ty sighed. "But what happens when the tree that falls was the one that should be left standing? What if the tree left standing isn't the strongest, just foolishly lucky?"

Somewhere in the back of his mind, the knight knew that wasn't what Abey had been getting at, but the thought dogged him all the same.

What do you do when the people who died were the ones who deserved to live the most?

For a moment, silence fell between the knight and the Sinti woman, the gurgle of the nearby waterfall serving as the only sound to break the stillness. Then, all of a sudden, Abey spoke.

"Would you be willing to do an experiment with me?" the woman questioned, smiling gently up at him.

Ty narrowed his eyes, at first offering only a cautious glance.

"What kind?"

"Just a thought experiment."

The man considered the proposal, then nodded hesitantly.

"Alright. What do you have in mind?"

"I want you to close your eyes."

Ty glanced over at her suspiciously, but Abey only sat there in patient silence, a light breeze wafting across the rice paddies and ruffling her feather-like hair. Finally, Ty sighed and did as he was bade.

"Now what?"

Though he couldn't see her, he could hear Abey shift, and he was keenly aware of her presence. Just as he was beginning to feel panic again, however, her words caught him off guard.

"Tell me, Ty. Whose place would you take in that last battle?"

The young man gave a start of surprise, his eyes snapping open to stare at the woman in front of him, but before he could get a good look at her face, Abey reached out, placing a hand over his eyes so that all he could see was darkness once more.

"Whose place, Ty? Who do you want to die for?"

Ty swallowed hard, unsure how to distinguish between the panic of his memories and the panic of the soft, feminine presence so close in front of him. His answer came in a hoarse whisper.

"Dion. Dion Aegis."

Abey let out a sound akin to a hum of approval, and Ty almost wished he had remained silent a moment longer as the woman slid her hand away from him. Something about that touch was mesmerizing, and he suddenly felt so much more alone with its absence.

"Alright," came Abey's voice. "You've died, Ty. You took Dion's place in that battle. He's alive. You're not. But you can still hear him from the Sea of Stars. What do you think he is saying?"

Ty paused again, unsure where Abey was going with this imagined scenario.

"Thank you?" he offered hesitantly.

"No," the woman replied, her voice gentle but firm. "He is saying, 'Why me? Why did you die and not me? Why am I alive and not you?'"

Ty felt his breath catch in his throat as he heard his own words spoken back to him. For a moment, Abey remained quiet, then she continued.

"For this moment, you can reply to him from the Sea of Stars. What do you want to say to him as you hear those questions?"

Reflexively, Ty clenched his hands into fists on his knees, working his jaw as he fought back the emotions that churned inside him. He flinched when he felt Abey's hands come to rest on his, a soft, reassuring touch amidst the turmoil.

"Let it out, Ty," came her gentle voice. "Cry. Scream if you need to. You're in a place where no one will harm you or criticize you for who you are or what you feel. Tell Dion, Ty. Tell him what you feel. Answer his question. Why was he allowed to live when you were not?"

As Abey's voice reached Ty's ears, it felt as though something inside him cracked. His voice came out in a tremor as tears began to slide down his face like the waterfalls that cascaded down the mountain and through the village below.

"Don't..." Ty sobbed, bowing his head under the weight of the emotions that were flooding out of him. "Don't do that to me. I only ever wanted you to have a future. My friend, you had so much life ahead of you. You deserved that chance. I would give my life a thousand times over to give you the future you deserved. So please...don't waste your life mourning for me. Don't throw away the chance I wanted to give you."

His voice felt distant, and for a moment, Ty didn't even realize it had been him speaking. But as his own words settled in his ears, his eyes blinked open, and he looked up into Abey's face. She gave him a soft, reassuring smile before leaning forward, until all Ty could see was a pair of doe-like brown eyes.

"If Dion could speak to you now, don't you think he would say the same?"

Ty's head felt as heavy as his heart, and without thinking, he let his forehead come to rest against Abey's shoulder.

"I miss them," he choked out. "I miss them so much. And their families...their families are alone because I wasn't strong enough to bring them home. How am I supposed to face that? How am I supposed to face *me*?"

Gently, Abey slid her arms around Ty's back, resting her chin against his shoulder.

"In the forest," she said softly, "when a great tree falls, its loss is acutely felt. It leaves behind a gap in the forest, but in its loss, the animals may find refuge, a seed may find sunlight, and the weak but foolishly lucky tree may find the nutrients it needs to become strong and carry on the legacy of its companion. But no seed naturally sprouts overnight, nor do wounds heal quickly of their own accord. You don't have to find all your answers right now. My only question to you is this: are you willing to become something new?"

5

A SHIELD FOR XANOM

12TH DAY OF OYNIS, AE 43

"Dismissed!"

With a chorus of affirmative shouts, ranks of men and women in crisp red and black uniforms disbursed from the training yard, heading out on their daily rounds with spears in their hands and swords strapped to their hips. The low hum of excited chatter broke through the still morning air, some discussing the day's assignments, some retelling tales of the previous night's escapades.

Among them, a young man of barely twenty moved leisurely through the crowds, the wind gently tousling his already unruly dark brown hair. Occasionally, a greeting of, "Morning, Percy!" could be heard from other guards as they crossed paths with him, and with a smile and a wave, he greeted them back, honey-brown eyes warm and welcoming. To any unfamiliar onlooker, he was just one of many young men among the ranks of the Xanomite city guard, handsome enough but, by appearance, not exceptional when alongside his peers. Only those who knew him would recognize him as Persius Lex, heir to one of the noble houses of the Xanomes Kingdom.

Now past the training yard entrance, the young knight found his way to a group of three others who waved him over when they spotted his approach.

"Ready to go?" the oldest of the three questioned, hardly waiting for Percy to come within earshot.

The young knight nodded.

"Ready."

"Alright. Fall out!"

Quietly, Percy glanced about at his comrades. Two of the three were his peers who had been knighted at the same time as him: a stern-faced woman named Brionna Acrisius and a shorter man named Denis Zoltar who made up in personality what he lacked in height. The older of the three was their team captain, a man named Estes Ophion. Percy knew very little about his three companions other than that they all hailed from the upper districts. And today, that fact was abundantly clear.

"It really is unfortunate that we're the new kids in town," Denis sighed as the four made their way past the buildings of the Military District and down the ramp leading to the Lower Ward. "I hate these rounds. The Lower Ward is always so dirty."

"What are you, a princess?" Percy smirked.

"Pretty sure the princesses aren't half as afraid of dirt as Denis," Brionna laughed in reply.

The young knight made a face at his two comrades.

"Yeah, yeah, laugh it up." Denis turned to look at Percy. "How are you so calm about having to work in the Lower Ward? You're a noble!"

Percy shrugged, casting his gaze up toward the clear blue sky as they walked.

"I used to help my mother in her flower garden when I was young. A little dirt never hurt me. But don't worry, we'll protect you. Wouldn't want to mess up those pretty little fingers of yours."

The sarcasm in Percy's voice was palpable, and Denis huffed indignantly as Brionna and Estes began to laugh.

"Oh, shut up."

The crunch of rough soil beneath Percy's boots was the first indication that the group was reaching the edge of the Lower Ward, and soon they had come to the ramp that wound down the hill from the Military District to the fields and thatch-roof cottages that marked the poorest parts of the city.

Xanom was a unique place, a settlement built upon a series of hills with sturdy walls surrounding them and the valleys that lay between. Long stone bridges spanned the distance between the hills, connecting the cobblestone streets and allowing members of the upper districts to pass over the Lower Ward without having to face the reality of what existed there. Still, narrow dirt roads wound their way down the hillsides from obscure corners and side streets, connecting the Lower Ward with the upper districts, only a faint reminder that they were one people despite being part of two very different worlds.

The Lower Ward was mostly farmland, and as Percy walked, only vaguely aware of his companions' banter, he observed the other people around him. Farmers in patched, thread-bare clothes worked the fields that flanked the tiny cottages they called home. The youngest children played in the narrow yards surrounding the ramshackle dwellings, some chasing chickens or each other, some quietly stacking rocks into little towers. A few of the older children sparred with sticks, buckets on their heads as though they were knights in plate armor. Here and there, old women sat in rocking chairs set just outside the doors of their cottages, churning butter or darning worn-out clothing while keeping a watchful eye on the nearby youngsters. It was a rough life, Percy thought, but charming in its simplicity. Certainly, it was different from the bustle and panache of the noble world in which he had grown up.

The group had just come around a bend in the road when Percy caught sight of an old woman sitting at a rickety table outside one of the cottages. A few odds and ends had been organized neatly about the table's scratched surface, possibly for the purpose of sale. For a moment, Percy paid no mind to the scene in front of him. The common people often set up such stands to collect a little extra income. He did pause, however, when he caught sight of something else: tears.

The old woman looked thin and fragile, slumped in her seat and staring for-lornly at the items set up on the table in front of her. The light of the early morning sun glinted off tears that streamed down her face, and she seemed to not notice the small contingent of guards coming up the road toward her. Before Percy knew it, his feet were carrying him in her direction.

"Percy?" came Brionna's confused voice.

He ignored the question in her tone, coming to a stop in front of the table and the old woman. There was a moment of pause as the old woman shifted, seeming to come out of a fog, but she gave a start of surprise when she noticed Percy standing in front of her.

"Oh, good day, officer," she said, hastily reaching for the few trinkets scattered about the table. "I suppose I've been out here too long. Wasn't meaning to be a nuisance. I should return home now. My apologies."

The woman's hands were clearly trembling, and as she reached for a small silver locket on the table, Percy quietly reached out his hand, gently placing it on her frail one. She froze, glancing up at him tentatively.

"You haven't done anything illegal," he reassured her. "People set up these stands all the time. I just noticed you were crying. Is everything alright?"

The old woman blinked back up at him for a moment, then lowered her gaze to the table and the items resting on its aged surface.

"It's...fine."

Percy's eyes narrowed. He had always been fairly good at reading people, and the demeanor of this woman was much more that of someone who didn't want to bother anyone else than someone who was truly "fine."

Rather than push the subject at the moment, Percy crouched down closer to her eye level, not wanting to tower over her with his spear and sharp uniform. He reached out, gently lifting the silver locket from the table.

"Do you mind if I ask your name?" he questioned, glancing up at the old woman.

She stared back at him curiously for a moment, then nodded.

"Aegis. Callia...Aegis."

Percy returned her answer with a bright smile.

"It's a pleasure to meet you. May I call you Callia? My name is Percy, by the way."

The old woman blushed slightly, and Percy had to bite back a grin of amusement as she placed her frail hands over her cheeks.

"Oh, yes, I suppose, if you'd like," she answered. "I haven't been called Callia since...since my husband..."

The blush in her face faded, and the tears returned. Percy's eyebrows knit in concern. Somehow, he knew what she was getting at without her having to say anything else.

"I'm sorry," he said softly, glancing back down at the trinkets on the table. "That was insensitive of me."

The old woman shook her head, wiping at the tears streaming down her wrinkled face.

"It's fine. I miss him, of course, but that's not really..."

Her voice trailed away as she seemed to become lost in thought again. Quietly, Percy flipped open the locket. The item was empty, but he could see a set of initials engraved in the tarnished surface.

"Forgive me for being pushy, but I get the sense you're not as fine as you would like to seem," he said, glancing over at Callia. "Has something else happened?"

The old woman nodded faintly.

"I will be losing my home tomorrow," she answered, her tone grieved but resigned. "I haven't been able to afford the rent since my husband passed away a year ago. My son passed away three years ago, so I don't have anyone left who can help me. I wish my old body would cooperate, or that I had some skill that could earn a living wage, but..." She glanced back at the items on the table. "Anyway, I won't be needing those anymore. I've been offered a place with a neighbor, so there's that. I just thought I would sell the last of my possessions. At least it will make leaving easier."

Percy's heart ached as he listened to the woman's words, partially speech, but partially a barely contained sob. Subconsciously, the young knight clenched his hands into fists. It didn't feel right. His mind spun. Three years ago...

"You don't have to answer this if you don't want to, but..." Percy said at length. "How did your son die?"

Callia wrung her hands together as the tears began to flow freely down her face.

"The morgrim," she choked out. "The morgrim took my boy at the Iron Vault."

It was just as Percy had suspected. Three years ago. He had heard about the tragedy. His father, Nereus, had been tasked with aiding in the recovery mission. Over three quarters of the knights on that mission had died. And it didn't take a diviner to understand what Callia Aegis was getting at. Her son had been one of those fallen knights.

Percy's body trembled with barely contained rage at the thought. Callia's son had given everything for the kingdom. But what had they given her in return?

He was so lost in thought that it took a moment for him to realize that Estes was calling his name. He looked up abruptly when a sharp, "Persius Lex!" reached his ears. Percy wasn't sure who was more startled by the outburst: him or Callia. The old woman turned terrified, wondering eyes on him at the sound of his given name.

"You're..." she barely squeaked.

Percy sighed, standing up straight and giving her a sympathetic smile.

"Don't worry," he said gently, tucking his rage away for later assessment. "I'm just Percy to you."

He gave her a playful wink, relaxing slightly when he saw the tension in her shoulders lessen and the vaguest hint of a smile reach her wrinkled face.

"Thank you for speaking with me, sir," Callia said, bowing her head. "Your kindness puts this old heart at ease, at least."

Percy gave her a nod, then glanced over at his bewildered companions.

"Well," he said, reaching into his pocket and pulling out a few gold coins, "I need to continue my rounds, but I'd like to buy what you have here. Would you mind holding onto it for me until I can pick it up tomorrow?"

Callia blinked back at Percy for a moment before looking down at the items on the table, just the locket and a handful of dented tin dishes.

"Are you sure? I mean...you're nobility, and..."

Percy slid the coins across the table toward her, the metallic clatter cutting her protest short.

"I'm sure." He smiled reassuringly. "I promise, I'll see you again tomorrow."

Then, with another wink, Percy turned to continue on his rounds. Inside, however, he seethed.

The door to the Lex manor all but crashed open with the force that Percy put behind his entry, startling his parents, Nereus and Julia, from their evening tea in the nearby sitting room.

"Percy?" Nereus called out, watching his son march by at a determined pace.

"I need your law books," the younger man called back, never faltering in his stride.

He could hear movement behind him, but still Percy kept marching, up the stairs and off to his father's study. Inside the room, he headed straight for a set of shelves containing copies of the heavy books that dictated the laws of the Xanomes Kingdom. Percy paused, scanning the spines of the aged volumes, and then he grimaced. He knew the basics of the Xanomite laws. Every knight did, especially those like him who had trained specifically for city defense. But if he was going to find something the average knight didn't know about, he would have to go through every single book to do so. And this...this was a much bigger task than he had anticipated.

The young man drew in a deep breath, closing his eyes as he tried to settle the anger and heartbreak that burned inside him. When he opened his eyes again, he was calmer. Then, he reached up, grabbing a handful of books off the shelf and stacking them up on the desk in the center of the room. He was hauling his fourth pile from the shelf to the desk when his father walked in, eyeing him curiously.

"Percy?" Nereus questioned. "What's gotten into you?"

The younger man pulled a fifth pile of books into his arms, somehow finding an empty spot on the desk to stack them with their brethren. He listened to the clunk as the heavy tomes came in contact with the desk's solid wooden surface, stared at the embossed leather cover of the lawbook closest to him, then looked up at his father.

"There's an old woman in the Lower Ward," he replied, trying to bite back the ache in his voice. "Her name is Callia Aegis. Her son was a knight who died three years ago at the Iron Vault. She lost her husband last year. She's disabled and can't work the fields, so she's ended up in debt. The debt collectors are going to evict her tomorrow. I know I can't do anything to stop it myself, but I want to see if there are any laws that could protect her."

Nereus leaned in the doorway, crossing his arms over his chest as he stared off into the distance. When he did speak, his voice was pained and quiet.

"That's one of the harsh realities of this life, Percy," his father said solemnly. "No matter how hard we try, we can't save everyone. This Mrs. Aegis...does she have a place to go after they evict her?"

Percy's shoulders sagged, and he sat heavily in the chair at his father's desk.

"One of the other families has offered to let her stay with them," he answered. "But the debt collectors are going to take everything. It just can't be legal...and it's definitely not right."

Percy glanced up at the sound of his father's approaching footsteps. Nereus placed a hand on his shoulder, giving his son a bemused smile.

"Well," he said, tapping one of the stacks of books, "it looks like you have some homework, then. I know better than to tell you it's a fruitless endeavor. You've always been stubborn. I'll have one of the maids bring you some coffee. You're going to need it."

He gave Percy's shoulder a light pat, then strode out of the room, waving over his shoulder as he went. Percy smiled after his father, then turned back to the stacks of lawbooks surrounding him.

"Thanks."

Exhaustion was evident in Percy's face as he hurried to the barracks the next morning, but his stride was one of a man who was both confident and determined. It had taken all night, but he had found what he was looking for. Now he could only hope he wasn't too late. The morning's address seemed to last a lifetime, and Percy realized he hadn't felt so anxious since he was a child. When at last the morning team had been dismissed, the young knight hurried toward the lieutenant holding the list of the day's assignments.

"Sir, I would like to request a brief reprieve from duties today," Percy said, keeping his shoulders straight and attempting an air of calm confidence. "I have updated information on the situation with Mrs. Callia Aegis, down in the Lower Ward."

The lieutenant's eyebrows knit together, visibly confused.

"Mrs. Aegis?"

The officer seemed to be thinking for a moment before he flipped through his list. He paused several pages in, then glanced up at Percy.

"You aren't on those rounds today." The lieutenant looked even more confused now. "Commander Rolan has already left to deal with that situation."

Percy could feel his heart drop at the mention of Commander Rolan, and he found his feet moving long before his mind caught up with them.

"Forgive me, Lieutenant!" the young knight exclaimed, racing for the gate leading out of the training yard. "I won't be gone long!"

The clip of his boots striking the cobblestone street echoed like war drums in Percy's ears as he dashed toward the ramp leading down from the Military District to the Lower Ward. All the while, his heart raced. He had to stop Commander Rolan before he made it to Callia's house. Of all the people to send after an old woman, why had they sent *him*?

Commander Rolan was a member of House Avram, a family known for their combat skills and no-nonsense personalities. But Rolan Avram was worse than most. The man had no compassion to speak of, and he did not have a reputation for being gentle.

The image of Callia Aegis' frail form in the hands of someone as gruff as Rolan Avram reignited the fury that Percy had felt the day before, and his legs burned beneath him as he charged down into the Lower Ward.

Heads turned as he darted past. He ignored them. Then there!

Up ahead, Percy could see the lonely little cottage surrounded by empty fields puddled from a late-night rain. Callia was sitting in her rickety old chair, head in her gnarled, bony hands as though waiting for the end to come. Percy could see, too, the rigid form of Commander Rolan leading a company of knights and debt collectors down the path toward the cottage.

Callia glanced up at the sound of people approaching, and when she spotted Commander Rolan, the old woman seemed to shrink into herself. Even from this distance, Percy could see the terror in her face. No one wanted to cross paths with Rolan Avram; not a knight, and definitely not a frail old woman.

As he ran, Percy's eyes darted across the surrounding area. He had to get to Callia before Commander Rolan, but the only way to do that would be to cut across the fields. He was guaranteed to get muddy, but it couldn't be helped.

Gravel skidded and hissed as the young knight took a hard left turn into the barren fields, ignoring the feeling of mud spraying up the back of his uniform as he bolted over the uneven furrows. Reaching the cottage just ahead of Commander Rolan, Percy skidded to a stop between the officer and the old woman, throwing his arms open as though to shield Callia from the cruelty that had been headed her way.

Commander Rolan and his company came to an abrupt halt at Percy's appearance, clearly surprised, and for a moment the world seemed to still. It was then that Percy realized how hard he was breathing, and how much his legs burned from his mad dash from the barracks to Callia's home.

"Percy?"

Callia's voice was timid and confused as it echoed up from behind. Percy cast a reassuring smile over his shoulder at her, then straightened his posture and turned a sharp gaze on Commander Rolan. By now, the older man seemed to have recovered from his surprise, and he crossed his arms over his broad chest, eyes narrowing as he stared at the young man's disheveled form.

"Persius," he stated coldly, "what is the meaning of this?"

It took all the willpower Percy had to still his heavy breathing and racing heart as he stared back at Commander Rolan.

"You can't take Mrs. Aegis' belongings, or remove her from her home," he began, but Commander Rolan cut him off.

"The law doesn't run on sentiment, boy," the older man snapped. "Now either get out of my way or get out of the military."

He took a step forward, meaning to push past Percy, but the young knight took a step toward him instead, until he was almost chest-to-chest with his superior. Percy wasn't a short man by any means, but Commander Rolan was far taller—and far broader—than even him, and as the older man loomed over him, Percy understood why so many people merely caved to Commander Rolan's iron will and imposing presence. But the younger man wasn't about to allow himself to be intimidated, so he stood his ground.

"You want to be court-martialed?" Commander Rolan hissed.

Percy's eyes narrowed.

"With all due respect, sir, that would go much more poorly for you than for me," the young knight answered evenly. "I and Mrs. Aegis are both protected under the law, and if you would listen, I could explain as much."

"What are you getting at?"

"In Volume 15 of the Laws of the Xanomes Kingdom, it states that on the 31st day of the month of Novis in the year ED 1016, King Evander signed into law that if a woman whose child served as a knight and died in combat was later widowed and incapable of sustaining herself, and if she had no living relatives to assist her, she would be entitled to the penchant of the child who died in combat in the same manner as the widow of a knight. Mrs. Aegis is the mother of a knight who died in combat at the Iron Vault three years ago. Her husband died last year and, as you can see, she is physically incapable of making an adequate living for herself. So this law applies to her, and I'm sure if you spoke with the experts of law at the palace, they would confirm as much. In fact, judging by the way the law is worded, Mrs. Aegis is not only owed her son's penchant, but she is owed back pay for the past year as well."

Commander Rolan's eyes seemed to narrow even further as he listened to Percy speak. When the younger man was finished, the commander's voice came back as a low growl.

"When did you become an expert of the law?"

Percy smirked, more with disdain than pleasure as he stared back into Commander Rolan's cold gaze.

"Last night," he replied evenly.

From behind the commander, one of the debt collectors laughed openly.

"As if you could understand all the obscure laws in the course of one night," the man huffed. "Who's to say you didn't simply misinterpret it?"

"I don't need to understand all the obscure laws in one night," Percy replied confidently. "I just needed to understand this one. I'll appeal it to the king if I have to, but I'm not going to sit by idly and watch you abuse someone who is protected by the law."

By now, a crowd of commoners had begun to curiously gather, all within earshot as they listened intently to Percy's words. Farmers in thread-bare clothes, craftsmen covered in soot and wood shavings, even a few children with skinned knees and muddy hands. And they all stared, bewildered, at the sight of the twenty-year-old city guard standing toe-to-toe with the most intimidating commander in the entire Xanomite military, the brother of the queen.

Commander Rolan took a glance around at the growing crowd, then stepped away and turned his back on Percy.

"Fine. This can wait a couple more days. But if you're wrong..." He glared back over his shoulder. "If you're wrong, you're going to regret crossing me, Lex."

Percy folded his arms across his chest, standing straight and staring back at his superior with a confident gaze.

"Guess you had better hurry then. Wouldn't want to keep my cellmate waiting."

Perhaps this wasn't the right time for sarcasm, but the words had already slipped out of his mouth before he could stop them. Commander Rolan glowered fiercely back at Percy for a moment longer, but when it was clear that the young knight wasn't going to budge, the older man turned and marched back up the dirt road that led out of the Lower Ward, a grumbling company of debt collectors at his heels.

Percy remained where he stood, feet planted and arms crossed as though he half expected Commander Rolan to change his mind and come back for a killing blow. It wasn't until he felt a tug at the back of his shirt that the young knight at last turned around. He blinked, suddenly realizing that there were several dozen commoners pressed in around him, staring at him with wide-eyed amazement. And there behind him, still clinging weakly to his shirt, was Callia Aegis.

"Is it true?" the old woman questioned cautiously as Percy turned to face her. "Is it true that the law would protect someone like me?"

Already Percy could see tears welling up in the woman's eyes, and he knelt on one knee in front of her, taking her frail hands and cupping them in his own.

"I'm confident of it," he answered, giving the woman a reassuring smile. "I poured over those books all night, cross-referenced everything I could find. There is no record of that law being repealed or altered in any way. Life should be easier for you from now on, if only just a little."

By now, the tears were freely falling from Callia's eyes, and shakily she reached out toward the young guard. Percy opened his arms to receive her, wrapping the old woman in a gentle hug as a murmur began to echo out through the crowd that had gathered.

"Thank you," Callia cried. "How can I ever repay you?"

Percy tightened his grip around the old woman, not enough to hurt her, but enough to provide a secure and comforting embrace.

"By living your best life, Callia," he said softly. "Think of it as my thanks for the sacrifices you and your family have made to provide a future for our kingdom."

Just then, the voice of one of the farmers caught Percy's ear.

"Persius Lex...I had heard that the heir to House Lex had joined the city guard, but...are you really a nobleman? You sure don't look or act like one."

Percy gently released his grip on Callia and glanced up at the man who had spoken. He was a middle-aged human male, and the dubious look on his face told Percy everything he needed to know about the man's attitude toward the nobility. The young knight tipped his head in acknowledgment.

"I'm the heir of a noble house, yes," he answered. "But I'm just a citizen of Xanom like the rest of you."

The farmer scoffed faintly at this.

"Really?" the man replied. "You really don't profit from this somehow?"

"How could I possibly profit from being at odds with the queen's brother?" Percy answered.

At his question, the crowd fell silent, so he continued.

"Ever since the last morgrim attack on Xanom, recruitment for the knighthood has fallen drastically," he stated, glancing about at the faces of those gathered around. "I've known that for a while, but now I understand why. People want to know their families are protected. That's why we become knights in the first place. But if I thought my family would only suffer because of my service to the kingdom, what motive would I have to risk my life like that?"

Percy watched as the people glanced about at each other, seemingly curious about the words that he had spoken. The young knight leveled his gaze on the farmer who had questioned him, and he smiled sympathetically.

"Sure, I was born a noble, but money, and power, and prestige don't make a man noble. They just make him comfortable. A noble is someone who uses what they have to protect the people who rely on them." He glanced over at Callia, placing a reassuring hand on her shoulder. "I can't do everything, but as long as I'm here, I mean to be a shield for the people of Xanom. This is my city, and these are my people. I will protect them, or at least I'll die trying."

6

— ⁂ —

RUIN

5TH DAY OF KUZAL, AE 48

"Damn, this place looks nightmarish."

The surrounding atmosphere was unnaturally gloomy as Harz crossed his arms over his chest, dark brown eyes examining the ancient archway and glowing sigil that loomed in front of him. Tendrils of corrupted aes wafted, tentacle-like, across the otherwise invisible barrier for which the sigil acted like a gate.

Nearby, a man clad in dark robes was pulling out a book and a slip of paper, preparing to set up a ritual.

"Of course it's nightmarish. It's the Nightwind Vale. What'd you expect? Sunshine and daisies?" the robe-clad man replied sarcastically, not even sparing Harz a glance.

Off to the side, another of their company, a rabbitfolk female clad in leather armor pieces, snorted derisively.

"Stay on your guard or *we* might be pushing up daisies before too long."

"Why so pessimistic, ears?" Harz laughed, leaning his back against the rocky outcropping behind him.

The rabbitfolk's long ears twitched at the man's words, her hands reaching for daggers at her hips.

"Call me that again and I'll stab you."

The man was unfazed, returning the threat with a teasing laugh.

"Threaten me with a good time, why don't you?"

The rabbitfolk looked like she was about to take him up on the offer when a red-scaled drakonite stepped forward to intervene.

"Harz, Clover, knock it off. We don't have the time for your bullshit. Remember, this is a job for Enigma. We can't afford to screw it up for the sake of petty grievances."

The rabbitfolk, Clover, flexed her hands once more before taking a step backward, signaling that she had heard and was obeying, though if looks could kill, Harz knew he would have been run through several times over by now. For his part, he merely shrugged and took to examining the dismal landscape around him.

The entrance to the Nightwind Vale was every bit as eerie as legends claimed. Nestled between mountain peaks at the top of a cracked and ancient road, framed by towering cliff walls and guarded by an intricate archway, it made perfect sense to Harz why the fallen kingdom of Ziz had chosen the place for its home. The location was easily the most defensible spot Harz had ever seen. Not that any of those natural defenses had protected them in the end. The magical dome holding back the better part of a sea of corrupted aes was proof of it. No one knew what had happened to Ziz. All that remained of it was rumor and legend, tales that spoke of horrors and riches in equal measure awaiting any who would dare to cross the barrier.

"How long will this ritual take, Mick?" the red drakonite inquired, leaning over the shoulder of the man in the dark robes.

"Fuck if I know," Mick retorted, spreading various spell components out across the ground. "Not like the cipher came with instructions. But it'll be a mess of a job if you keep hovering over my shoulder like that."

"Nah, Krex just likes the view, bookworm," Harz snorted sarcastically.

Both the human and the drakonite shot their companion pointed glares.

"You've got a snarky comment for every occasion, don't you, asshat?" Krex grumbled in exasperation.

Harz shrugged.

"You know you love me."

The comment elicited a slew of curses and grumblings from the man's companions, but no one outright disagreed with him, and Harz chuckled to himself as he watched the facial expressions playing across his companions' features.

This party was a strange composition, he had to admit. But then, one could hardly expect a group of thieves to be conventional. And of course, that's what they were, in one respect or another. No two had the same goals, motivations, or skills. Practically the only thing they had in common was a loose loyalty to the organization that gave them purpose.

Harz had been born in the earlier years of the alliance known as the Free Cities of Nor to a poor farming family living on the outskirts of Arcanum. With an alcoholic father who died early in his life and an all but absent mother, Harz had grown up with little hope for a future. He had started stealing things at an early age, maybe seven or eight. What started as a means of survival quickly became a habit, and at the age of twelve, it might have ended in imprisonment and a flogging if not for the intervention of Krex, who took Harz under his wing and eventually invited him to join the organization he was a part of: the Gray Ravens.

The Gray Ravens were small fish in a much larger pond that was crime in the port city of Arcanum, but what they lacked in resources, they made up for in talent. It was Mick who had infiltrated the Crystal Archives to gain access to the cipher said to allow passage through the barrier. Harz had little talent in the intellectually heavy work, but he was notably talented in combat. And gods knew there was likely plenty of combat on the other side of that barrier.

It was difficult to sense the passage of time here at the entrance of the Nightwind Vale. The day seemed to come only in shades of shadow, and despite being surrounded by cliff walls, sounds were muffled. The first couple of hours passed with little progress and a lot of cussing on the part of Mick. And so the other three whiled away the time with idle chatter.

"You think Danton's fallen asleep yet?" Harz mused, glancing at the cracked road that wound its way down the mountainside. "Swear the halfling's part cat the way he just falls asleep wherever he is, and you know he's got to be bored watching the path all by himself like that."

"He better not have," Krex retorted, taking a long draw on his pipe and breathing the smoke out through his draconic nostrils. "We can't afford to get caught by any snoopers, not with Enigma for an employer."

The drakonite seemed to consider the possibility a moment longer before turning to Clover.

"Yo, go check in with Danton. Hate leaving him down there by himself but he's the only one who can really get into those nooks and blend in."

"Yessir."

The rabbitfolk gave the drakonite a firm nod before bounding at a nearly supernatural pace down the path and out of sight. Krex cast half a glance in Harz's direction.

"You tell your boy goodbye before you left?"

Harz diverted his gaze at the question, idly sifting through his pack as he shrugged.

"He left with Desirae about a week back. No chance. Not that it matters. I'm not much of a father type."

He idly lifted a potion vial skyward, as though the dim light above would reveal some sort of secret within the viscous liquid. Krex took in a deep draw of his pipe, still eyeing Harz.

"Boy thinks the world of you, though."

Harz scoffed lightly at the notion.

"He was a mistake. Just like the girl in Avannon. Just a fool mistake by a fool of a man too drunk out of his wits to know the difference." He shoved the vial back into his pack. "Kid would be better off without me to drag him down anyway. Des is a bit of a mess herself, but she's better with kids than I've ever been."

"Well, if we make it out of this job, we just might make enough coin to change that," Krex replied, knocking out his pipe and standing to stretch. "Gods know I'm getting too old for this work. And you got a good kid out there. A chance to do something for him that your old man never bothered trying." He shook his now-empty pipe at Harz for emphasis. "Don't become your old man."

Harz laughed.

"Since when did you get all preachy and sentimental?"

"I may be a thief, but I've got my code," Krex answered. "You're still young, even for a human. You got a chance to make a difference in the kid's life."

"Yeah, yeah. I get it." Harz waved him off. "Anyway, shouldn't Clover be back by now?"

Krex inclined his head in the direction the rabbitfolk had disappeared.

"It's true. She's usually faster than this..."

The pair exchanged glances. It could have just been paranoia, but Harz could feel something heavy lingering in the air. It didn't feel right. Krex appeared to have the same thought, and the drakonite moved in the direction of the road, only to take an alarmed step backward as a blur of gray bolted into view.

"We gotta clear out!" Clover gasped, voice low and secretive. "There's a whole contingent of Xanomes knights headed our way!"

Harz pushed himself to his feet, his expression concerned as he hurried to join his two companions.

"Xanomes knights? What're they doing all the way out here? This is way past their usual territory."

"Like I'm supposed to know that?!" Clover exclaimed. "But you know they'll ask questions if they find us here, and I'm not about to tangle with a whole brigade of reds."

"Where's the pipsqueak?" Harz questioned, glancing down the path.

"Left him in the dust," the rabbitfolk shrugged back. "He'll get here when he gets here. But we need to get moving before the knights find us."

Krex spun on his heels, marching in the direction of Mick.

"Mick, we need to speed this process up."

The mage heaved a frustrated sigh as he struggled to continue the ritual he was currently conducting.

"You don't just speed up a fucking arcane ritual," he snapped. "And this one is tough. The cipher is written in Zizian. You know how hard it is to read Zizian? And that's without adding magic into the mix."

"Well, figure it out fast or you'll be reading that damned cipher in the afterlife. Neither Enigma nor the Xanomes knights are known for their empathy."

Mick cursed profusely under his breath before flipping a page in his spellbook.

"Fine. But we'll probably end up regretting this."

Rolling up his sleeves, the mage began to hastily cast the spell. As he worked, the sound of hurried footsteps and a short stride caught Harz's ears, and he turned to see Danton wheezing up the road.

"Knights...hurry...get away," the halfling panted.

Clover, who stood tapping her right foot with the speed of a starving woodpecker, jumped several feet in the air and whirled at the sound of her companion's voice.

"Great. Now the dunce squad is together. If you imbeciles don't hurry this operation up, I'm leaving you to be pincushions," the rabbitfolk fumed.

As she said that, a crackling sound caught the group's ears, and the others turned to see arcane energy arching up from symbols and components surrounding Mick. The sigil guarding the entrance to the Nightwind Vale flickered and distorted, tendrils of darkness beginning to leak through the arcane cracks. It occurred to Harz then that even though he wasn't educated in the use of magic, something looked terribly wrong with this spell.

Before he could say anything, however, a force pulse rippled outward, sending Mick flying backward and the others scrambling to stay on their feet. The sound of something ripping followed, and when Harz at last regained his bearings, he found himself staring into a gaping, dark hole. The arcane symbols of the sigil guarding the Vale had been torn and distorted, though he could tell that the magic was attempting to mend itself.

"Is...is it supposed to do that?" Danton squeaked, recoiling from the shock of the magic pulse.

"Fuck no, but too late to ask questions," Mick replied, scrambling to his feet again and dusting the debris from his robes. "Let's go!"

The five companions wasted no time darting through the tear in the barrier. Harz was the last through, and no sooner had he stepped foot past the barrier than the tear sealed back over, the sigil's incantation a jumbled mess in comparison to what it had been before. For a moment, no one spoke, staring at the sigil from the other side. Clover blinked rapidly several times.

"How...do we get back, exactly?"

Krex regarded the sight blankly only a moment longer before spinning about on his heels, turning his back on the sigil and archway and focusing on the Vale beyond.

"We'll worry about that later. Give the knights time to clear out. Let's go find what we were sent here for and get the fuck out."

Harz listened to the crunch of the drakonite's heavy footfall disappearing further into the darkness and, one by one, the sounds of the others following. Only Harz remained a moment longer, staring back the way he had come, back at that seal that somehow looked unmade. It gave him a bad feeling about the whole thing, but who was he to question it? Krex had been more of a father to him than the man who had sired him, and Harz was more than aware that he was not the smartest person in the group.

Just then, the first of the Xanomes knights crested the incline, and quickly Harz darted out of sight. Pushing all concern to the side, the man slipped through the shadows to rejoin his companions. If they were lucky, they'd find what they were looking for and get out of the Vale before anyone was the wiser.

Harz had heard all the ghost stories, the tales of a dead land haunted by shadow and dread. It didn't take long for the man to realize that no rumor could compare to the horrors that stalked what he was certain was the most cursed region in the known world.

Though the entrance to the Vale had indeed seemed dark, passing through the barrier had placed Harz and his companions in what could only be described as a perpetual twilight. Even in what should have been daytime, Harz knew he had worked on moonless nights that were brighter. Nighttime was terror incarnate.

Phantasmal forces and monstrous shadows seemed to haunt every corner of the crumbling ruins that dotted the length and breadth of the Vale, the withered remains of ancient crops standing twisted and bent in their cracked fields as the burnt amethyst light of corrupted aes pulsed like a heartbeat through the gaps. The remains of a river cut through the heart of the Vale, but even that was mostly dry, save for a few stagnant pools rank with disease and unholy vermin.

At the beginning, torches had been lit to guide their way through the gloom, but even those barely cut through the thick atmosphere, and the group quickly realized that the light acted as a beacon for all the evil that haunted the Vale. Mick took to sacrificing some of his arcane power to grant the group the ability to magically see in the dark, but that had left him less capable of holding his own in combat. There was now the unspoken question between them all: would only five be enough to survive the horrors of the Nightwind Vale?

It was odd, Harz thought. The further they traveled into the Nightwind Vale, the more relaxed he became. He had always been the sort to laugh at things others would deem inappropriate to laugh at, but here, everything was starting to seem just a bit funnier than normal. He cared less, too.

But while Harz had increasingly found himself at home amidst the menacing twilight and twisted ruins, the others had not fared so well. Mick was a paranoid mess, acting as though the others were bound to rob or murder him at any point. His concerns weren't exactly unjustified. They were, after all, a band of thieves. Convincing him to continue casting the darkvision spell was becoming increasingly tedious, however, and that was a real nuisance.

Krex had become angrier—anything was bound to set him off—while Clover spooked at every hint of movement. Although, Harz thought, that wasn't so far outside her natural behavior. Danton was the biggest concern, though. He wasn't just relaxed like Harz here in the Nightwind Vale. He had taken to wandering. It was only a matter of time before he disappeared entirely.

By Harz's calculation, it had been somewhere around three days since they had entered the Vale, though time was strange in this place and it never really felt like they covered any new ground. Now stopped for a rest inside the ruins of an ancient courtyard, the five comrades had set themselves apart to do what they wished for the short respite.

Quietly, Harz hummed a familiar, cheery tune to himself as he worked through a pack of rations and fiddled with some odd trinkets—a ring and an oddly lustrous silver half-mask—that he had found during their journey through the Vale. Strange. He no longer remembered the name of the tune he hummed or where he first heard it, though it felt as though it was something he had known for a long time.

Well, it hardly mattered. It was a pleasant tune. He didn't care about anything beyond that.

Nearby, Krex snapped at him.

"Harz, shut the fuck up! Or do you want the whole fucking Vale to come find us?"

The outburst caused Clover to jump several feet skyward.

"Krex!" the rabbitfolk squeaked, gaze darting back and forth like a hunted thing. "Don't scare me like that."

"Fuck off," the red drakonite responded. "You jump at your own shadow."

"Relax, old man," Harz said, chuckling. "You'll get an ulcer."

Krex stood to his full seven-foot height, squaring his shoulders as he leveled his gaze on the human leaning lazily against a cracked pillar.

"How about I give you an ulcer," he snarled. "Tear a hole in your gut and leave you to whatever wanders this gods-forsaken shit-hole."

Harz replied with a dismissive wave.

"Yes, yes. Absolutely terrifying."

With a draconic roar, Krex stormed forward, snatching Harz up by the front of his shirt and driving the point of a dagger into his skin, enough to draw blood but not enough to do lasting harm. Nearby, Clover and Mick cowered in their corners. Danton stared off into space. Harz let out a maniacal cackle.

"You actually did it," the man laughed loudly. "Look at all that blood! And it's mine!"

The others stared back at him in disbelief. Even the rage that flickered through Krex's reptilian eyes was dampened with confusion at what was now occurring. Harz felt a tremble in the drakonite's grip, and he dropped the dagger as he took a step away from him. Taking another step backward, Krex grabbed at his head with both hands.

"What is happening...?"

Harz reached down to the wound on his abdomen, wiping his fingers across the dark stream and lifting his hand into view. The wound stung, but the man didn't flinch. Instead, he merely laughed. How absurd everything seemed.

Just then, the ground beneath his feet began to rumble. The others froze, looking frantically around them for the source of the disturbance. Harz cocked his head to one side, casting a languid glance at the archway to his right. The others followed his gaze, and Clover let out a terrified squeak.

"What in Abyss...?" Krex growled, recoiling.

Not more than fifty feet away from them stood Danton, motionless, craning his neck to stare upward until he surely at any moment would topple in a heap on his back. And there, looming above him, framed by the dim light of the twilight-infused sun, was a monstrosity the like of which Harz could not have fathomed even in his worst nightmares.

Standing as tall as a building, the creature dwarfed the halfling staring up at it. Mangey hair covered a vaguely dog-like body and gnarled hands that could easily have been human. Its neck was long like that of a horse, but its head was nearly reptilian, all supported by hunched shoulders and sunken withers. Within the reptilian face, pupilless eyes glowed from angled sockets, rows of dagger-sharp teeth lining the monster's giant maw. A long, thin tongue slithered out between its teeth, like a snake testing the air for scents.

There was a moment of pause, of absolute silence. Or, Harz thought, maybe it was just the strange perception of time and space that existed in the Nightwind Vale. He didn't really care. All the same, however, he watched as the beast shifted, eyeing the halfling standing in a daze in front of it. And then...

CRUNCH!

Clover screeched. Krex roared. Harz cackled.

"All in one bite!" the man crowed.

The monster before them—maybe a morgrim, maybe just the twisted remains of what had once existed in the Nightwind Vale—turned its orbless eyes on the other four and, on impulse, Mick launched a massive gout of fire in its direction. The flames licked almost harmlessly off the monster's mangy form and, with a roar, it lept in the direction that Harz and his companions stood.

For a moment, sanity returned to Harz, enough to tell him that he needed to move, and the four rogues dodged away as the beast's massive body struck the crumbling ruins, sending shards of stone scattering in all directions with a thunderous snap.

With an enraged roar, Krex drew a pair of daggers from his belt, flying at the creature with a blind fury Harz had never seen in him. Righting himself, Harz pulled his spear into his hands, flinging it at the monster's neck. The weapon struck what should have been a jugular vein, but instead of bleeding, the wound began to leak shadow. The creature roared, reaching one twisted forepaw up to the spear and snapping it in half.

Arcane bolts zipped around Harz at the same moment, striking with some effectiveness against the monster's matted hide. The creature ignored the onslaught, leaping over Harz's head and landing heavily on the other side. The man whirled on his heels, readying himself for another attack, but only just in time to hear a crunch and a pained squeak. Now it was only him, Mick, and Krex.

A stream of draconic flames erupted from Krex's mouth as he charged at the monster, throwing himself at the creature's hind leg and digging both of his daggers hilt-deep into its flesh. The monster shook him off with one pointed kick, but again the drakonite threw himself with fury at the creature, entirely unfazed.

From off to the side, other shadows descended on the trio, the battlefield falling into bloody chaos. Harz could feel his mind slipping even as he drew his daggers. Sometimes he understood what and who he should be protecting. Sometimes, he could only feel the disillusioned amusement that pervaded his thoughts. And the more he fought, the heavier the atmosphere became.

Mick quickly got torn in two, his robes offering little resistance against the attacking monster. Harz didn't even remember who he was in that moment, laughing at the bloody mess strewn out before him.

The monster turned its attention to Krex next. Something snapped in Harz at the sight. Why did the drakonite look so angry? Where even were they? He felt like he should be remembering something else, but it was all clouded in the recesses of his mind. Still, he didn't like that look on the monster's face.

"Over here, bastard!" the man shouted, stabbing at something smaller that descended on him as he grinned menacingly up at the primary threat.

His body moved with practiced skill, instinct kicking in. Killing wasn't his area of expertise. It wasn't even his interest. But that didn't negate the years of combat training he had undergone over his years with the Gray Ravens.

His taunt worked. The monster turned its attention to him and, with it, swung one gnarled hand backward with lightning speed. Harz ducked, managing to dodge the greater part of the promised strike but failing to entirely escape that monstrous paw, which clipped him soundly on the side.

The impact sent him flying several dozen feet backward, his back striking the stone rubble behind him and knocking the wind out of his lungs. His daggers scattered with a sharp twang across the cracked stone foundation. The man's vision spun as the ground below him trembled with every footstep the monster took. In the blur, he heard a familiar roar followed by another crunch, and then...silence.

Reeling with pain, Harz fell into a fit of laughter, rolling onto his knees and holding his head with one hand as he struggled to stand. But for that moment, memory returned.

"Damned," he cackled. "I'm damned. This whole job, damned from the start. The fuck were we thinking?"

Still disoriented, he fell with his back against a cracked stone wall, turning to look up at the monstrous creature approaching him. It didn't seem in a hurry, stalking him, toying with its prey. Harz sneered up at the creature. They both knew there was no escape.

Just then, a crackling whisper caught Harz's ear. Or...was it actually inside his head? He could hardly be sure at this point.

Come, the voice hissed. *Draw me from my resting place, and I can make all your nightmares disappear...*

The man felt a nearly supernatural pull to his right, his dark brown eyes landing on a jagged black spear only a few feet away and buried several inches deep in the ground. The weapon crackled with a shadowy energy that licked out towards him, beckoning.

Nearby, the monster was almost within biting distance.

Come, the disembodied voice called again. *I am power. I am vengeance. Or do you wish to die?*

A moment longer and Harz knew he would be dead. The concept made him laugh. He didn't feel afraid, even though he knew he should. Maybe, though, he had always been dead. What did it even mean to live? But still...

He turned to look up at the creature now looming over him. Bloody saliva dripped from its toothy maw, landing on Harz's face in heavy, putrid drops. If a creature like that could sneer, the man thought it did in that moment, knowing it had him disabled and cornered.

He sneered back.

"Fuck you."

In what seemed like the same moment, the monster lunged for him, but Harz rolled out of the way. The creature's head struck the stone wall the man had been leaning against, crushing it with the impact. The monster reeled back, angered by the mouthful of stone it had just consumed, and swung its massive head in the direction Harz had gone. At the same time, the man grabbed for the spear.

Then he screamed.

Something akin to fire the color of burnt amethyst roared up the shaft of the spear as his fingers clasped it, burning its way up his arm and face. For a moment, Harz thought he really would lose consciousness this time. But no. He wouldn't allow it. He would survive. Whatever horrors the Nightwind Vale could concoct, he would persevere. That had always been his way. It didn't matter if he wasn't alive. He existed, if for no other reason than to spite the world that had used and abused him.

Yes, yes, good, the ethereal voice crooned, a cackling laughter echoing through Harz's mind. *You're strong. You will be a perfect vessel.*

Almost as though something else had taken control of his thoughts and movements, Harz felt his right arm arch backward, and as the monster before him turned for another strike, he launched the spear in its direction.

The weapon sailed through the air at a dizzying speed, and the man watched as lightning the color of burnt amethyst appeared around it, starting at the tip and sizzling down the shaft. The weapon easily found purchase in the massive, mangey form, and the creature reeled back at the impact with a blood-curdling screech. The spear lingered in the beast's body for only a moment before reappearing in Harz's empty hand.

Go! the voice commanded. *A little ways off is my brother. You will be a good match for us both.*

Harz couldn't begin to comprehend the meaning of the echoing words, but he had no interest in questioning them now. Allowing the power coursing through him to guide the way, the man made a dash for the other side of the ruins, gaze instinctively landing on the form of a black dagger abandoned in the debris. He dashed forward, snatching it up just in time for the monster pursuing him to make a flying leap in his direction. The man only barely managed to evade the bulk of the attack, though not before taking a nasty strike to his side from one of the monster's claws.

Good, the ethereal voice crooned. *Now, run! I sense a weakness in the barrier. I will exploit it and we will escape this place.*

It sounded like a good enough plan to Harz, and quickly he turned, allowing his instincts—or those of whatever entity was speaking to him—to lead him back the way he had come. Shadows became little more than a blur as the man made his retreat. Some things moved. He stabbed whatever got too close. Then there, up ahead, he caught sight of the sigil marking the break in the Vale's barrier. It flickered strangely, patches of it opening and closing like a creature gasping for air, the arcane lettering a buzzing, flickering jumble.

At the same time, the spear vanished from Harz's hand, and for a moment he slowed to glance around, wondering where the strange weapon had gone.

Move! the voice commanded.

A rumbling behind Harz told him that he was not alone, that the monster hunting him was still on his heels. Still bleeding, his head reeling, Harz made a dash for the gaps in the barrier, stumbling through only a breath of a moment before the arcane symbols reorganized themselves, again sealing the Vale and its darkness away.

The man paused, blinking at his surroundings. The world around him was dark and gray, just beginning to shift with the light of dawn that would be crossing the sky beyond the angry storm clouds above. Harz glanced up, the sting of cold rain striking his throbbing head. It was a welcome relief, and the man fell into a fit of maniacal laughter along with it.

A pained groan caught his ear then, and the man turned in the direction of the sound. It was then that he realized that he was surrounded by bodies. He cocked his head. At first, it was difficult to tell who the people here had once been, as torn up as most of the bodies were.

Harz crossed the distance between himself and the source of the groaning. It looked to be a young woman, lying face-down in a pool of her own blood. He tucked the tip of his boot under her, using it to roll her onto her back, and he watched in wonder as a silvery radiance began to shimmer out from a gaping wound in her gut. Her dark brown hair began to shift, turning white, with only a trace of the darkness that had once been there.

The glint of metal caught Harz's eye then. A signet ring and a medallion. He knelt on one knee, examining the icons cast into the metallic objects. He wasn't sure about the signet ring, but he recognized the medallion. Xanomes knights? What were Xanomes knights doing so close to the Vale?

All of a sudden, the dark, arcane burn on his right side began to pulse, the mysterious voice again echoing inside his head.

Kill her! it snarled. *Don't let her open her eyes! Look at that ring. What did she do to deserve it? Kill her, and take it as a trophy!*

Harz grimaced, holding the side of his head with one hand and shaking it.

I'm not a killer. I'm a bad man, but I'm not a killer.

But you want to try it. You thirst for it. For vengeance...and power...against a world that has done nothing but wrong you.

As the voice hissed inside his mind, Harz felt his right arm begin to burn, forcing him to reach outward against his will. At the same time, the silver mask inside his satchel pulsed. The burn subsided before growing in strength again. Shadow seemed to coalesce in Harz's outstretched hand, the form of that jagged black spear materializing from it.

Take the girl's life. Feed me her soul, and I will give you a gift you could only dream of.

As the voice spoke, Harz reached his free hand into his satchel, fishing around for the mask. The resistance had been only slight, practically imperceptible, but it was there. And what little reason was left inside the man's broken mind knew he only had one chance.

Harz let out a derisive laugh as he stared at the menacing weapon in his hand. "So that's what happened! Who knew a spear could have so much power?"

Of course I have power! I have more power than you will ever know!

"Tell me then," Harz smirked. "Whom do I serve?"

A menacing cackle echoed through the man's mind.

I am chaos. I am storm. I am fury. I am war. Those who see me call me Ruin.

"Ruin..."

Harz yanked the mask from his satchel, pressing it up against the dark burn on his face. The voice in his head screeched.

What are you doing?!

The fury with which the sentient spear reacted was enough to make Harz's head spin and his vision nearly go dark. Instead, however, he steeled himself, turning his back on the Xanomes knight who was beginning to stir. The darkness burned into his flesh clawed at him, as though beckoning him to turn around and run the girl through, but instead he took off at a sprint down the road.

I don't know what you are. I don't know why you demand what you do. But while even a fraction of me exists...if it's war you want...this is a war I will wage...

7

THE BLACK CAT

14TH DAY OF ZHAYAN, AE 49

"Hey, please tell, oh wishing well, what can a young man do? What can he say at end of day? A devil's hunting you..."

The lute strings hummed out a haunting tune as Ehren Carpenter strummed the chords, his sonorous voice coupled with the snap of the campfire and cheers of the other travelers in his company. As he sang, the half-elf cast flirtatious winks and animated smiles at the company's fairer companions, eliciting many a blush or embarrassed giggle.

The ballad the man now sang was as good as any ghost story, entertaining his audience with laughter and surprised squeals. His songs were as much acting as music, and with the Ruins of Taj dipped in moonlight behind him, the song he now sang seemed to cast a special sort of magic over those gathered around.

With the last strum of the lute, the song ended in a soft finale, leaving with it a feeling of unresolved mystery that set the audience to chattering quietly amongst themselves.

"How true do you think that story is?" one young man questioned of the girl sitting next to him.

"I certainly hope not at all!" the girl replied emphatically. "Can you imagine having the cursed soul of a dead person hunting you throughout your life?"

"It's just a moralistic tale," an older man shrugged, taking a swig from his whiskey canteen. "The story starts with the young man killing another man. That's why he gets haunted. Just a caution against anger and hatred. Things like that don't happen in real life."

Holding the neck of his lute in one hand, Ehren threw his arm around the other man's shoulders.

"Ah, but you forget," he said, using his instrument to point at the crumbling ruins scattered across the distant horizon. "We're very close to the Ruins of Taj. Anything can happen here."

A couple of the younger women had gathered around by now.

"What do you mean by 'anything'?" one questioned.

Ehren smirked mischievously.

"You know, they say that souls from the Lost Era wander the ruins at night," the half-elf teased, advancing with a bit of a swagger in the girl's direction. "Dumb beasts gain sentience, stones walk, mortals might even become gods. But all the while, the lost, tormented souls of Taj wander the shattered remains of their once great home, searching for a body to consume and become their own."

As he finished his sentence, Ehren leaned forward, placing his lips only a fraction of an inch from the girl's ear and allowing his breath and voice to linger there. He smiled with amusement as he listened to the girl's breath catch in her throat, a rosy blush spreading up her neck and into her scalp.

"Oh? Is that so?" she replied, swallowing back what Ehren could guess to be a sigh.

A heavy hand landed on his shoulder then, interrupting the moment, and the half-elf glanced back to see several of the other men glaring fiercely at him. He laughed, shrugging off the warning and backing away with a showman's flair.

"Well, that's what the legends say."

Nearby, the leader of the caravan clapped his hands together.

"I think we've had quite enough ghost stories for one night, yeah? Everyone, get some sleep while you can. We break camp at first light. Watches, take your positions."

Ehren stretched lazily before turning to put away his lute, chuckling to himself when he overheard the caravan leader whisper to another of the party, "Keep a particular eye on the bard. We don't need him getting any friendlier with the women than he already has."

The watchman grumbled back a reply, but Ehren paid little mind to it, rolling out his sleeping mat and settling down for the night. He didn't blame them for their concerns, though in truth he wouldn't have tried anything particularly intimate without ample invitation. He had at least that much dignity left.

Pulling his blanket up to his chest, Ehren stared at the sky above, running one hand aimlessly through his shoulder-length, jet-black hair. It had been twenty-four years since that fateful night, the night he had accidentally betrayed his troop and nearly cost the Free Cities an alliance with Dulin and Saffir Sarth.

Some of the wounds of that moment had been mended. At the very least, history had largely forgotten about him. The alliance was prospering, and the Free Cities of Nor seemed stronger than ever. What remained was a wound against his pride, a wound against his character, and the pervasive reputation that he was a loafer and a womanizer.

That wasn't what had been meant that night, but it was an identity Ehren had accepted. Certainly, he couldn't call himself a soldier, and while the Free Cities had chosen not to punish him in the end, Ehren had chosen a punishment that seemed appropriate for his failures: to accept the reputation that the rumor mill had conjured. He would live up to the expectations set out before him. It was easier—and probably safer—than telling people he was easily deceived and, just in general, a proper fool.

The sky was clear tonight, as clear as it had been that day over two decades ago, and quietly Ehren traced constellations in the stars with the tip of his finger. Who knew that someone could be so lonely while surrounded by so many people? He snorted to himself. The irony was, at least, amusing.

Somewhere in the midst of his thoughts, Ehren found himself drifting off into slumber, lulled to sleep by the gentle rhythm of the autumn breeze and the chirp of crickets nearby. How long he had been dozing the half-elf couldn't be sure, but he was startled awake by the shouts of some of the night watchmen. With a groan, Ehren rolled over on his side, squinting in the direction of the noise.

"Having fun without me?" he called jokingly, stifling a yawn.

"You call this fun?!" one of the watchmen hissed, voice strained in an attempt to keep from waking the others. "Something small and black just scurried under one of the carts! I swear it! If it's a morgrim, we'll be in trouble."

The second watchman sighed dramatically.

"We've looked all over the camp already," he replied. "There's nothing here. If it were a morgrim, I think it would have tried to take a bite out of someone by now."

Almost as if on cue, one of the girls screamed, bolting upright and looking frantically around. The two watchmen rushed to the girl's side. Ehren pulled himself out from under his bedding, sauntering over to see what all the fuss was about.

"What happened? Are you injured?" the first watchman inquired.

The girl blinked up at him, then shook her head.

"No, but...something just ran across my chest."

Ehren smirked at the statement, but a sideways glare from the second of the watchmen kept him silent. Instead, he knelt on one knee next to the girl, taking one hand in his and offering her a charming smile.

"Worry not, my lady. We shall ensure your safety."

The girl blushed and, for added effect, Ehren placed a kiss on the tops of the girl's fingers. Immediately he felt two hands reaching down, grabbing him under the arms and hauling him away. With a laugh, the half-elf held up both hands in surrender.

"I get it, I get it," he declared, backing away. "But it does sound like we have a mystery friend wandering the camp."

The others glanced between themselves, clearly nervous.

"You're not just saying that because of your little ghost stories, are you?" the more reasonable of the two watchmen queried.

He sounded hopeful. Ehren motioned toward the girl still sitting nearby, looking around the dark camp warily.

"She seemed to think that whatever it was was quite real."

The watchmen seemed to consider the possibility before nodding.

"We should make another thorough sweep of the camp. I hate to admit it, but we could use your help, Ehren. I don't want to wake the whole camp if it's nothing to worry about, but an extra pair of eyes would be useful, especially since you can actually see well in the dark."

"Hm, well, being a half-breed does have its perks, doesn't it?"

Ehren cast a flirtatious smirk in the direction of the girl nearby, who blushed and hid her face behind the edge of her blanket. Then, before he incurred any more wrath from the watchmen, the bard gave them a flourishing bow and set off to make a round of the camp.

Now further away, the half-elf dropped his facade, his smirk fading into a frown. The watchman had been wrong earlier when he said that a morgrim would have attacked by now. While it was true that many of the more common varieties were that aggressive, he had traveled enough to know that there were other varieties far more cunning.

Starting with the location that the girl had earlier indicated, Ehren traced his way around the circle of wagons, sharp elvin eyes examining the marks pressed into the earth. With over two-dozen individuals of various races comprising their little caravan, coupled with all the horses and wagons, it was no easy feat to differentiate between footprints. It had been some time since the region had seen rain as well, leaving the ground around the campsite fairly hard-packed. As Ehren worked, however, his eyes picked up on a shape that didn't match any of the others.

A cat footprint?

The half-elf stood up straight, glancing around at the people searching the other areas of the camp, as well as at those who still slept, blissfully unaware of any potential peril. There were no catfolk in this party, and the prints pressed only faintly into some churned-up earth left over by the footfall of a draft horse were too small to be one anyway. It had to be a domestic cat, but he hadn't seen any domestic cats in the caravan, and being so far away from civilization, one would think that they would have discovered a stowaway ages ago. Both Greyhaven and Xanom were a good three to four days away, and even the settlement surrounding House Froura, the fortress that guarded the road between Greyhaven and Xanom, was too far away for a cat to wander of its own accord.

Now quite curious, Ehren returned to the faint pawprint, tracing its trajectory until at last he came to a wagon loaded down with dried meat and covered with a heavy canvas. All was silent. Cautiously, the half-elf lifted the canvas to take a look inside. No sooner had he done so when a hiss and a shrieking yowl split the still night air, the flash of white fangs glinting in the moonlight. With a yelp of his own, Ehren dropped the canvas, bounding back a pace as his hand flew to the hilt of his rapier.

"Ehren! What happened?!"

The bard could hear the sound of footsteps rushing up behind him. Without answering, he drew his rapier, using the tip of the blade to flip the canvas up and over the crates and barrels. Again came the hiss and shrieking yowl, but Ehren was ready for it this time, and when at last the canvas landed with a heavy flutter on the other side of the cart, the half-elf found hunched before him a little black cat.

For a moment, a stare-down ensued, with the little cat backed into a corner, tail and hackles standing on point as those gathered around stared at it in disbelief. Then, Ehren doubled over, his laughter echoing across the otherwise quiet camp.

"There's your morgrim," he said when at last he had regained a measure of his composure.

He sheathed his rapier as he wiped tears from his eyes. The others exchanged glances before laughing and shrugging along with him.

"Who knew you'd find a stray cat all the way out here," one of the watchmen chuckled. "Better shoo it away before it gets into the product, though."

Ehren glanced over at the cat who, seeing that the strangers' attention had been diverted, was in the process of attempting to slink away.

"Here kitty, kitty," the half-elf called softly, holding his hand out slightly to get the creature's attention.

The cat froze at the call, turning to look at him as it flattened its ears against its head.

"'Here kitty, kitty' yourself, asshole."

Ehren paused, blinking back at the cat in disbelief. The words had garnered the attention of the two watchmen still standing nearby as well.

"Did that cat just...?" one of the watchmen questioned.

Cautiously, Ehren reached into one of the nearby crates, taking out a piece of dried fish and tossing it in the cat's direction.

"Hey!" the watchmen began to protest, but Ehren motioned for them to be quiet.

The unfamiliar voice had most certainly come from the cat—a sound much like a young male—and the poor creature was hardly more than skin and bones. Now that Ehren had gotten a better look at the cat, he noticed something concerning. There were dark gashes cut across the creature's body, crusty with dried blood, and it limped badly.

"You're injured," the half-elf said.

The cat eyed him warily, looking torn between his desire for the dried fish and his fear of the unwelcome audience he had suddenly acquired.

"What was your first clue?"

Unfazed by the sharp response, Ehren kept his gaze focused on the injured feline.

"Will you allow me to help you?"

By now, hunger had won over, and the cat carefully limped forward, sniffing at the offering the half-elf had tossed to him. He seemed satisfied, all but inhaling the morsel. Then he looked back up at Ehren.

"How will you help me, exactly?"

"I can do a bit of healing with my lute," Ehren explained. "Get you some food. Clean up some of that blood. I promise you'll feel better."

The cat hesitated a moment longer, then cautiously limped to the side of the cart, allowing Ehren to lift him out of it. He stiffened as a crowd began to gather, but the half-elf cradled him closer, using his own body to shield the cat from some of the onlookers and offer him a sense of safety. Just to be sure, he cast a cautioning glance in the direction of the other members of the caravan and, seeing him serious for the first time since the beginning of the trip, the crowd quickly disbursed.

Quietly, Ehren carried the cat to his mat by the campfire, setting him gently on the soft bedding. He then picked up his lute, running his fingers along the strings as he sang a few arcane lines under his breath. Light the color of the aurora from which the island had received its name danced along the strings, springing outward and suffusing the cat's body in its ethereal glow. When the light faded, the cat's wounds had been completely healed over. The only sign of injury now was a bit of dry blood matted into the creature's fur.

The little feline visibly relaxed as the pain of the wounds dissipated, and he sat down on his haunches, looking at Ehren curiously.

"You're the first two-legged who hasn't been afraid of me," the cat noted. He sounded impressed and disappointed all at once.

Ehren laughed lightly at the comment.

"Well, you certainly put forth your best effort there at the beginning. Nearly had to change my pants after that."

It was hard to read the cat's face, but Ehren thought he heard the faintest hint of a snort as the little creature swished his tail. The half-elf offered his feline companion a gentle smile, then reached for his pack.

"How about some food next? We can get that blood out of your fur afterward."

"Thank the gods, yes!" the cat replied, ears swiveling forward at the suggestion. "I haven't eaten in centuries!"

"That, I am quite certain, is an exaggeration," Ehren laughed, offering the cat a selection of dried meat.

The little creature puffed out his chest indignantly before happily gorging himself on the food.

"I would never..."

For a moment, Ehren allowed the cat to eat in silence. Then, when at last the little creature seemed satisfied, he reached for a rag and his water skin.

"Shall I help you get some of that old blood out of your fur now?"

The cat pinned his ears against his head.

"How, exactly?" he questioned warily.

"I'll just put a small amount of water on this cloth, just enough to moisten it, I promise. I know that cats don't like water."

The cat tipped his nose in the air.

"I am perfectly capable of grooming myself, thank you."

"Of course you are. But is that what you want to be doing all night when you're already so tired?"

The cat considered the question before letting out a reluctant sigh.

"Fine. But *not too much water!*"

Ehren chuckled lightly as the cat stepped forward, sitting down in front of him. While he presented his back to the half-elf, the cat still kept him in his peripheral vision.

"So, a talking cat, huh?" Ehren mused at length, gently working at the matted patches of fur that covered the cat's body.

"So, a talking human, huh?" the little creature mocked in return, ears flicking back in annoyance.

"Technically, I'm only half human."

"What's the other half? Stupid?"

"Now, now. Is that any way to talk about your rescuer?"

In response, the cat flicked his tail but said nothing.

"Do you have a name?" Ehren ventured. "Or should I just keep calling you 'cat'?"

There was a moment of pause before the feline replied, "I think...my name is Loki."

"Loki? That's an interesting name. Where did you get it?"

Again the cat flicked his tail.

"I don't really remember. All I remember is waking up in the ruins over there."

Ehren glanced up, off in the direction of the Ruins of Taj.

"That explains a few things," the half-elf nodded. "I've heard of animals gaining sentience there, although I must admit, a cat that actually talks is a new one for me. How did you end up so injured, though?"

Loki pinned his ears back and hunched down at the question.

"There are a lot of awful things that stalk those ruins. One tried to eat me after I woke up, but I escaped because of some weird magic powers I have."

Ehren paused, tilting his head curiously as he examined the little black cat.

"You have magic powers?"

The feline nodded faintly.

"I don't know how to use them intentionally, but when I get scared, sometimes it happens."

"What do your powers look like?"

Loki considered the question for a moment.

"It depends. Sometimes, I can just feel it working in my mind. But there was one time that I accidentally summoned dark purple chains. That was interesting."

The statement was so strangely casual that Ehren couldn't help but laugh.

"Oh, is that all?"

The cat tipped his head at him.

"Is that not normal for two-leggeds?"

Ehren laughed heartily at this.

"Not in the slightest," he replied. "That sounds like quite the talent."

Loki flicked his ears, seeming to consider the bard's words. Then, if a cat could shrug, Ehren thought the little black feline might have done so then.

"Well, I suppose I'm just extra special. Not that I wasn't special to start with."

Ehren imagined the cat doing a hair flip and doubled over laughing. When at last he recovered his composure, he found Loki staring back at him, unamused.

"You should have been a bard," the half-elf smirked.

"Why?"

Ehren paused to consider the question. He could hardly say it was because of his own reputation.

"No reason," he replied coyly. "Regardless, it sounds like you have quite the story to tell."

At this, Loki fell silent for a time. When he spoke again, his spunk was significantly more subdued.

"It's hard to remember what I knew or experienced before I woke up, but...I had a brother. I remember that. Have you seen him?"

Ehren shook his head sympathetically.

"No, sorry. You're the first cat I've seen in several days."

"I see..."

For a moment, the pair lapsed into silence. It was then that Ehren noticed that a heavy fog had begun to creep in from the north. The air around him felt a little colder, and in the distance he could hear the faint sound of skittering. Quickly, Ehren bounded to his feet, drawing his rapier into his hand. The sudden movement startled Loki, who bolted for cover under a nearby wagon.

"Hey!" Ehren called out to the watchmen who stood chatting in hushed tones several paces away. "On your guard. I think we have company!"

The guards turned to give Ehren a skeptical look, as though they expected him to pull a prank, but the outburst stirred several others in the camp from slumber.

"What's the meaning of all this racket?" someone nearby grumbled.

One of the watchmen from earlier moved around to where Ehren stood.

"Find another cat?" he laughed, clapping the half-elf on the back.

Hearing more skittering, closer this time, Ehren ignored the teasing, turning to face the direction of the sound. The reaction sobered up the others, who scrambled for shields and weapons. Another moment of stillness, another faint, almost imperceptible movement in the fog, and then...

SCREE!

A blood-curdling screech split the still night air as a gangly shadow dashed from the wall of dark gray mist. Even knowing that danger was near could not have prepared the travelers for the horrific speed at which the monster moved. Before Ehren could even register what had happened, the creature was in the center of the group, a dark, towering mass with six long, claw-tipped appendages glinting in the dim light of the nearby campfire. The narrow, elongated, eyeless face made for an especially eerie sight, and when it shrieked, its jaw dropped as though entirely unhinged, revealing rows of needle-like teeth.

With unnatural speed, the monster tore into Ehren and the two others who were near him. The watchman who had been teasing him collapsed almost instantly in a bloody heap, his pained wail quickly snuffed out. It was impossible to tell at the moment if the man was dead or if he had simply fainted from the pain.

Two appendages reached for the second watchman but he ducked out of the way, taking only the slightest of glancing blows. Ehren mirrored his movements, avoiding one set of claws but taking a nasty strike to the back of his shoulder with the maneuver.

"What in Abyss is this thing?!" the surviving watchman exclaimed as the rest of the caravan scrambled for weapons or cover.

"Big, bad, and damned ugly!" Ehren exclaimed back. "There's an opening! Flank it!"

As he shouted his command, the half-elf shifted around the monster, which was still in the process of recovering from the flurry of strikes it had just delivered. With his training as a soldier, it was clear to Ehren that, while deadly, the creature was awkward once it lost its momentum. They had to take advantage of whatever opportunity they could find.

The nearby watchman was the first to bring his sword around, both hands fiercely gripping the weapon's handle as he cut a gash in the monster's back. He brought the sword around for another strike but the creature darted nimbly out of the blade's path.

Angered by the watchman's previous blow, the creature began to wheel around for another attack. Memories of the night his company had been slaughtered filled Ehren's mind, and with it, a dark energy began to form.

"Go back to the shadows from whence you came, you vile monstrosity," he snarled.

As he spoke, the air around him began to distort, and the creature before him winced, though it didn't have half the impact Ehren had hoped. The mind-warping effect was a power he had gained after the tragedy that had ruined his career as a soldier, one that had been quite useful against humanoids. But clearly, whatever sort of monster stood before him now was nothing like the humanoids he had fought.

This wasn't an orc, or goblin, or any of the other sentient beings that made a habit of assaulting travelers east of the Dragonspine Mountains. It was something altogether different, and as the creature's jaw sank into a gaping snarl of its own, the half-elf thought he heard something akin to a laugh amidst the awful sound that emanated from that cavernous maw. This was a morgrim. It had to be. The dark spawn of a fallen kingdom of fae. Mind magic would have little effect. Well, the rapier would have to do then.

"It seems that the blade will have to suffice," Ehren called out to the nearby watchman, maneuvering around their target to get a better angle for the strike. "Don't die on me now, friend."

He flashed an impish smile around the monster and toward his comrade on the other side. The watchman grimaced, hardly inspired by the remark, but focused on his swordsmanship all the same. At the same moment, Ehren heard a hissing yowl emanate from under the cart that Loki had retreated to. Instantly, chains of dark magic energy erupted from the ground between Ehren and the watchman, battering the monster before them from all sides. As the chains assaulted the creature, a necrotic aura seemed to pulse out from them, only to be repelled by an energy equal to it that pulsed out of the monster with each strike.

Almost as though spurred on by the chain attack, the monster spun around to face the watchman who had gone in for another strike. One clawed hand lashed out, catching the man by the wrist and wrenching the sword out of his grasp. At the same time, two more claws tore gashes into the watchman's chest, and Ehren watched in horror as the other man collapsed into a bloody heap alongside his previously fallen companion.

By now, the other fighters in the group had rallied themselves and, with battle cries, they converged on the monster, weapons glinting in the firelight. A few strikes missed as the dark monster ducked and swerved, its multiple arms attempting to fend off the sword strikes. Still, several of the attacks found purchase, shadow leaking out of the wounds left in their wake.

Taking advantage of the openings left by the onslaught, Ehren darted forward, driving his rapier through one side of the monster and out the other. In the same movement, he loosed a dagger from his belt, dragging the blade along the creature's side and leaving in its wake a deep gash that leaked a combination of burnt amethyst and shadow.

No sooner had his dagger left the flesh of the monster when an undulating bolt of sickly green energy flew a few inches above his head, breaking into a viscous liquid upon impact. The monster screeched, writhing in pain as the concoction—acid by all appearance—seemed to eat at its flesh from the outside in and, a few seconds later, the last vestiges of it dissipated into smoke and shadow. Only a handful of bloody bodies lying on the ground nearby stood as testament to the horror that had been there only moments before.

For a moment, everyone stood in silence, panting heavily as they stared at the spot where the monster had been. Then, quickly, Ehren turned to the two watchmen lying on the ground nearby. He didn't have time to check if they were alive or dead. He had to try something, and try it now.

Dropping his weapons on the ground at his side, Ehren grabbed for his lute nearby, repeating the tune and arcane words he had used earlier to heal Loki. The same light as before emanated out, suffusing the bodies of the fallen watchmen. As the music faded, there came a moment of pause. Everyone seemed to be holding their breath. And then, slowly, the watchmen began to stir, groaning and looking around at their surroundings. With all attention focused elsewhere, Ehren let out a nearly imperceptible sigh of relief. There would be no repeat of two decades ago. That, at least, was something.

As the others of the group rushed to help the wounded watchmen, Ehren turned and moved in the direction of Loki, who had tucked himself into a ball of fur behind the wheel of the nearby wagon. As he walked, Ehren noted that the fog had also retreated back toward the ruins, the starry expanse above again glimmering brightly.

"Everything is fine now," the half-elf called to the little black cat. "The monster is gone."

Cautiously, Loki slunk out from his hiding place, tail poofed, hackles up, ears back, but seemingly willing to trust Ehren's judgment.

"That was the thing that tore me up in the ruins," the cat noted, still keeping a close eye on what was happening around them.

"You're the reason?" came an angry voice from nearby.

Ehren and Loki turned to see one of the watchmen glaring fiercely at the little black cat. His words attracted the attention of the others, who began to form a crowd behind him.

"You led that thing here?" another of the crowd questioned furiously.

Loki hunched back, ready to run from the crowd's wrath.

"How was I supposed to know it would follow me all the way out here?"

"You could have gotten us all killed!"

At this, Ehren stood up, placing himself between the crowd and the terrified cat.

"You're scared and angry. I get that," he said. "But that's the risk of the ruins. It could have been anyone. Would you want someone to be angry with you if you were in his place?"

A murmur spread through the crowd, some of the anger dissipating as the group considered the bard's words. Still, there were a few amongst them not so easily placated.

"You know, black cats *are* bad luck. Kill it or get it out of here before it gets us all killed."

The speaker took a step forward. Ehren flashed him his most charming smile, attempting to tap into the well of magic within him.

"Now then, friend, I suggest you leave the cat be for the remainder of the trip."

The man paused only a moment before turning his glare on Ehren.

"Be glad we're not in the Xanomes Kingdom, *friend*. Using magic on an unwilling target is a criminal offense. And don't think I'm unaware of the kind of magic bullshit you like to pull."

At that, Ehren dropped his friendly facade, his gaze hardening as he positioned himself within reach of his weapons while still guarding Loki.

"I won't allow you to harm an innocent life," the half-elf warned. "I do not wish to fight you, but I will if I must."

"If you want to protect that *thing*, then leave. We can't afford to have you endangering the whole caravan."

"If it weren't for me, you all would have been ambushed in your sleep."

"If it weren't for that cat, we wouldn't have needed you at all."

Ehren clenched his hands into fists, biting back the anger welling up inside him as he plastered an amicable smile onto his face once more.

"These are a lot of what-ifs. How about we avoid further conjecture and finish our rest for the evening?"

His opponent remained unmoved.

"Give us the cat, or get out."

Just then, the sound of Loki's voice echoed through Ehren's mind.

It's fine. You need your people. I'll leave so I don't cause any more trouble. I know when I'm not wanted.

The amicable smile on Ehren's lips faltered, becoming more melancholy and bitter. He didn't know how the cat was speaking into his mind, but it was certainly more convenient than baring his soul in front of the whole assembly.

That won't be necessary, the half-elf thought, focusing in on that mental connection he had felt when the cat spoke to him. *We make quite the team, you and I, don't you think? What do you say? Just two outcasts on the open road, seeing what adventure awaits us.*

The man who had been after Loki frowned further at Ehren's smile.

"What's so amusing, bard?"

After a short pause, Ehren heard Loki's voice in his head again.

Really? You really want to travel with me?

Why not?

One more pause, then, *I...would really like to not be alone anymore. I guess you'll do.*

Ehren laughed audibly at the feigned disinterest. Quietly, he turned, sheathing his weapons and gathering his belongings before offering a hand to Loki, who jumped up lightly to perch on the top of his rucksack. Then Ehren turned to face the other members of the caravan.

"Well," he said, offering them one last smile, though he could feel the disdain lingering in it, "I suppose we'll be off then. It's nice to know the kind of people I've been traveling with. May the gods treat you as you have treated us."

Several in the crowd shifted uncomfortably at the bard's words but he paid them no further mind. With a flourishing bow, the half-elf did an about-face, continuing on down the road in the direction the caravan had been traveling that day.

When they were finally out of earshot, Loki at last spoke aloud again.

"Hey."

"Hm?"

"What if...I really am bad luck?"

Ehren glanced over his shoulder at the little black feline perched atop his pack, then laughed openly.

"Well," the half-elf answered, turning his eyes back to the dark road ahead of them, "then we can be bad luck together. It will be nice to not be alone in that endeavor."

8

THE KID

7TH DAY OF KUZAL, AE 50

"Hmm...no. That doesn't seem like it'll go anywhere. Maybe...this way? Gods, that's a tall cliff. Ah, well, why not?"

Xerxes reached for the gauntlet extending up his right arm, channeling arcane energy into the gem on the back of his hand. He watched as the pale blue stone glimmered briefly before a wave of magic rippled across his body.

"There. That should do it."

He reached out toward the slick surface of the cave wall in front of him, grinning with satisfaction as he felt his gauntlet adhere to the place it touched. He reached his other hand up, just a bit higher, and nodded approvingly as he felt the leather glove on that hand also stick to the cave wall. Yes, that would do nicely. Thank goodness for magic.

By appearance only a boy of ten years, Xerxes knew he must have made for quite the sight as he scrambled over cavernous crags and debris from the ancient ruins that dotted the subterranean depths he now traversed. A pair of oversized goggles had been pulled down over his eyes, and his small frame was clad in adult clothing that had been tacked and tied to fit his lithe frame. Even he had to laugh at himself.

As he climbed, Xerxes thought back over the series of events that had led him to this moment. He wondered if anyone back at the Crystal Archives would believe it if he told them. Well, probably they would. They were no strangers to the bizarre happenings of Aurora, and even less to the eccentric behaviors of their resident inventor. It would just be one more thing to add to their "Proof that Xerxes is an Oddball" checklist.

They had one of those, right? Most likely.

It didn't bother him, though. Rather than worry about what other people thought, it was always Xerxes' method of operation to let others be their own person, in whatever form that took, and he would be his. Unless someone was hurting someone else, there was no reason for him to worry about what other people thought or did.

Actually, from Xerxes' perspective, it was all quite amusing. By the most technical of terms, he was a man of twenty-eight, with years of research experience under his belt. But it had only taken one strange little stone in the Ruins of Taj to change all of that. Physically, touching that stone had de-aged him by almost two decades. To anyone who didn't know him, he was just a young human boy with a wild mop of brown hair and curious teal eyes. And that...that was hilarious. Just imagine what he could get away with if people thought he was a child!

Well, if nothing else, being in the body of a child had been useful as of late, especially while attempting to escape that strange tribe of green-skinned elves residing in the northern Dragonspine Mountains. Now that he thought about it, Xerxes wasn't sure they had been true elves. Some unknown race left over from the Lost Era, perhaps? It was possible. There were a lot of things even researchers such as himself didn't understand about the time before explorers began to arrive on the shores of Aurora.

Regardless, Xerxes' curiosity had not been warmly welcomed and, in an attempt to escape some angry warriors, he had gone underground. Gods knew how long he had been down in these twisting tunnels. All the boy knew was that his rations were running low, and this adventure was quickly getting old. There should be an exit soon, though. The tunnels were dotted with ancient ruins older than Taj itself, and surely the previous inhabitants had come and gone from the surface somewhere.

By this point, Xerxes had managed to pull himself over the cliff edge, and he paused to wipe some of the dirt off his gauntlet and glove. When he looked up to check his surroundings, however, the boy froze, staring in wide-eyed wonder at what caught his eye.

There were no ruins in this part of the cave, but he could clearly see the marks of pickaxes scoring the stone walls, cut between veins of aes crystals that glowed with ethereal light, in every color and variety Xerxes could think of. Half in a daze, he lifted the goggles up to rest on his forehead and rubbed his eyes, just to make sure he wasn't hallucinating or falling prey to an illusion. Still the image remained, and quickly Xerxes lifted his gauntlet, activating the gem set inside it. He watched as dozens of symbols lit up the polished surface like symbols on a compass, moving as he moved. Conjuration, evocation, restoration, chronurgy...the list went on.

"Unbelievable," he breathed. "Talk about a jackpot!"

The sound of Xerxes' small feet padding along the cavern floor echoed loudly in his ears, but if there was anything to disturb at this moment, the possibility had yet to cross the boy's mind. To find even one aes crystal was a rare stroke of luck. To happen across an entire cave system of them? If money had been a factor, Xerxes knew he could live like a king.

To him, though, these crystals served a much more valuable purpose, one that money couldn't buy. All arcane inventions relied on aes crystals to power them, and even the most mundane of crystals could cost well over a year's wages for the common person. Of course, Xerxes was far from common at this stage in his life, but with how many inventions he was already pursuing—and with how often he had a tendency to blow things up—a cave full of aes crystals was a boon he could hardly afford to ignore.

For a moment, the boy fumbled with his bag and the baldrics and belts that crisscrossed over his hips and chest. He wasn't a miner, but he had his fair share of tools and gadgets to work with. After assembling a satisfactory collection kit, Xerxes turned to the walls lined with aes crystals and began to pick at the soft stone around them. The first stone he freed was a transmutation crystal. Those were especially useful for his type of work and the research he had quietly dedicated his time to in the background.

While he wasn't sure what kind of stone he had happened across in the Ruins of Taj—and it had disintegrated before he could study it—he was fairly certain that it had been either transmutation or chronurgy that had reduced him to the body of a child, and it would take an equally powerful magic to restore him to his original form.

When he was through enjoying the pleasures of youth, of course.

These stones would be saved for a later date. And in any case, that little detail aside, transmutation was good for animating constructs, a topic of research that was quite up his alley as well.

Next, he worked on extracting some of the nearby evocation crystals. Those were especially good for creating weapons. Not that Xerxes was himself much of a fighter, but combat skills were useful for survival in a place like Aurora, especially when one explored the ancient ruins that dotted the landscape.

Little was understood of Aurora's original inhabitants, but from what Xerxes had studied, they had been powerful entities, combining magic and science into frightening examples of what those schools of study could be when united. Few in Aurora paid an overabundance of attention to the scientific side of things. Magic was more than enough to satisfy the needs and wishes of the general populace. But Xerxes had always been fascinated by the world of the mundane—which was no mundane thing, to be sure—and he was even more fascinated by the prospect of combining the two. The ancient Aurorans had understood and appreciated that line of thought, and so that which remained of them was where Xerxes wanted to be most.

His mind mostly focused on the task at hand, Xerxes failed to notice the beginnings of a tremor beneath his feet. It was the crack of the nearby wall that caught his attention. The boy paused in what he was doing, leaning back to look at the earthen gash curiously. Out from the crack, a stony formation only vaguely in the shape of a humanoid emerged, turning a pair of angry red orbs on him. It stared. He blinked. Then it occurred to him: this was an earth elemental, and a very angry one at that.

"Well, shit."

The words had hardly escaped his mouth before the entity in front of him lunged forward, stony fists swinging. The boy ducked, thankful that he was naturally closer to the ground right now, and bolted between the elemental's legs in the opposite direction from which he had come. There was no exit that way. Best thing to do was head forward...right?

Another sharp crack resounded at Xerxes' feet as he darted down the hall, a stony hand striking out from below and only narrowly missing the boy's foot.

There were more of them?!

He ducked just beneath the reach of yet another elemental that had sprung from the wall and slid between the legs of a fourth.

"Of course there are more of them," the boy huffed to no one in particular as he dashed blindly down the cave hallway, now with at least half a dozen elementals on his heels. "There are always more of them. That collection of crystals was massive! What did you expect, Xerxes? You'd just find aes crystals easy and free? Nothing is ever easy and free. Why is nothing ever at least easy?!"

He skidded around a corner, realizing far too late that there was a chasm between him and his path of escape, the remnants of a shattered stone bridge serving as the only indicator that anything particularly civilized or sentient had ever resided here. If he tried skidding to a halt, he would no doubt end up going right over the edge anyway. He was fast running out of options, and he knew it.

"Oh well. Here goes nothing."

In the five or so feet he had between himself and the edge of the dropoff, Xerxes reached for his gauntlet, activating the stone set inside. As the first of his boots hit the edge of the chasm, he launched himself forward. A burst of arcane energy radiated out from the gauntlet and down to his feet, propelling him forward with a velocity that defied nature. He landed heavily on the other side of the chasm, stumbled, rolled, then continued his retreat.

Smack!

Xerxes had just come around a corner when he ran headlong into a figure even smaller than himself. The impact was enough to knock his feet out from under him, and with a pained grunt, he landed heavily on his backside. The boy glanced up at the figure he had just run into and blinked. A gnome? His teal eyes scanned the room into which he had run. One, two, three...there had to be at least two dozen pickaxe-wielding gnomes in here, all staring blankly in his direction.

He didn't have time to wonder about it though, whirling at the rumble of the cavern floor as something large seemed to be coming up from below. Xerxes let out a defeated sigh, then activated his gauntlet again. Right...earth elementals could travel through stone. So much for running.

Wind and fog curled in a menacing vortex, all but consuming two figures kneeling together over a tiny candle. The gnarled branches of aged trees pressed in around them...twisted, dead, monstrous. Somewhere in the midst of the fog, eerie howls split the heavy air, and eyes that glowed with the angry burnt amethyst of corrupted aes peered through the gloom. Each time they appeared, however, a third figure moved to strike them away with a blind fury, dispersing the threatening shadows into smoky ether.

The younger of the two kneeling figures, a half-elf girl with wavy, dark brown hair loosely braided over her shoulder, held her small hand out around the candle flame. Together with a young woman of strikingly similar appearance, the girl swayed lightly back and forth, singing a soft lullaby as they shielded the candle together. Every now and again, the child tried to turn, attempting to observe her surroundings or look for the sources of the eerie sounds; each time, the older of the two reached out with her free hand, shielding the little girl's eyes and ears and directing her gaze back to the candle.

"What is happening, Weiss?" the child questioned, looking up into the face of her older twin.

"Don't worry," Weiss whispered, her voice still a hum. "Madra is protecting us. We're alright, Hope. Just focus on the candle. Don't let the candle go out."

Life was little more than a confusing blur for Weiss, a haze of images and voices, memories that were hers but not hers and thoughts that were familiar yet unfamiliar. Sometimes she was herself, Weiss. Other times, when stress or danger pushed her to a breaking point, there was Madra, her protector, who forcefully ushered her into the background, taking the lead in this disembodied experience she had grown so accustomed to. Consciously, she understood only that Madra had appeared to defend her after the loss of her family. That Weiss and Madra were one in body and spirit was something only the deepest, most untapped levels of her consciousness understood.

There was another, too. Hope, the innocence of childhood, but together Weiss and Madra kept her shielded away. It wasn't safe. It was better to let Madra handle things. Madra was stronger, braver, so much better equipped than any of the other identities that existed in this clouded labyrinth. If Weiss had known Madra the day the morgrim attacked her clan, maybe...just maybe...

But she didn't dare think of it further, retreating into the fog, back to shielding Hope, and allowing Madra to take her place.

From an outside perspective, Weiss was a tall young half-elf with long, wavy, dark brown hair and violet eyes, clothed in simple garb of neutral tones. Originally a member of the Wiyota Sinti, she still carried with her the fetishes of three of the Droma spirits: the bear spirit Enyeto, the star spirit Stea, and the water spirit Nashtera. It was an odd mix of spirits to follow, even for the average Sinti. But then, to the rest of the world, Weiss was an odd individual regardless.

To the group of adventurers Weiss currently traveled with, it had been clear from the beginning that her mind was broken. Weiss was a healer, a non-combatant and teetotaler, completely lost with a blade in her hand. Her primary alter, Madra, however, was fierce—blindly so—and didn't so much as flinch at the suggestion of a tavern brawl or drinking competition.

Though the group had extended what aid they could, even attempting divine restoration, nothing could truly mend the split voices inside the young woman's mind. Never quite able to predict which personality would be at the forefront at any point in time, the adventurers had settled for keeping their distance. Weiss was a good person. That, at least, was certain. She was powerful in a fight, too, both as a healer and a combatant depending on the persona in charge, so the headache her personality switching caused had so far been worth the price paid.

For her part, Weiss was aware that she wasn't a whole person. Where Weiss ended and Madra began, she was unsure. But she *was* broken. That much she understood. At one point, the group had suggested she write her thoughts in a journal so that her personalities were, at the very least, properly communicating with one another. It hadn't changed much. She found the disjointed scribbles to be more confusing than helpful. But she could at least keep her distance, aiding the group as they aided her but staying far enough away so as to not be a burden to them.

The earth elemental attack was a surprise for everyone, and it had been disorienting as Madra shoved Weiss back into the recesses of their mental fortress in response to the sudden threat. The Madra side of her wasn't truly sure what they had been doing before. She didn't remember arriving in the gnome-dominated city of Seneschal, located along the southern coast of the Free Cities of Nor. Madra wasn't even sure how long they had been in this place. All she knew was they were being attacked, and she had to protect Weiss and Hope. She had to shield them from harm. They couldn't again experience the horrors of combat. Not again. It would destroy them both.

Joining forces with the group's Thalan fighter, an ex-Drakewarden named Sekhet, Madra raised her shield and rapier, aiming for the vulnerable joints that held these animated rock formations together, weakening them as Sekhet brought her greatsword down to crush them with the sheer force of her blows.

Sekhet was the only member of the group that Madra paid any attention to. She knew the names of the others—vaguely—but Sekhet was a brawler and a drinker, a friendly but brash personality with whom Madra could identify, and they made for an excellent combat team. But really that was where the connection ended. Weiss liked Sekhet well enough. She was tolerant and seemed to pay no mind to the brokenness the young Wiyota endured. But largely it seemed that was because Sekhet really didn't care about much other than alcohol and fighting.

And that was something Weiss simply had no interest in. Not when Madra wasn't in charge.

Somewhere in the midst of Madra's blind fury—the desperate fight for survival from which her persona had been born—Sekhet's sword landed heavily on the last of the earth elementals, crushing it and sending bits of stone ricocheting across the town square. At last everything slowed, and Madra braced herself, looking around for more enemies to fight. There were none; just an array of terrified onlookers half her size, poking their heads out of windows and doorways and even over the edge of the nearby well.

The silence seemed to summon the town's mayor, a wiry old gnome with a perpetually wary expression etched across his face. One of the team turned to him as Madra remained on the alert.

"Is it normal for earth elementals to attack the city like this?" she heard them ask the mayor.

"Oh, well, we get a rogue elemental here from time to time," the mayor replied. "But never this many at once. I can't imagine what would cause a surge like this."

Almost at the same moment, a din of angry voices caught Madra's ears and she whirled, prepared for another fight. Coming from the direction of what looked to be mines in the distant hills, the half-elf could see a mob of gnomes and halflings dragging a slightly larger figure along with them. From this vantage point, it looked like a human child, and Madra's eyes narrowed.

What the fuck?

It didn't take long for the mob to enter the town square and, seeing the mayor, they surged forward, shoving the child forward to stand in front of their leader. He was a disheveled mess of a kid, with unruly, dark brown hair and bright teal eyes, wearing clothes much too big for him that had been tacked and tied just to stay on.

What struck Madra as particularly odd, though, was the random assortment of belts and baldrics he wore, all filled with pouches, pockets, and latches overflowing with bizarre items, ingredients, and glass vials. Stranger still was the metallic gauntlet the boy wore on his right hand, a glowing, pale blue aes stone embedded on the dorsal side of the contraption which was, without doubt, far too big for such a small hand. Madra had never seen anything like it.

She wasn't sure what exactly the mob was saying as they yelled furiously at the mayor, each straining their necks a bit further, projecting their voices a pitch louder to be heard above the shouts of their companions. Madra was just about to get involved, because there was no way she was going to let a child get assaulted by an angry mob, when the mayor managed to calm the noise enough for the half-elf to at least hear him above the uproar.

"They say they found you disturbing the mines," the mayor began, clearly addressing the human child who stood looking bewilderedly around at the individuals who had dragged him into the town square. "That you...caused the elemental attack?"

The mayor looked as confused as the group of adventurers watching the whole scene unfold in front of them. The question caught the boy's attention, however, and he turned back to look at the gnome with a sheepish grin.

"Ah, yeah, that was me. Sorry," he replied, rubbing the back of his neck with his gauntleted hand.

The mayor blinked at him for a moment, eyebrows narrowing in confusion.

"Where are your parents?"

It was a very valid question, and Madra was more than a little perturbed at the idea of a child wandering around and possibly getting himself killed simply because he didn't have parental supervision.

The boy raised an eyebrow, cocking his head like a curious puppy as he considered the gnome's question.

"Um...my father is back in Yasil. In the Thal Sultanate. Why...?"

Everyone around seemed to give a start of surprise at his words.

"The Thal Sultanate?" Sekhet questioned from nearby. She had been leaning languidly against a nearby wall, arms crossed over her chest, but she perked up at the mention of her homeland. "What's a little kid like you doing all the way out here by yourself? You're a long way from home."

The boy almost looked offended at the term "little kid" until he did a dou-ble-take, glancing down at his appearance. A light of realization crossed his face then, and he suddenly burst out laughing, eliciting more than one baffled look from the others around him.

"Oh, this?" he motioned up and down at his body. "No, this is a...shall we say, a magical mishap? I'm actually almost thirty." He held his gauntleted hand out toward the mayor. "Name's Xerxes. I'm an arcane inventor from the Crystal Archives."

Madra narrowed her eyes suspiciously but bit back a grin at the air of noncha-lant confidence the child was exuding amidst the angry mob and the disbelieving stares.

No way in Abyss that's a grown man, the half-elf thought. *But this little shit is crazy. I like him.*

All at once, the mob's protests started up again, no doubt wanting something to be done to punish the boy for his transgressions, and Madra squared her shoulders, marching forward.

Kid is gonna get himself killed. Can't have that. Fuck these gnomes.

The half-elf took Xerxes by the shoulder, shoving him behind her and using herself as a shield between him and the angry mob. The sight of the six-foot-tall warrioress looming over them with a glare that could kill was enough to silence the vast majority.

"Leave the kid alone and no one gets hurt," she snarled, baring her teeth in an almost animalistic fashion.

"Well, I'm not actually...okay..." Xerxes began to say from behind her, though one look from Madra silenced his protests entirely.

The gathered mob grumbled discontentedly between each other but, with an encouraging word from the mayor, they did at last disburse. With that settled, Madra did an about-face to take another look at her new charge. The boy visibly flinched, eyebrows knitting in concern as though he was expecting her to stab him in the process. When she didn't, however, he cocked his head as he stared up at her, that same look of innocent curiosity playing across his face and again reminding Madra of a puppy.

"Thanks for the help," the boy said, holding his gauntleted hand out toward her. "I'm Xerxes. What's your name?"

Already, the rest of Madra's group was moving past the pair, clearly having lost interest in the whole charade. Before the half-elf could offer a reply, the dwarf of the group interrupted.

"That's Madra," he noted as he walked by, clearly headed to the tavern. "Give it a minute and you'll meet Weiss."

Xerxes turned in the direction the dwarf was walking, visibly confused.

"What do you mean?"

The dwarf laughed over his shoulder.

"Stick around and you'll figure it out."

Madra didn't take the boy's hand, and she didn't bother offering any kind of response to the dwarf's quip. Weiss and Hope were safe, and she had fulfilled her duty to protect the innocent around her. She still wasn't sure what to make of this boy named Xerxes. She definitely wasn't convinced he was an adult in a child's body. But there was one thing she did take note of, and that was the look of innocent wonder that glimmered in the boy's bright teal eyes.

She had seen that look once, a long time ago...back before the tragedy that took away her family...back before she, Madra, first gained consciousness...back when *they* were whole. And it was for this reason she couldn't help herself. She had to protect this crazy human child. She had to protect that little glimmer of hope and life she so rarely saw in a world torn apart by the horrors of the morgrim.

She'd be damned if she let anyone, or anything, hurt this kid.

9

Trials of Khul

19TH DAY OF KUZAL, AE 50

The snap of the nearby campfire and an occasional soft snore were the only sounds to break the stillness as Xerxes sat crosslegged on his bedroll, fiddling with an odd assortment of metallic pieces stretched out over a sheet of canvas. Between the campfire, his arcane gauntlet, his leather glove, the rolls of fabric tucked and tied to make his clothes fit, and the goggles pulled down over his eyes, the boy hardly noticed the chill of the nighttime desert as he worked. Only the occasional puff of moon-silvered breath served as a distraction and a reminder that the desert did, in fact, get very cold at night.

It had been just shy of two weeks since Xerxes had first run across the rag-tag group of adventurers in Seneschal. Traveling together more out of necessity than friendship, especially as they made their way out of the relative safety of the Free Cities of Nor and into the deadly Wailing Desert, few in the group had paid much mind to the eccentric little tinkerer tagging along with them. The only real exception to that was the rapier-wielding half-elf everyone called Weiss.

For a moment, Xerxes paused to glance over at the young woman who had cocooned herself in her bedroll. Of all the adventurers he had been traveling with, she was by far the most interesting. In times of calm, she was Weiss, a kind and gentle healer who invested herself heavily in the well-being of the others, regardless of their attitudes toward her. In times of danger, she became something else, taking on the persona of Madra, a terrifying and yet fascinating figure of reckless protectiveness.

Xerxes hadn't quite figured her out, but he found the whole situation intriguing. He appreciated the times she had reached out to him or attempted to protect him. Certainly, she seemed to take her role of group defender quite seriously. Still, sometimes he wondered...for a person with more than one personality, why did it seem as though she never left any room for herself in that equation?

The snap of embers nearby pulled Xerxes' attention away from Weiss and back to his current project, a flying contraption he had been working on for several years. Anything with wings fascinated him, and he had always wondered what it was like to see the world from a bird's eye view. Magic could theoretically make anything fly, but it was expensive, volatile, and too easily dispelled. What Xerxes was looking for was a way to combine the magical *and* the mundane, to blend the strengths of both into one reliable, awe-inspiring invention. Succeeding would put him well on the path to becoming a master at the Crystal Archives, too. It was an honor rarely granted to someone as young as him, even before the incident that turned him into a child. But that was the beauty—and the consequence—of the intense curiosity that defined him.

For a moment the boy glanced up, his gaze stretching across the waves of sand and off toward the dark, jagged teeth of the Dragonspine Mountains in the east. In the silver light of the full moon, he could just make out the form of a pyramid in the distance, tucked between the mountain foothills and rolling dunes. The Pyramid of Khul, it was called. Believed to be the cursed tomb of an ancient fae king, the pyramid was said to be a place of magic and mystery that had lured more than one adventurer to their doom. Legend claimed that if one ever *did* survive the "Trials of Khul," untold blessings and riches awaited the victor on the other side. Xerxes didn't really buy into the rumors of curses and treasure, but he had often wondered if there was any ancient technology lost inside those sealed doors.

He considered the prospect only a moment before letting out a quiet huff, his breath puffing out into a small cloud. It probably wasn't worth the risk. At the very least, curious though he was, he wasn't about to wander in there by himself. No sane person would ever think of it.

Xerxes had just gone back to assembling his contraption when, all at once, a shrill scream split the still night air. The boy just about came out of his skin at the sound, whirling around to see Weiss sitting bolt upright, eyes wide and bloodshot, a look of panic etched into her face. The scream had definitely been hers, if her distraught expression was any indication.

The sound startled the rest of the group awake as well, and everyone turned in Weiss' direction as the young woman sat there shivering and on the verge of hyperventilation, arms wrapped around her chest in a protective self-hug.

Cautiously, Xerxes crossed the distance to where the half-elf sat. He wasn't sure what was going on, but it was clear that something was wrong.

"Weiss, hey, you alright?"

The woman grabbed the sides of her head with her trembling hands, letting out something between a whimper and a growl.

"Mercury. Where's Mercury?"

Xerxes blinked back at her, then glanced about at the rest of the adventurers who had gathered around. If he remembered correctly, Mercury was the frogfolk that had been traveling with them, a simple-minded fellow with a penchant for trouble that far exceeded even Xerxes' dangerous levels of curiosity. While the boy hadn't paid much mind to who came and went from the camp before, now that Weiss mentioned it, he didn't see Mercury anywhere.

Xerxes' gaze caught that of the nearby Tekula druid, a wolflike humanoid clad in simple leather armor, and the druid nodded, turning to search the camp. There seemed to be an unspoken understanding in this group. It was almost expected that the frogfolk called Mercury would get into trouble at some point. Out here in the Wailing Desert, though, that could be a death sentence even for a native creature. That was doubly true for someone as far from home as Mercury, who hailed from the Mir Archipelago off the coast of Tallan.

It only took a moment for the druid to spot the little amphibious footprints in the soft sand just outside of camp, and his canid ears swiveled backward as his gaze trailed up toward the pyramid in the distance.

"You can't be serious..."

By now, Weiss had pulled herself from her bedroll, and the look on the druid's face seemed to be the final trigger. Xerxes watched as the half-elf stumbled, almost flinched, then grabbed her armor. Her facial expression hardened, became more determined and detached, and the force behind her grip as she snatched up her shield and rapier told him that Weiss had again retreated into the background.

"So...Madra now, right?" he questioned, cocking his head curiously.

The woman only gave him half a glance as she marched past.

"Just stay here, half-pint," she said, her voice a pitch lower than Weiss's ever dropped. "I'll go find the frog."

For a moment, the group watched as the half-elf stepped out into the dark desert, slowly fading into the distance with the moonlit pyramid framing her silhouette. A frigid wind kicked up loose sand behind her, her footprints quickly fading and forgotten. Xerxes frowned. It made for a very lonely picture, and something about that thought stung.

Nope. That wasn't going to happen. He was curious about the place anyway, and he wasn't going to let Weiss disappear into the darkness alone. He knew what it felt like to be alone in the dark. He couldn't imagine someone actually enjoying it.

Nearby, several of the others flopped back on their beds, pulling warm bedding tighter around them.

"Nice knowing 'em," one muttered, throwing his arm over his eyes as though blocking out the reality of what had just happened. "No way I'm going to suicide myself into that."

A few of the group exchanged questioning glances between each other. It was hard to justify letting one or two of the group simply walk into their own doom, but it was also difficult to justify leaving the relative safety of the roadside. No one came back from the Temple of Khul. Everyone knew that.

The group's concerns were wholly lost on Xerxes, however, as he bundled up his gear and trotted off after the wayward half-elf. The danger of the pyramid and the Wailing Desert was only a peripheral concern to him. He couldn't get that lonely image out of his mind.

"Mercury, if you're not already dead, I swear I'm going to kill you before the bitch can heal you and bring you back!" came a frustrated bellow from the half-elf up ahead.

Definitely Madra. "The Bitch" was Madra's way of referring to Weiss. It was one of the easiest ways to tell which personality was currently in control.

It took a moment for Xerxes to catch up with the woman, and more than once he cursed the fact that his legs had become so short, forced to pause to catch his breath as the half-elf forged ahead with her determined gait and long strides. Damn, but she moved fast! She was already just about at the sealed door leading into the pyramid.

"Hey! Wait up!" he shouted, trying to get Madra's attention.

The half-elf visibly jumped, whirling to meet the voice that called to her with one hand on the hilt of the rapier at her hip. The tension in her shoulders eased when she recognized Xerxes.

"I told you to stay in the camp, half-pint," the woman huffed as the boy trotted up to her side.

Xerxes let out a hum of acknowledgment, but his curiosity had already gotten the better of him as he examined the ancient door before them.

"Canopic runes..." he muttered, standing on tiptoe to get a better look at some of the inscriptions located much too far above his head. "I'm not an expert on them myself, but I've read that they're used in a lot of ancient arcane puzzles. The people who lived in the Wailing Desert during the Lost Era seemed to favor things like that. Some scholars believe it was as much a religious practice as a social one."

"Well, at least you're useful," Madra sighed. "Alright. So how do we find Mercury? His tracks lead up to the door and disappear."

Xerxes cocked his head to one side, rubbing his chin with his gauntleted hand as he considered the woman's question.

"It would be somewhat unusual to open a door like this accidentally, but...if the frog *did* enter the pyramid, the most logical thing to do would be to find the pattern in the canopic runes, which would be..."

He traced his finger through the air, searching through the patterns among the ancient script. The boy poked at a few of the symbols and, with a flash and a rumble, the door to the pyramid began to recede upward, further into the structure.

"Too easy!"

Xerxes cast an impish grin in Madra's direction, and the woman let out a heavy sigh.

"Fine," she said. "Just...stay behind me, half-pint? That way if anything comes out swinging, it'll punch me first. Alright?"

Xerxes' expression contorted at the notion.

"I guess..."

He still didn't like the idea, and he definitely didn't understand why it was that Madra was so adamant about enduring harm in the place of others, but he knew better than to argue with her. Weiss was easier to reason with. Madra wouldn't take "no" for an answer.

By now, the door had opened enough to peer inside, and the pair paused, blinking, at what lay ahead. The interior of the pyramid was pitch dark, a seemingly endless black void filled with shards of glass that floated ominously in the ether. Madra glanced down at Xerxes.

"You know anything about that?" she questioned.

Xerxes cocked his head, puffing out his cheeks.

"Nope," he replied at length. "That's new."

"So...what? We break the glass?"

Xerxes pursed his lips, thinking hard on the question before shaking his head.

"Glass in the ancient ruins of Aurora is often associated with arcane power. I'd leave it alone if I didn't need to damage it."

Madra shrugged.

"Alright, fine. Let's get the frog and get the fuck out."

Xerxes watched as the half-elf turned resolutely toward the void, hardly hesitating as she marched into the darkness. It was a fascinating effect, Xerxes thought, as he watched her first footstep land on the fathomless expanse within. It might as well have been the night sky she stepped into, but her touch caused the darkness to ripple like water on a still pond. The woman moved with a deftness that defied her brusque demeanor, and as Xerxes wandered nonchalantly after her, he couldn't help but be impressed. And with his attention elsewhere, he didn't notice the glass shard so close to his forehead.

The light tap of the shard was little more than a prick, but the pulse of arcane power that coursed out from it caused Xerxes to yelp, dropping to one knee as the worst pain he had ever known seemed to tear his mind to pieces. Flashes of imagery raced through the back of his consciousness, a confusing array of visions and voices that he couldn't quite make sense of. A lush tropical paradise, fae and fauna he had never seen, aes crystals growing out of the ground like fields of flowers...

By the time Xerxes regained consciousness, Madra was holding him by the shoulders and looking panicked.

"Hey, you alright, half-pint?"

Xerxes reached for his head as he felt fluid trickling from his nose and ears. He wiped his gloved hand across the sensation, and when he brought it back into vision, he could see clear bloodstains on the glove.

"Damn. Don't touch the glass," he groaned in reply.

Seeing that the boy was steady sitting up, Madra dug around in the satchel at her hip, producing a vial of viscous liquid.

"Here. Drink this. I dunno, it's supposed to be helpful. The bitch made it."

Xerxes gave her a pained chuckle as he gratefully accepted the vial held out toward him. He had seen Weiss make that healing potion only a couple nights before. But of course, she wouldn't remember that in Madra mode.

"Thanks," he replied, making a cheers motion before downing the concoction as fast as he could. He winced at the bitter taste that washed over his tongue, but a moment later the headache subsided and the bleeding stopped.

Seeing that Xerxes was, at least, not going to die on her right that moment, Madra stood back up, glancing around the space.

"Alright, don't touch the glass. Guess it's a good thing I didn't smash it. Mercury! Where the *fuck* are you?!"

Xerxes glanced back the way they had come. There was no door, no night sky, just an endless black void filled with floating shards of faintly glowing glass. Were they...trapped? He doubted it would be beneficial to tell Madra about that right now. Well, he had heard of the Trials of Khul. Maybe if they completed those trials, they would escape just fine when all was said and done. Yes, he was optimistic about their chances. No need to worry for now.

Shrugging off the concern for the time being—it did no good to stress over it anyway—Xerxes turned his attention back to his companion and the task at hand. In the distance, the dark corridor opened up into a doorway, and from it, the familiar croaky voice of the group's resident frogfolk echoed through the chamber.

"I am over here!"

It was a call of greeting rather than distress, and Madra and Xerxes exchanged glances at the sound.

"Well, he sounds like *he's* having a good time," Xerxes mused.

Madra cursed under her breath as she marched in the direction of the voice, being careful to avoid the shards of glass suspended in the atmosphere around them. Xerxes scrambled to his feet, hurrying to catch up with her, though he also made it a point to stay as far away from the shards as possible this time.

Passing through the doorway was like passing into another plane entirely. Perhaps it actually was. Where the first chamber had been suspended in a surreal void, this room looked as one would expect of an ancient ruin: a stone corridor with a heavy layer of dust and debris coating the floor, ornate alabaster pillars supporting the structure's heavy ceiling. Ancient paintings covered the walls and pillars, all intermixed with canopic script. Xerxes slowed to a stop, taking in the scene in wide-eyed wonder.

"Wow! Imagine what the Master of Archaeology and Linguistics would think about this place!" he mused aloud.

If Madra heard him, she made no note of it, and the next thing Xerxes heard echoing down the hall was, "Mercury! There you are. Are you alright, you little fucker?"

"Hello. I am fine," the frogfolk croaked back. "Look what I found!"

"What the...where did you...?"

The commotion caught Xerxes' interest and he trotted over to where the pair stood, the six-foot-tall half-elf leering over an unconcerned Mercury, who was only half Xerxes' size. The frogfolk held a platter of food in his tiny, webbed hands and was hoisting it up toward a very bewildered Madra. Xerxes cocked his head curiously.

"Where'd you get that?" he questioned.

"I just thought about being hungry and it appeared," Mercury replied nonchalantly. "This place is fun! You think about things and sometimes they happen!"

"Oh, yeah?" Madra growled. "So what if I think about strangling you?"

A motion caught Xerxes' attention from the corner of his eye, and he turned to look at the wall, watching as the images shifted to depict a beastly woman strangling a frogfolk.

Well that was...fascinating.

"Hey, have a look at this," Xerxes called to his companions nearby.

He motioned toward the display that had appeared on the wall. Madra glanced up, her face twisting with confusion when she spotted the image.

"Wait...that really works?"

Already, Xerxes was moving along the sides of the chamber, examining the pictures and glyphs decorating the surfaces. If Madra could just think about something and change the art, what other thoughts might have altered the images? Their own trio aside, had there been people who came before, influencing the pictures and patterns the way Madra had just done?

A few of the images were clearly of Mercury's origin, Xerxes thought, if the depictions of candle-lit ponds and banquet tables laden with food were any indication. One, he realized, was his own: the image of a flying contraption. A man in a tattered green cloak perched atop the artificial wings, surrounded by birds and clouds with the sun shining brightly in the background. When had he thought about that project? Oh well. He knew himself well enough to understand that he wasn't always attuned of his own thoughts and feelings. Maybe the pyramid was more aware of his inner workings than he was. Which was...fascinating and terrifying. The boy resolved to pay closer attention to what passed through his mind. Just in case.

Further down the corridor, Xerxes found images that were entirely foreign to him, and to some extent, they looked older. The polished alabaster walls were littered with pictures of terrified adventurers retreating from armies of undead and crystalline constructs, some lying in pools of blood as they were trampled beneath the horde. Crystals, most likely aes in origin, featured heavily in the depictions there, but all the images led to one conclusion: there was a reason no one came out of the Pyramid of Khul alive.

Xerxes paused in front of one of the extensive murals, rubbing his chin with his gauntleted hand and cocking his head as though somehow a different angle would change his perspective on the impending outcome of their little misadventure. If no one came out of the pyramid alive, how could anyone know about the Trials of Khul? No, the more he thought about it, the more illogical the whole thing sounded. There had to be a way, and he meant to find it.

"Hey, half-pint!" Madra's voice interrupted his thoughts. "We found the frog. Let's get our asses out of here."

Xerxes paused, blinking back at the woman as though only now remembering where he was.

"Oh, yeah, about that..." he replied matter-of-factly, "you can double-check, but I don't think we can leave right now."

"The fuck do you mean we can't leave?"

Xerxes and Mercury padded along after the half-elf as she marched back into the room with the shattered glass. They had hardly reached the door when a string of cursing echoed through the chamber and Madra stormed back in toward them. At first glance, she looked furious, but there was a hint of terror in her eyes as well.

"Now what?" the woman fumed. "There a lever or some shit we can use to open the damn door? Isn't that how this usually works?"

Xerxes turned to look back at the walls. Amidst the depictions there, the consistent images were of a mummy and two crystalline guardians. The patterns surrounding them were geometric, as though herding those who entered into a particular direction.

"So, there's this legend about something called the Trials of Khul, right?" the boy mused, skipping forward lightly before turning his bright teal eyes on Madra. "It's simple. We complete the trials, we get out of the pyramid."

"It's never that simple."

Xerxes shrugged.

"Won't know 'til we try."

He watched as Madra stiffened, almost as though she was bracing herself for the inevitable. For a moment, the two stared each other down, bright teal versus dark amethyst, but at last the half-elf sighed audibly.

"Fine. So what's your idea?"

Time seemed not to exist inside the Temple of Khul. Or, perhaps, it was simply that the sensation of it felt distorted amidst the winding passages that funneled Xerxes, Madra, and Mercury further into its depths. Aside from a few simple traps, the experience had felt rather mundane, but even Xerxes wasn't fool enough to think it would stay that easy.

The boy's mind was just beginning to wander when the trio turned a bend in the hall, stepping into a room filled to the brim with treasure. The floor was carpeted with a deep layer of gold and gems intermixed, with alabaster pedestals on which sat a varied selection of weapons, armor, and accessories. Magical torchlight flickered out of gilded braziers, casting dancing shadows across the room.

Immediately, Xerxes and Madra ground to a halt while Mercury let out an excited croak and bounded forward, all but diving head-long into the piles of gold. The other two turned to look at each other, wide-eyed.

"This can't possibly be real," Madra stated.

Quickly, Xerxes lifted his gauntlet, channeling magic into the gem in its center and watching as various symbols began to appear inside it. The sheer quantity of magical items in this room was phenomenal, and slowly the boy began to wade in after the frog, glancing around in wide-eyed wonder.

"Evocation, abjuration, divination...transmutation..."

He muttered the various schools of magic aloud until his gaze caught sight of a small, pale crystal nestled amidst the sea of gold. It glowed with an arcane light Xerxes had never seen before and, like a moth to a flame, he felt drawn to it. He gave a start of surprise when a firm hand landed on his shoulder.

"Hm? What?" the boy questioned, glancing up at Madra.

Her grip on his shoulder tightened ever so slightly.

"Don't touch shit," the half-elf huffed back. "You don't know what it'll do to you."

"But...it's got a strong transmutation signature to it," Xerxes protested. "From the looks of it, it's some form of aes gem, but its aura is different from anything I've ever seen."

"Doesn't transmutation turn you into...you know...weird stuff?"

Now Madra looked even more distressed.

"I mean...not all the time. Transmutation can serve a variety of purposes."

Immediately, the boy launched into an explanation of the various uses of transmutation magic, and the more he spoke, the more distressed Madra seemed to become, her voice rising in pitch, her protests becoming progressively louder and more frequently filled with bouts of cursing until at last she bellowed, "Don't fucking touch *anything*! You're the only one with the big brain thing going for us here!"

Xerxes paused, blinking up at the half-elf looming over him. She was red in the face, fists clenched at her sides, but in her eyes he could see that same look of panic that he had caught glimpses of in other moments of intense stress. The boy sighed heavily, glancing back over at the crystal. He really wanted to take a look at it, but he couldn't exactly argue with Madra. She was determined to protect him, and he had to respect her commitment if nothing else. She would sooner knock him out cold than let him do something potentially harmful to himself.

Seeing that Xerxes had given up the fight for the time being, Madra's shoulders visibly relaxed and she plopped a hand down on his head.

"Look, mini-brains, if you really want the damn thing, let *me* touch it first. At least that way if something happens, you'll still be in one piece, yeah?"

Xerxes frowned back at her.

"But what about you? If we get attacked by something, we'll need *you* in one piece. I'm not much of a fighter myself."

"If something happens to me, you might be able to put me back together. If something happens to you, we're all screwed. I don't know how to get through this damned trial."

For a moment, Xerxes stood still, quietly observing Madra as she spoke. He didn't like the nonchalant attitude she maintained when talking about harm coming to herself.

You really won't protect yourself at all, will you? he thought, letting out an audible sigh.

No. As much as it pained him, if his only options were to argue with her or put her in danger, he wouldn't go for the crystal. Not right now. Not while there was a chance of her getting hurt. If she wouldn't protect herself, he'd do it in her place. It was one thing to take a risk for the sake of research. But if he was going to take that risk, he wasn't going to let someone else take the hit for him. It didn't feel right.

Just then, something seemed to catch the corner of Madra's vision, because her head snapped up as her gaze shot across the room.

"Fucking frog, I just got through saying not to touch anything!"

Xerxes stifled a chuckle, the heavy clink of gold coins echoing in his ears as Madra marched in the direction of Mercury, who was currently reaching for something on one of the pedestals. With the woman now thoroughly distracted, Xerxes slunk toward the mysterious crystal, pocketing it before anyone could notice.

Sorry, Madra, but I can't pass up this chance, and I can't have you getting hurt because of me.

By the time the half-elf had removed Mercury from the pedestal, Xerxes was already back at her side, examining the canopic runes scattered about the room.

"Alright, now that the damn frog isn't trying to blow himself up, what about it, half-pint? Want me to get that crystal for you?"

"Don't worry about it," Xerxes replied, his voice sing-song. "Anyway, we've got a trial to solve, right?"

Madra eyed him dubiously.

"You sure...?"

The boy hummed in reply before cocking his head at a series of nearby canopic runes. The more he thought of it, the more he realized that the runes had become weirdly familiar since coming into contact with the glass shard in the first room.

"This script..." he muttered, eyebrows narrowing in thought. "The central room contains a powerful undead, and this room contains tools with which to defeat it. But...don't take more than one item or—"

The boy didn't get to finish his sentence as the whole room began to quake around them.

Madra whirled at the sensation, and Xerxes didn't need to ask what happened when he heard the half-elf bellow, "Mercury! What the *fuck*, you damned frog!"

The gold coins on the floor began to clink together as something beneath them rose to the surface, and as Madra grabbed their resident frogfolk by the collar of his armor, the form of two crystalline golems emerged from the sea of treasure, eye sockets glowing with crimson light. For a moment, time seemed to still around them. And then, as the crimson light began to glow brighter, Madra's voice split through the heavy atmosphere.

"Run!"

The half-elf threw Mercury in Xerxes' direction as she grabbed for the rapier at her side, rushing to place herself between the constructs and her companions. Nearby, the frogfolk let out a frightened croak as he sprung for the door leading out of the room, Xerxes only a pace behind him. The boy paused, however, when he reached the doorway.

"Madra! What about you?!"

"Get the fuck out of here, half-pint!" the woman yelled back. "I'll be right behind you!"

Already Madra was fending off attacks from the crystalline golems, backing toward the exit but never so much as to give the enemy an opening to the other two. Xerxes hesitated but, seeing the determined look that glimmered in the half-elf's dark amethyst eyes, he knew she would stand her ground and die so long as he remained within range of the threat. The boy bit his lower lip, then spun on his heels and darted for the hall.

You better follow, dummy, he thought as he dashed back the way the trio had come. *Or I'll come back for you.*

He doubted that Madra could hear his thoughts, but if she could, he hoped she understood that he was just as committed to seeing her make it out alive as she was to seeing him and Mercury survive. He was just slowing down and turning to go back for her when he spotted Madra skidding around the corner, a crystal dart whizzing just a hair's breadth past her head and shattering against the alabaster wall on the other side. Xerxes relaxed visibly. Alright. At least they were all back together.

"The fuck are you waiting for!" Madra roared, regaining her footing and charging in Xerxes' direction. "Keep running, damn it!"

The boy needed no further prodding, turning and taking off as fast as his little legs could carry him. The trio turned another corner, Madra nearly running Xerxes over as he skidded to a stop and doubled back.

"Back up, back up, back up!" the boy exclaimed, the sound of shattering crystal echoing in his ears only inches from his head as he darted away from another crystalline construct.

Back and forth the trio ran, each time only narrowly escaping an angry golem. The longer they ran, the more winded they became, and by the time they found a room with doorways that were too narrow for the constructs to follow, all three were doubled over and gasping for breath.

"Did...did we make it?" Xerxes panted, wiping sweat from his forehead with one sleeve.

Almost as if in answer, an eerie breeze began to stir inside the chamber, picking up granules of sand and swirling it around them in a slow yet menacing vortex. Behind them, a stone slab slammed shut over the doorway. Madra whirled, cursing violently until a mocking laugh began to echo through the chamber, and the trio turned to see a humanoid encased in linen wrapping apparate in front of them. Immediately, Madra placed herself between the new arrival and her companions.

"Who are you?" the half-elf demanded. "What do you want?"

The being replied in a language Xerxes couldn't even begin to recognize, the sound echoing as though in a cavern. He had heard about the mummies that haunted the ruins of the Wailing Desert, but Xerxes felt his skin crawl at the sound that this one made.

The mummy lifted its hand, flicking its wrist swiftly as arcane runes and sigils filled the air with an ominous light. A wave of necrotic energy washed through the room, and all three of the adventurers staggered under the weight of its draining effect. Madra was the first to regain her footing, letting out a battle cry that echoed off the chamber walls as she threw herself at the enemy before her. Nearby, Mercury raised his tiny bow, loosing arrows with an accuracy that defied the whirlwind that tore at them.

Sand whirled up from the ground, buffeting Xerxes' bare face. Only the goggles pulled over his eyes guarded his sight from the debris. With his gloved hand shielding his face from some of the assault, the boy raised his gauntleted fist in the air and yanked downward. A pulse of light emanated from the gem in the center of his gauntlet, and with it, glossy metal scales began to flow out like liquid over his small form, encasing him in protective armor.

Now he was ready.

Though tired from his earlier sprint through the pyramid corridors, Xerxes took off again, pausing only a moment to release a bolt of arcane energy in the mummy's direction before darting away. The enemy had a clear advantage here, but he could at least force them to work for whatever damage they dealt.

As he moved, a warm sensation began to form at his hip, emanating from the small satchel in which he had tucked the mysterious aes crystal earlier. It wasn't the kind of heat he was accustomed to feeling at the forge, and certainly not the kind he was used to feeling before something blew up in his face. It had a healing aura to it, and almost instinctively, Xerxes reached for the crystal, pulling it out with his gloved hand.

"Please don't blow us up," he muttered to himself, holding the crystal out and channeling just enough arcane energy into it to activate it.

He had no idea if what happened next would be a bane or a boon to their fight, but he was used to trusting his instincts, and his instincts told him now was the time to use the crystal.

A silvery light pulsed out from his hand with the release of the energy, settling on Madra and Mercury as they continued their fight with the mummy. Xerxes watched as their strikes became a little more sure, their movements swifter, almost as though they were divinely guided.

Dark, soulless eyes snapped in Xerxes' direction, and the boy shivered as the being began to chant something in a language he couldn't understand. Starting at his feet, a sensation not unlike a river of spiders crawling up his legs began to reach up his body, though there was nothing visibly there. As he felt his muscles begin to lock up, Madra turned ever so slightly, mostly in preparation for another strike of her rapier, but for a moment their gazes met, and he saw in that feral, battle-frenzied glance a hint of hesitation, an internal battle between the desire to fight the enemy and the desire to rescue him from whatever condition was now beginning to affect him.

That desperate, terrified glint that flickered behind a facade of fury...it didn't suit her. Whether in the guise of the loud, brash, bull-headed Madra or the gentle, nurturing Weiss, Xerxes knew that all he wanted was to see her thriving, not scared. Especially not because of him. The look was enough to snap him out of the magical influence that was attempting to overtake his mind. Planting his feet firmly, the boy leveled his gauntlet at the mummy, unleashing another bolt of arcane force in the being's direction. The bolt struck a gem glinting out from between the burial wrappings that encased the undead form, and the mummy shrieked, stumbling slightly with the impact.

"The gem!" Xerxes shouted, waiting for his gauntlet to charge up for another shot. "Aim for the gem in its chest!"

Seeing that Xerxes was unharmed, Madra refocused her attention, lifting her shield and flinging herself back into the fight. From the side, Mercury unleashed a volley of arrows, and Xerxes swung around to the opposite side of the room to keep the enemy's attention split.

There were no facial features to speak of, but the screeching bellows and rapid, discordant movements indicated that the mummy was becoming increasingly angry as the trio backed it into a corner. The creature lashed out at Madra, and Xerxes could see the woman bite back a scream as dark tendrils reached out from where the enemy had touched her, scorching her with flames of burnt amethyst. The mummy recoiled slightly, seeming surprised its attack hadn't had more of an effect, and Xerxes took the opportunity to dart in, activating his gauntlet as he moved.

"I got ya," he said, placing a hand on Madra's arm and releasing a pulse of healing magic into her. The arcane burns the mummy had left on the woman's shoulder healed over, and she gave a slight nod of thanks as she threw herself back into the fight.

A couple of times, the mummy launched attacks at Xerxes. Each time he ducked and dodged, shrugging off some of the more ambient magic as it tugged and tore at his muscles and mind. He was tired. There was no doubt about that. Only the magic energy thrumming through his arcane armor kept him light on his feet.

Xerxes was just beginning to think they had worn the mummy down enough to get at the gem embedded in its chest when, all at once, the sand kicked up again, forcing the adventurers to pause in their offense and brace themselves. Amidst the sandstorm, Xerxes realized only too late he had lost sight of the target. It was a pained croak that told him where the enemy had gone.

Xerxes heard Madra's enraged scream long before the sand cleared enough for him to see what was happening nearby, turning just in time to see the mummy rip Mercury's heart out of his chest. The frogfolk fell limply to the floor, and Xerxes watched as Madra flung herself at the cursed undead. The entity seemed to have underestimated the coordination and speed with which the half-elf was capable of moving, because a split second later she buried her rapier hilt-deep into the mummy's chest, missing the gem core by only a hair's width as it turned to escape her attack.

"Xerxes!" Madra roared.

"Got it!"

The boy leveled his gauntlet at the gem, unleashing another gout of raw arcane energy. Madra didn't even flinch, keeping the mummy pinned to her rapier as the pulsing ray struck its target, narrowly missing her.

A burst of magic erupted from the spot on which the mummy had been standing, the ground quaking beneath Xerxes' and Madra's feet. Sand swirled in a rending torrent, and for a moment Xerxes wondered if the temple would collapse around them. When at last the quaking stilled and the sand settled, he looked up to find himself back outside the pyramid, with Madra at his side and Mercury's lifeless body at their feet.

The aes gem in Xerxes' hand pulsed as he stared down at the frogfolk, almost as though tugging him toward the fallen adventurer. Next to him, Madra stood staring at the gory scene blankly.

Xerxes stepped forward, kneeling next to Mercury's body and holding the crystal over the open wound. The motion seemed to activate the pale stone, and the boy watched as silvery light sealed over the gaping hole in Mercury's chest. For a moment, he felt a tug, as though the gem was calling the frogfolk's soul back to his mortal form. He felt a sense of hesitation, another tug, and then...the sensation vanished. The light in the crystal faded, and again Xerxes found himself and Madra alone in the darkness of a desert night. Somehow, the boy knew that Mercury had chosen not to come back.

He frowned. Bastard. After all of that? After the lengths Madra had gone to in order to save him?

A wail of rage and anguish broke through the still night air, followed by a loud crack, and Xerxes glanced up to see Madra standing in front of the door leading into the pyramid, fisted hand pressed against the stony surface and bleeding from the impact of her strike. Her eyes held the fire of fury, but tears streamed down her sand-caked cheeks.

"Why?" the half-elf fumed. "I tried. I tried so hard. But again..."

Xerxes glanced down at the now inert crystal in his hand and sighed before pocketing it and trotting up to where Madra stood. He reached up, taking her bloodied hand and pulling it away from the pyramid door as he activated his gauntlet. For a moment, the pair stood in silence as the last of the healing magic stored in the pale blue stone washed through Madra's wounds. Then, the woman's legs gave out beneath her, and she collapsed to her knees in the cold sand. The hard edges of her face softened as tears flowed freely down her face, dark amethyst eyes staring blankly in front of her.

"We...did everything we could. We finally gave it our all. But it still wasn't enough..."

Her voice was soft and distant, like a child lost in the dark. Quietly, Xerxes squatted down in front of her, his hands still holding hers.

"Weiss?" he questioned.

The woman turned toward his voice, her eyes refocusing to make contact with his.

"Yes?"

Xerxes offered her a sympathetic smile.

"Welcome back," he said softly. "How about we get out of here, yeah?"

The half-elf hesitated, then slowly nodded, allowing the boy to help her back to her feet. Her gaze shifted toward Mercury's lifeless body and she swallowed heavily.

"Yeah. Let's get out of here."

10

REFORGED

20TH DAY OF KUZAL, AE 50

Weiss' mind was a confusing jumble, flashes of horrifying images scattered in the fog that only vaguely separated her from Madra. The lines between the two had become blurred, but only enough for Weiss to know and remember the horrifying truth. She had failed to protect Mercury, and she had watched him die a truly awful death. Madra had done everything she could. *Weiss* had done everything she could. They knew that. They had given that fight everything they had, but it still hadn't been enough. And here, among her comrades in a bar in Eisell, surrounded by laughter and music and boisterous chatter, Weiss couldn't pretend that she was okay. Even the lights in the tavern felt dull.

"Hey, Weiss, you alright?"

The voice was familiar, and the half-elf gave a start as she turned to look at Xerxes sitting next to her. The group had chosen a booth in the corner of the tavern, and the boy had taken to kneeling on the bench to prop himself up high enough to write in his book. It never ceased to amuse Weiss. The book seemed almost as big as he was. She was fairly certain at this point that she believed him when he said he was actually a grown man stuck in the form of a child, but that didn't change the fact that he had every bit the demeanor she would expect from an innocent youth. Still, that searching look in his teal eyes made her feel vulnerable, and quickly she turned back to the apple cider she had been nursing for well over an hour.

"I'm fine."

She could see him cock his head out of the corner of her eye, one of his quirks that always made him look like a curious puppy, but the boy didn't press and, with a shrug, he turned back to his book.

Weiss let out a quiet sigh that was quickly lost amidst the din of the tavern. No, she wasn't fine. She hadn't been fine for a long time. But she couldn't tell him that. The last thing she ever wanted was to be a burden.

For a moment, the young woman sat in silence, a somber figure amidst the otherwise boisterous crowd. Subconsciously, she glanced back over at Xerxes, and she did a double-take when she noticed a unique drawing of a butterfly surrounded by scribbled notes. The butterfly didn't quite look natural. Most likely the drawing was schematics for one of the boy's inventions. Still, for a machine, it looked beautiful. Weiss had never considered the possibility of combining nature and mechanics together. To her, those fields of study had always been two wholly separate entities. And yet here was Xerxes, blending them in his designs not only effortlessly but with a sense of artistic beauty she had never imagined possible. It wasn't in Weiss' nature to snoop or look at other people's private work, but somehow she couldn't seem to tear her eyes away from that design.

It wasn't long before Xerxes noticed Weiss' gaze, his teal eyes flicking up at her curiously, and quickly the woman diverted her attention elsewhere, attempting to bury herself in her mug as a feeling of embarrassment and shame washed over her. It really was impolite to look. She knew better.

A light scraping caught her ear then, the sound of something sliding gently across the table, and Weiss glanced over to see Xerxes pushing the open book toward her, providing a better view of its pages. He scooted closer ever so slightly, enough to adjust for the change so that he could continue with his work, flashed her a friendly smile, then went back to sketching.

Weiss blinked back at him for a moment before glancing down. The book was now clearly in front of her. She couldn't avoid looking at it. Her grasp on her mug tightened, and Weiss swallowed back the tears that were threatening to fall. In all her time as an adventurer, in all those years since she had lost her family to the morgrim, she had always at best felt tolerated. But now here was Xerxes, not only tolerating the fact that she had been looking at his work without asking but actively inviting her into his world.

Quietly, Weiss set aside her mug, leaning over to get a better look at the designs scrawled across the pages in front of her. The butterfly design contained sketches from multiple angles, the notes surrounding the images a smattering of various languages. Weiss could read the ones in elvish and trade speech. There were others there, too, though. If she were to guess, she would think the scripts and patterns matched draconic, dwarvish, and gnomish. Some of the notes mentioned sources, but all of the various scripts were so tightly packed together that sometimes it was difficult to know where one note ended and the other began. Xerxes clearly had not wanted to waste even a fraction of the space available to him.

From there, Weiss' gaze trailed over to what her companion was currently working on. The schematics on this page consisted of a set of gauntlets with gemstones on the backs of the hands.

"Working on an upgrade for your gauntlet?" the woman ventured.

Xerxes paused only long enough to flash her an impish grin.

"Not quite, but you'll see."

"Oh...alright."

She turned back to the butterfly design. It didn't seem that he wanted to talk about his newest project, and Weiss didn't want to bother him with questions about the butterfly. No sooner had she thought that, however, than she heard Xerxes' cheery voice break through the din of the tavern again.

"Pretty neat, huh?" he said, pointing to the butterfly design with his free hand as he continued to sketch out the gauntlet schematics with the other. "I haven't had a chance to test my theory on it yet, but if my calculations are correct, I might be able to make that one fly. I've added a chamber in the abdominal piece that should be able to release a healing concoction on a target it touches. None of my alchemical formulas have really matched what I'm looking for, though, so I might have to take a gander into herbalism."

He paused before looking up at Weiss, his eyes fairly glittering.

"Actually, now that I think of it, you're pretty good at herbalism. What do you think of the idea? Would that be something you could do?"

Weiss blinked back at him for a moment before turning to stare at her reflection in the mug of apple cider. There was a part of her that doubted that she could be helpful to someone as insanely intelligent as Xerxes. What could she possibly do that he couldn't? But a voice deep inside of her called out a hint of encouragement.

You can do it, Weiss. Just remember what ina *taught you. Our mother taught us everything!*

A slight smile crept onto the half-elf's face, bittersweet and gentle.

You're right, Hope. Ina *was the best at that, and she taught us everything she knew…*

Weiss glanced back up at Xerxes, nodding shyly.

"A healing vapor, maybe? I can think of a few combinations you could try."

The boy's eyes lit up even more at the woman's words.

"Perfect! I'll be counting on you!" He stood up on the bench seat, scooping up his oversized schematics book in the process. "In that case, I've got some work to do. Want to come with me? I can even teach you the basics of using the forge if you'd like."

Weiss blinked back at him.

"You…want me to come with you?"

"Well, I won't force you, but I wouldn't mind the company if you're interested."

The half-elf glanced once more at what remained of her drink before looking back up into that eager, boyish face and sparkling teal eyes. His vivaciousness touched something deep inside Weiss' soul, and she couldn't help but let out a light giggle of amusement.

"Sure. I'll come with you."

"Awesome!"

With one more impish grin, Xerxes bounded off the bench and trotted in the direction of the door leading out of the tavern, pausing only long enough to be sure he wasn't leaving Weiss behind.

Halfway to the door, the girl glanced over her shoulder, back at the group she had been traveling with for months. No one spared her a glance. At the tavern exit, however, Xerxes stood patiently waiting. It felt natural to follow.

Outside, the heat of the day had given way to a palpable chill, partially because of the environment of the desert to the west, but partially also because of Eisell's position inside the mountain pass that connected the Free Cities of Nor to the Wailing Desert and the Thal Sultanate that claimed most of that barren territory. As a major connecting city, Eisell stayed busy, and even at this late hour, Weiss could see all manner of humanoids coming and going from taverns and shops. The lights of the city winked between the throngs of travelers like the stars in the sky above, and Weiss raised her gaze upward, watching as her breath formed into a pale vapor that mimicked the scattered clouds curling around the mountain peaks.

Next to her, she could hear Xerxes going on about the project he currently had in mind.

"The best place to go would be the Temple of Kuz. They always have excellent forges."

He paused in thought before glancing up at Weiss.

"You wear three symbols. Are those the gods you serve?"

The half-elf inclined her head slightly.

"Yes and no. The symbols I wear are of three of the Droma nature spirits. My people, the Sinti, serve the Droma, though each tribe..." She swallowed hard at the thought before continuing. "Each tribe tends to favor one above the others. Mine...followed Nashtera, the spirit of flowing water. She is believed to most often take the form of a naiad and is often associated with the ebb and flow of life's rhythms. This is her symbol here."

Weiss pointed to an image depicting moving water before pointing next to one of a bear.

"This is Enyeto, a bear spirit. It is usually depicted as a black bear with white lightning in its fur. Those who follow Enyeto are considered very war-like, but also fiercely protective of their loved ones. This is Madra's favored spirit."

The woman paused in her explanation, considering her own words. When had she met Madra? Or...she wondered...when had she first become aware of her? There was still a blur of memories and thoughts and feelings wheeling around inside her mind, but ever since the battle in the Pyramid of Khul, she hadn't felt quite so...lost. Madra was, at least, sharing some of her experiences with her. Still, it was confusing, trying to understand the other voices around her, trying to put all those disjointed pieces together.

Xerxes' laughter broke Weiss from her thoughts then.

"Madra really is a mother bear," the boy laughed, casting a bright smile up at the half-elf. "That spirit definitely sounds like it suits her."

Weiss blinked back. She was broken, and Madra was, somehow, a part of that brokenness. Weiss understood that much. Yet...how was it that Xerxes could so easily just accept them for what they were? The boy seemed oblivious to her confusion, however, as he pointed to the third and final symbol that she wore, the image of a star.

"What about that one?" he questioned.

Weiss glanced down.

"That's Stea...the guiding light for those who are lost..."

Xerxes tipped his head, humming lightly as he considered this most recent fact.

"Interesting...that might be a fun addition..."

Weiss raised an eyebrow, staring at the boy curiously.

"What do you mean?"

At her question, he flashed her his signature, impish grin.

"You'll see."

Weiss sighed.

"You keep saying that."

Xerxes' only reply was a light laugh and a hum, mischief flickering across his features as he all but bounded up the road toward the temple of Kuz, god of craftsmen. For a person of such short stature, he certainly had a lot of spirit, Weiss thought as they reached the temple entrance. She watched as Xerxes threw open the doors without a hint of hesitation and strode inside. There wasn't an overabundance of people in the temple at this time of night, but those who were present all did double-takes when they spotted the odd pair making their way toward the forges.

"Excuse me, may I help you?" a rumbling voice questioned, its source stepping over from a secluded workstation to intercept the pair.

Weiss froze at the sight of a burly minotaur who stood well over eight feet tall. The half-elf had only rarely met someone who could claim to be taller than her, but this one looked like he could crush her with his gaze alone. The surprise and alarm were enough to trigger a hint of a tug at the back of her mind, the familiar presence of Madra hovering just out of reach. It was Xerxes' cheerful voice that snapped Weiss back to the present moment.

"Evening! I'm here to borrow one of the forges."

The minotaur glanced between the half-elf woman and the human child dubiously.

"Is this...your son?" he inquired.

Weiss blinked back at him.

"Um...no...he's my..."

She paused to look down at Xerxes who was heaving a frustrated sigh at the question.

What exactly are you to me? she wondered.

"My name is Xerxes," the boy said, oblivious to Weiss' dilemma as he fished out an insignia from his bag and held it up as high as his small arms could reach. "I'm from the Crystal Archives. I know, I know. I look like a kid. Magical mishap. Things happen. Anyway, you can check with High Priest Murzak if you need to. I've been through here before."

The minotaur leaned over to get a better look at the item the boy held up towards him—a rectangular silver tag attached to a lanyard via a marble-like gemstone—then glanced back over at Weiss. She shrugged faintly. She couldn't deny they made for an odd sight.

After another moment of hesitation, the minotaur stood up straight again, giving the pair a shrug.

"Alright, well...the forges are this way. If you need me to show you how to start them..."

"I've got it," Xerxes interrupted, giving the minotaur a dismissive wave as he bounded off again. "Oh, Weiss doesn't know, though."

Still largely focused on the task at hand, the boy launched into a detailed description of the process of forging an item, complete with the different levels of heat produced by various fuel sources, as well as the types of metals and the temperatures they required to forge and produce various results.

As far as Weiss was concerned, it might as well have been a foreign language. Next to her, the minotaur blacksmith stared at Xerxes with wide-eyed wonder before shrugging.

"Even I didn't know half of that. I wonder how..."

He seemed baffled as he wandered back to his workstation deep in thought.

Weiss turned to follow after Xerxes. The boy was already digging things out of his pack, scattering tools and scrap metal across the workbench. Curious, Weiss leaned over to examine the odds and ends her companion had deemed necessary for his work. None of it seemed especially beautiful or valuable. Twisted pieces of tarnished metal had been stacked into heaps along with fragments of aes crystals that glowed only faintly in the dim light of the workshop. It was all just a random mix of broken things. What could Xerxes possibly make with little more than trash?

She glanced up at her companion again. The boy hummed an off-key tune as he scurried about the forge, tossing fuel into the fire and pumping levers. While it all seemed bizarre to Weiss, it was clear that Xerxes was at least confident in his work. The half-elf considered asking him what he was doing but then thought better of it. He would probably just give her the same answer as before: "You'll see."

A short while later, the forge was burning brightly, and the boy set to work with tools and scrap to get his project started. Weiss glanced about, looking for a place to sit. Seeming to notice her wandering, Xerxes motioned to the stone workbench nearby.

"Feel free to sit wherever," he said, his voice filled with laughter. "This'll take a little while."

"Oh, alright."

Sheepishly, the half-elf took a seat on the far corner, still attempting to stay out of her companion's way. After a long moment of silence, Weiss ventured a question.

"Where did you learn to use a forge?"

She watched as a soft smile appeared on the boy's face.

"Oh, my father taught me. He's a blacksmith in Yasil, a small village just west of the Crystal City. I've been doing this sort of work most of my life."

Weiss felt a twinge of pain in her heart but swallowed it back, nodding.

"That makes sense. You must be very close to your father."

"I am. He was my best friend growing up."

"What about your mother?"

Xerxes paused at the half-elf's question, a more somber look crossing his face before he mustered a half-hearted smile and dove back into his work.

"My mother passed away when I was born. I never knew her."

"Oh. I'm...sorry..."

The boy shrugged, reaching for another piece of scrap metal and placing it strategically into the coals.

"It's fine. It's hard to miss something you've never known, anyway. What about you? What's your family like?"

The mention of her family made Weiss' head spin. Flashes of memory, dark and terrifying, wove a tangled web of emotions through her mind, and she quickly found herself panicking involuntarily. There came a tug at the back of her consciousness, Madra preparing to take over, to protect her from the horror of her memories, but the woman's head snapped up quickly when she felt a gentle touch at her elbow. She looked up to see Xerxes, who had paused in his work to check on her. He looked perplexed, unsure what to do as Weiss began to notice tears streaming down her own face. But still...he was there.

The boy cleared his throat awkwardly and looked away, holding his canteen of water out toward her.

"Sorry," he muttered. "Didn't mean to break you. Forget I asked. Just...don't get dehydrated or anything."

Realizing that he was trying to comfort her, Weiss sheepishly accepted the canteen. She didn't really feel like she needed water, but she appreciated the gesture all the same.

I'm alright, Madra. I think I'm safe with Xerxes.

There was a hint of lingering resistance, then Madra released the pressure on Weiss' mind.

Yeah, half-pint's alright.

Quietly, Weiss took a swig of the water, mostly to humor her companion before holding the canteen out to him.

"Thanks, Xerxes. I'm alright now, though."

He gave her a hesitant look as he took his canteen back, watching her as though watching for signs that she wasn't as alright as she claimed. The half-elf offered him a weak smile.

"It's hard. I can't always talk about it but...I feel like I can this time."

She drew in a deep, shaky breath, steeling herself as she searched for the words to explain to him what had happened.

"My people, the Sinti...we're nomads who travel the Rahan Wilds. Of course, the Rahan Wilds are always dangerous but...one day...one day a hoard of morgrim flooded into camp. There were so many of them...I watched my family get torn apart, one by one, and I...I ran."

Weiss squeezed her eyes tightly shut, fighting the tears that poured down her face as she clenched her fists.

"I didn't do anything to help them. My mother was a healer, and she taught me to value all life, to do no harm. To fight...it's against our creed, I suppose. And I was so scared. All I could do was run. That was when...everything started getting foggy. That was when I first remember meeting Madra. It's still a bit confusing to me. I...don't always know what's going on, but...it's strange. Up until that fight in the pyramid, I kept thinking that if I had just been stronger...or braver...if I had just done a little bit more...maybe I could have stopped what happened to my family. But now...something feels different. I actually...remember what happened in the pyramid. And I remember, after Mercury died...and as Madra...as I...as *we* struck the mummy...I remember thinking...we finally did everything we could, and it wasn't our fault. All this time, I've been thinking that what happened with the morgrim...that it was somehow my fault, but..."

Her voice trailed away as she stared at her hands clenched tightly in her lap. For a moment, only the sound of the snapping embers in the forge broke the silence around her. Then, a motion caught her attention, and she glanced up to see Xerxes hop up to sit next to her. The boy leaned back, bracing his hands behind him and staring up at the ceiling of the building that served both as a workshop and a temple. He drew in a deep breath before he spoke.

"I won't pretend to know what you went through or what happened back then," he said softly. "I wasn't there. But still...with everything I've seen of you, I'm gonna venture a guess that you did everything you could have done in that moment."

He cast a gentle smile in Weiss' direction, bright teal eyes reflecting the firelight from the forge nearby. His glance was brief, gaze trailing back to the forge. He paused before continuing.

"Can I...tell you a secret?"

Weiss cocked her head, watching the boy curiously.

"Sure?"

Xerxes paused, working his jaw.

"This," he motioned up and down to his small form, "is actually the result of some research I've been doing on the side. Some research on time manipulation and longevity."

The boy leaned forward, placing his hands in his lap and staring down at the gauntlet that trailed up his right arm.

"My father was on the older side when I was born, and he's started to really show his age in recent years. It's difficult for him to continue the work of a blacksmith, and honestly, I don't really know how much longer he can keep up with everything. He's all I've ever had, so..." He cast a sheepish smile in Weiss' direction before looking away again. "I've kind of been looking for a way to de-age him. Just...I'm not ready to lose him, you know?"

Weiss reached out, placing a gentle hand on Xerxes' shoulder. He returned the touch with an appreciative smile.

"Thanks for putting up with me," he said, letting out a slight laugh.

Weiss smiled back.

"You know, strangely enough, it really has been a pleasure," she replied. "If I may suggest though, perhaps take just a little more caution in the future? I really appreciate your curiosity, but sometimes exercising a measure of wisdom isn't such a bad idea."

Xerxes laughed at the comment before flashing Weiss his signature, impish grin and bounding off the workbench.

"What do you mean? I'm the wisest person you'll ever meet!"

The sarcasm was palpable, and Weiss let out a deep, genuine laugh as the boy made a flourishing bow and all but twirled on tiptoe back around to the forge.

From there, the pair lapsed into a comfortable silence, Weiss watching with fascination as Xerxes did his work. Slowly, the hammering of metal and the hissing of embers turned into a comfortable rhythm, and Weiss felt her eyelids begin to droop.

Just a moment of rest and then I'll be fine, she thought, leaning her head back against a nearby pillar.

A moment turned into hours, and when Weiss stirred from a heavy, dreamless sleep, she opened her eyes to the first light of morning seeping in through the temple doors, which had been left open a crack, most likely due to the heat of the active forge. The half-elf turned her head, blinking, to find Xerxes just finishing his project. The boy let out a hum of satisfaction, holding up a pair of gauntlets to view them in better lighting.

Quietly, Weiss stood and stretched. Her movement caught Xerxes' gaze, and he cast an amused smile in her direction.

"Morning, sunshine."

Weiss returned the greeting with an embarrassed smile of her own.

"Sorry, I guess I fell asleep."

Xerxes replied with a light shrug.

"No need to apologize. You looked like you really needed the rest." He tossed the new gauntlets in her direction. "Here. Try those on for size."

Weiss cast a quizzical look at her companion before cautiously obliging, slipping the gauntlets onto her hands. She wasn't exactly sure why he would ask her to try on gauntlets he made for himself; but then, Xerxes was a bundle of energetic mystery, so who knew?

The half-elf cocked her head as she flexed her hands. Strangely enough, the gauntlets seemed to fit her perfectly. Even if they were magical and capable of self-adjusting to fit their bearer, she didn't feel any give or magical transition.

Curious, the woman turned her hands to take a look at the reverse side of the gauntlets. There, nestled in the center, were a pair of identical aes stones. Weiss blinked. Those stones looked similar to the one Xerxes had picked up in the pyramid. And then something else caught her gaze. Encircling the stones on each gauntlet, tracing a delicate pattern across the metal plate, were the symbols of Nashtera, Enyeto, and Stea.

Weiss looked back up at Xerxes.

"What...?" she began, but the impish look on the boy's face told her everything she needed to know. "Wait...are these...for me?"

"Mhmm," her companion replied, looking at the gauntlets on Weiss' hands with clear satisfaction. "Turned out to be a good fit, if I do say so myself."

"But...why? What are they for?"

Weiss was still dubious. All that work...all those hours Xerxes had spent crafting these intensely magical items...she could only imagine how much the gauntlets were worth. And he did all of that...for her?

Seeing her hesitance, Xerxes bounded up onto the workstation, leaning over slightly to be on eye level with the tall half-elf.

"They're to protect you, silly," he replied, bracing his fists against his side. "You say I need to exercise a bit more caution, but you're always throwing yourself in harm's way to protect others. So if you won't protect yourself, something's gotta make up the difference."

Weiss blinked back at him, dumbfounded. Oblivious to the emotion churning inside her, Xerxes continued.

"The metal is a special alloy that comes from the Ruins of Taj. I've never managed to recreate it myself, but it accepts and conducts aes especially well. And the stones," he pointed to the aes gems on the backs of Weiss' hands, "are from that stone I found in the pyramid. They're a bit difficult to split and refine, but they store magic like nothing else. The gauntlets will give you some magical defense if you ever end up in danger again, and I'm not sure, but they might be able to take other enchantments eventually, too."

He paused in his explanation, a look of concern tracing its way across his boyish features, and it was only then that Weiss realized she was crying. Though Xerxes had used a much more complex and roundabout method of saying it, Weiss still understood his underlying meaning.

You're important. You're worth protecting. I'm here for you.

For so long, Weiss had felt lost and alone, both physically and mentally. How many people had she crossed paths with in the years since leaving the Rahan Wilds? How many had merely accepted the role she had assigned herself: that of a tool to be used until no longer needed? How was it possible that this quirky, bright-eyed boy could see past the broken pieces and believe in her as a person worthy of protection? But then, weren't the gauntlets an answer to that? She had seen the materials Xerxes had used to create them. Dirty, gnarled, rejected, broken pieces of metal and stone. And yet he had looked at what others would have deemed trash and said, "I can make something beautiful and powerful with this." Maybe, Weiss thought, just maybe, Xerxes' real gift was seeing the beauty in the broken. The thought alone sent her into a throe of messy sobs.

Somewhere in her peripheral, Weiss saw Xerxes stand up straight, still perched atop the workbench as he ran his gloved hand through his mop of unruly brown hair.

"And...I broke her. Again..." he muttered.

A laugh slipped through Weiss' tears and she reached up, dragging the boy off the workbench and into a crushing hug. He seemed surprised, even a little startled at first, but eventually he eased into the embrace, wrapping his arms around her warmly.

"Thank you," Weiss said through her tears.

She could feel the boy nod slightly, giving her an awkward grunt of acknowledgment as he tightened his arms around her ever so slightly. When at last Weiss let go and stepped back, her sobs had died down, and a sense of peace she hadn't felt in a very long time began to wash over her.

Still looking awkward, Xerxes reached into a pouch, holding out a handkerchief, and Weiss laughed at the perplexed expression plastered across the boy's face. The woman smiled through her tears, gratefully accepting the gesture.

"Really, Xerxes," Weiss said at length, "I can't begin to tell you how much this means to me. I'll treasure the gauntlets. I promise."

The boy looked back up at her, his shoulders relaxing, and he smiled broadly.

"I'm glad you like them," he replied. "Hey, Weiss. Do you have plans after Eisell?"

The half-elf blinked back at him for a moment before shaking her head.

"Not really. I think...after what happened at the pyramid...this adventuring group will probably part ways. I don't know where I'll go from here. Why?"

"You wanna go to the Crystal City with me?"

"The Crystal City?"

Weiss considered the offer. She had heard a lot of good things about the Crystal City, but in all her time traveling she had never been that far west. She glanced back at Xerxes.

"It sounds interesting, but I don't want to be a bother..."

The boy's eyes lit up at her answer and he reached for his pack, gathering up the last of his tools and materials.

"You're never a bother, Weiss," he replied as he worked. "Actually, I can get you into the Crystal Archives. I think you'll like it. They've got a massive collection of herb lore there and a whole department dedicated to apothecary and medical studies. I bet with your knowledge, you could teach them a thing or two as well. What do you say?"

He swung his pack over his shoulders and glanced up at Weiss again. The woman's expression gentled, and she smiled back at him.

"I think...I'd like that. If you don't mind..."

"Not at all!"

Weiss gave a start of surprise as Xerxes grabbed her by the hand, pulling her in the direction of the door leading out of the temple with all the energy of an excited child.

"Let's just get a bit of rest and then find a caravan heading north. This'll be fun!"

The boy's excitement was contagious, and Weiss found herself smiling back excitedly at the thought of this new adventure ahead of her.

For a moment, the woman glanced back over her shoulder, toward the forge where Xerxes had created her gauntlets. As she turned, some of the cooling embers snapped, sending bright sparks arching upward. The motion triggered something deep inside of her, casting her back into a familiar, foggy void. This time, however, she kept her focus on the sparks.

The tiny orbs of light danced through the darkness, leaving faint, luminescent trails in their wake, and as they moved, Weiss noticed the vortex around her begin to still and the fog start to retreat. Like fireflies on a clear summer night...or had the sparks actually become fireflies?...the light bobbed its way toward a half-elf woman and a child of identical appearance protecting the flame of a tiny candle. Madra...and Hope...

Weiss watched the sparks encircle the flame, and Madra and Hope stood back as the fire lept forward, the candle transforming into a warm campfire in front of them. With the fog now disbursed, the trio found themselves standing in a quiet forest. No longer did the trees look dead, gnarled, and foreboding. No longer did an angry wind howl. No longer did the fog place an impenetrable veil between them.

Hope let out a giggle of glee, chasing after the sparks that had become fireflies amidst the peaceful forest. Nearby, Madra took a step back, resting one hand on the hilt of her rapier as she cast her gaze upward. Weiss followed her gaze, up to a bright night sky blanketed with stars.

"Hey," Madra's voice called to her, breaking through the stillness. "You find it? What you were looking for."

Weiss turned to her, blinking. Then she glanced down at the gauntlets on her hands and she smiled.

"I think...I did," she responded at length. "For the first time in so long, I feel...whole."

Madra grunted.

"What does that mean?"

Weiss contemplated the question before pressing her hands to her chest, closing her eyes as she processed the emotions swirling inside and around her. She could feel the rhythm of her own heartbeat there, but one hand felt warmer than the other, and when she opened her eyes again, she found herself blinking in the early morning light, hand-in-hand with Xerxes as he prattled on about the Crystal Archives. Somewhere in the back of her mind, Weiss could still feel the presence of Madra and Hope. Perhaps they would always be there, but she no longer felt lost and disoriented because of it.

So many people had asked her to change, had tried to "fix" her in her brokenness. But here was Xerxes, happily inviting her into his life, not asking her to change, just offering to share the journey with her as they looked forward to what the future might have to offer.

Weiss smiled, then laughed slightly.

What did it mean to feel whole? It meant knowing she was broken and yet also understanding that by her side was a person who could look at the broken things and see all the potential they had in store. It was the most peace she had felt in years, and in this moment, the future had never felt so bright.

11

CAVALIER ROMANCE

31ST DAY OF MOLNAR, AE 50

The roar of the cheering crowd mixed with the sharp singing of metal against metal as Oriel Shiloh brought his sword up to deflect his opponent's blow. The force of the two blades colliding sent a rush of wind across the young man's face, mussing his dark brown hair that had been cut short and slicked back from his forehead.

Brown eyes flitted across the form of the rival in front of him, analyzing the weak points the blow had opened up. At Oriel's shoulder, the insignia of a knight of the Xanomes Kingdom clinked lightly in his ear, a faint but soothing sound echoing amidst the roar of the crowd in the seats surrounding the arena and the clash of weapons engaged in combat.

The rough sand below the young knight's boots crunched and hissed as he rounded on the man in front of him, bringing his own blade down in an arc, targeting his opponent's unguarded shoulder. He brought the sword to a halt as he felt metal meet armor, just as the bellow of a horn echoed across the open arena—a critical strike, which ensured that he would win that round. To Oriel, the world began to still then, though the roar of the crowd only grew.

For a moment, the young man and his opponent stood rooted to their spots in the arena, breathing heavily and processing what had just happened. And then they both laughed, reaching out to shake each other's hands.

"Damn, Oriel, you're as good off a horse as on one," the other man laughed, shaking his head as he accepted the reality of his defeat. "So much for being 'just a cavalier,' huh? Well, good luck in the next round."

"Thanks. That was a good fight."

The sound of musicians broke through the din of the crowd gathered in the tiered seats surrounding the arena, diverting the audience's attention away from the recently finished fight to yet another type of entertainment, and quietly Oriel and his opponent slipped into the men's dressing room to freshen up before the next fight. Oriel had barely made it through the door before a small towel smacked him squarely in the face. Instinct made him reach out quickly to grab the rough cloth before it fell, and when he glanced up, he saw a handful of his other comrades gathered around and grinning broadly.

"Congratulations, Oriel!" one of the other knights, a young man by the name of Hector, greeted energetically. "That was an incredible fight. You've got to be one of the most skilled knights in all of Xanom!"

Oriel laughed at his friend's words, using the towel he had been bombarded with to wipe the sweat from his face.

"Thanks, but that's a bit of an over-exaggeration when you only have maybe twenty knights actually in the tournament."

"Yeah, yeah," Hector sighed, waving his friend off. "You know, you could stand to be a bit less humble."

Oriel shrugged sheepishly.

"I suppose."

The discussion was interrupted when another of the knights suddenly burst through the door, exclaiming, "Adonia Kallis is up! If she wins this bout, guess who our man Oriel will be fighting next!"

Oriel only barely had time to grab his waterskin before he found himself swept up in his comrades' excitement, and they all piled out into the seating area next to the dressing room. Out in the arena, Oriel could see two people who could not have looked more different if they tried, both facing off with the other and circling each other like animals waiting for a kill. The most notable of the two was a large man with sinewy arms covered in scars. Definitely not a knight, Oriel thought. He was too unkempt. Maybe an adventurer? They got those in Xanom from time to time. The other contestant...

Oriel's eyes scanned the distance between the large man and the person he faced off against. The second opponent was a young woman, most likely in her mid-twenties, clad in the armor of a Xanomes knight but wearing a tasseled cloak that marked her as a member of the country's nobility as well. Her dark blond hair had been loosely braided and tossed over her left shoulder, eyes analyzing her opponent like a tactician. She bore an air of confidence that Oriel had rarely seen, even in the most haughty of knights, and he wondered if it was because she was a noble or if it was because she really was that good. Considering her reputation and the fact that she had already come this far in the competition, Oriel was inclined to think the latter. This *was* the infamous Adonia Kallis, and by reputation alone, Oriel couldn't help but feel sorry for the foreigner about to trade blows with her.

The Kallis name was, in and of itself, nothing to underestimate. Descended from one of the original founders of the Xanomes Kingdom and the closest friend of the country's first king, the members of House Kallis were all but living legends. Among them were two of the kingdom's most elite warriors, the Xanomes Crimson Knights named Leona and Rosaria. And from what Oriel knew, the girl now facing off with the adventurer in the arena was the daughter of Leona Kallis.

Almost as if triggered by that thought, Adonia and her opponent rounded on each other, the clang of clashing swords marking the beginning of their fight. The more the pair fought, the more Oriel found himself leaning against the railing in front of him, observing the competition in wonder. He watched as loose strands of the girl's blond hair whipped and danced about her face and shoulders, determination burning in her eyes. Despite the heavy chain mail she wore, Adonia moved with a level of grace that defied the armor's natural restrictions. Oriel couldn't help but feel entranced.

To some degree, Adonia Kallis reminded him of a horse, the way her hair whipped and flowed with her skilled movements. She was strong...and she was beautiful...and yet there was something wild and dangerous about her, too.

Realizing how odd of a thought that must be, Oriel tucked it away in the recesses of his mind and leaned back in his seat, but it was at that moment that his comrades' chatter caught his ears.

"The Kallis women are terrifying," one of the other young knights was saying. "Did you hear that Adonia put a hole in a man's foot once?"

"She did *what*? *How*?!" the second knight exclaimed, looking aghast.

The first knight nodded solemnly.

"I heard the fellow was trying to woo her. He got a little too cozy and she was wearing really tall, thin heels. She stomped her heel clean through his foot. Some rumors say she even burned him with divine energy in the process!"

Oriel couldn't help but snort at the story he had just overheard. Sounded a bit far-fetched, but this *was* Adonia Kallis they were talking about. And clearly, it sounded like the man in question deserved everything he got.

The humor attracted the attention of Oriel's companions.

"Laugh while you can, friend," one of the other knights said, glancing back to the arena. "You're next."

Oriel turned his gaze back to the fight, only to see Adonia sweeping the legs out from under a man easily a foot taller than herself. A cloud of dust erupted with the impact of the man's fall, and Oriel let out a bemused sigh. Yes, somehow he knew there was a good chance he would end up in the dirt, too.

The young knight glanced up when he felt a pat on his shoulder, only to find Hector grinning impishly at him.

"Nice knowing you," the other knight said, giving Oriel a teasing smirk before heading back toward the locker room. "Ale, anyone? This is going to be a show! *If* it lasts that long."

A chorus of laughter and affirmative shouts followed.

Oriel watched as the adventurer in the arena, very clearly embarrassed after being solidly beaten by a girl half his size and age, stood to his feet and sulked off to the dressing room. Then the young knight turned and headed for the entrance to the arena. He had gotten enough of a feel for Adonia Kallis' style to know this was going to be one hell of a fight, but he couldn't leave room for defeat in his mind. It was a possibility, sure, but it wasn't something he was going to allow himself to think about.

Upon his approach to the arena entrance, a half-elf glanced up from the list he was holding.

"Oriel Shiloh?"

Oriel nodded, and the half-elf marked something on his list before opening the gate next to him.

"Good luck out there."

"Thanks."

There hadn't been an interlude between the last fight and this one, so Adonia still stood in the middle of the arena, stretching as she waited for her next opponent to arrive. She glanced up curiously as Oriel took his place in front of her, and her hazel eyes brightened at the sight of him.

"Glad to see the top competitors are both knights today," the girl grinned, crossing her arms over her chest and eyeing Oriel up and down.

The young man honestly wasn't sure if she was sizing up his combat ability or his body, and he gave her a hesitant but equally curious look in return.

"Well, I just got lucky, I suppose."

Adonia's grin broadened.

"Humble *and* handsome," she teased. "Ok, I'll play."

Somewhere in the distance, Oriel heard the sound of his and Adonia's names being announced, followed by the bellow of a horn signaling the beginning of the fight. Adonia drew her sword at the sound, and Oriel did the same. Though both blades were equally dull, meant only for the competition, the metal from which they had been forged still sang sharply as they were pulled from their sheaths.

As she had done in the previous match, Adonia began to circle, keeping herself on the defensive. For a moment, Oriel watched where those bright hazel eyes traced. She was searching his form, looking for weaknesses in his stance, body structure, and technique. He couldn't afford to give her the opportunity to find them.

With that thought, the young man launched himself forward, his plate armor clanking noisily with the force of his advance. He could see the surprise in Adonia's eyes, no doubt because she was accustomed to her male opponents hesitating at crossing swords with her. The Xanomes Kingdom was accommodating to female warriors, but Oriel knew that some instincts, and some attitudes passed down from their people's original homeland, were not so easy to erase. Still, he couldn't afford to see her as a woman in this moment. She was a soldier, his opponent, just like any he had fought before. If he wanted to win, that was all he could allow himself to focus on.

The surprise was effective, but Adonia was just as quick, and Oriel only managed to land a glancing blow against the young woman's shoulder before she brought her shield up to deflect the blade slicing across at her.

The force of the shield blow knocked Oriel's sword arm backward, leaving his right shoulder open, and Adonia took the opportunity to land a strike of her own. The tip of her sword pricked him, but he leaned away from it, bringing his own shield up to defend.

The pair arched their eyebrows at each other as they circled around for another bout, and Oriel was certain that Adonia was as impressed with the traded blows as he was. Across the way, the girl openly smirked, eyes sparkling gleefully. Whoever won the tournament today, it was clear that both parties were enjoying themselves.

Up in the stands, the crowd roared, a din so loud that it was impossible to tell who the favored combatant was. Oriel sprung in for another round, channeling all the strength and speed he could muster into the technique. Adonia was tough, and by Oriel's estimation, for the purposes of the tournament, their skills were just about on par with one another. If the girl did possess divine power, she wouldn't be allowed to use it here, which was to his advantage, but he strongly suspected that Adonia didn't need divine assistance to be a worthy opponent.

One, two, three, four times he struck out with his blade. Adonia managed to block two of the strikes, but the other two hit home. The girl wasn't fazed, pitting her strength and speed against Oriel's. Soon the fight became like a dance, their power and agility equal in every way.

The only problem for Oriel was his armor. The plate that protected him from sword blows was also heavy and cumbersome. While the chain mail Adonia wore wasn't by any means favorable to excessively speedy movements, it still allowed for a measure of dexterity. And as they fought, Oriel realized he had made one very vital error: he had wanted to defeat her quickly, and he had played his hand too soon. Adonia was conserving her strength, biding her time, allowing Oriel's own armor to weigh him down and become his undoing.

The realization came far too late.

Halfway through a series of shield blocks and sword strikes, Adonia shifted her footing, somehow slipping past Oriel's shield until she was practically chest-to-chest with him. The young man blinked, at first wondering what she could be doing; she wasn't going to get a hit in that way. He watched a nearly impish expression cross Adonia's face, and in that moment, Oriel felt his heartbeat stutter.

"Shit."

No sooner had the word come out of Oriel's mouth when he felt his feet slip out from under him. The world around him spun—the screaming crowd up in the stands, the bright blue sky above, the fluttering red banners of the Xanomes Kingdom—and for a breath of a moment, he found himself airborne. The impact that followed knocked the wind out of his lungs.

It took a moment for Oriel's mind to process what had just happened, but when the dust cleared, he found himself staring up at Adonia, one boot pressed to his chest and the tip of her sword biting into the tender flesh beneath his chin. She grinned broadly, hazel eyes dancing.

The roar of the crowd in the stands was deafening, even from this distance, and Oriel couldn't help but accept the truth. He had been squarely beaten by Adonia Kallis.

Sword still at his throat, Oriel watched as Adonia leaned forward, resting the elbow of her shield arm against her knee. She stared at him curiously. Then she said the absolute last thing the young knight expected to come out of the girl's mouth.

"You're cute," she said, her grin broadening. "How about drinks after this?"

Oriel blinked back up at her, for a moment absolutely dumbfounded. Then, he started to laugh. It was the most heartfelt laugh he had experienced in a very long time. He raised an eyebrow at her and glanced between her face, her sword, and the boot still pressed to his chest.

"May I at least get out of the dirt first?" he asked.

Now it was Adonia's turn to pause.

"Oh! Right! Sorry."

Oriel relaxed slightly as the girl's boot lifted from his chest and the sword slid away from his throat. He sat up, bruised and covered in sand but also highly amused by the girl who stood unabashed in front of him. Meanwhile, the shouts of the crowd had eased into an excited hum, and a quick glance through the stands revealed more than one blushing face as girls giggled between each other and young men smirked. Off in the seats next to the men's dressing room, Oriel could see his companions talking excitedly amongst themselves and sending him teasing glances. He could only imagine how that must have looked.

"Hey."

Oriel glanced up at the sound of Adonia's voice, only to find her hand outstretched, offering to pull him up off the ground. He smiled, grateful for the assistance under the weight of his armor and the disorienting impact he had just endured.

"I think I'm going to have sand in my armor until I retire," Oriel laughed sheepishly, rolling his shoulders and listening amusedly to the hiss of sand raining down his back.

Adonia laughed in return, a rich, open sound that made the earlier defeat feel less chafing.

"You're welcome for the souvenir," the girl said, placing a hand on the young man's shoulder and leaning into him slightly. "Something to remember me by."

She gave him a flirtatious wink, then stepped back as a referee came to fetch her, motioning for her to follow him to a dais set up above the arena to accept her reward as the winner of the tournament. As Adonia turned to walk away, however, she called over her shoulder, "Crimson Shield! Sunset!"

Oriel smiled back and nodded.

"I'll be there!"

For a moment, he watched after the woman's retreating form: her confident stride, the wave of her tasseled cape, the dance of her dark blond hair in the faint breeze that managed to waft its way over the arena walls. Then he turned, heading for the men's dressing room. He hadn't even cleared the doorway when he was met by a host of his comrades.

"How'd it feel, lying there under her boot, huh?" Hector teased, elbowing him as he began to unstrap his armor.

"Oh, shut up," Oriel sighed, though he bit back a laugh with every hiss of sand that came with it. "I've heard about Adonia Kallis, but she's got way more presence in person."

"Presence is one way to put it," another of the knights chimed in. "By the way, it looked like you two were having a nice chat when she had you pinned down like that. You've got to tell us what she said."

Oriel paused, feeling the heat of a blush rising into his cheeks at the memory. Then he glanced up at the curious gazes hanging on the silence, waiting for his response.

"Actually..." the young man chuckled, nervously rubbing the back of his neck, "she asked me out for drinks this evening."

"She what?!"

The outburst was so perfectly in tandem that it was a wonder the group of young men hadn't rehearsed it for decades. It was quickly followed by a tangled volley of questions, and several minutes had passed before Oriel managed to calm everyone down.

"You know we were teasing, right?" Hector pressed, eyes wide as he stared at his friend. "I mean, what kind of girl just asks a man out for drinks while she's *standing on him*?!"

Another of the knights leaned against a nearby wall, his expression a complex mix of emotions.

"Damn," he muttered, "if that were me, I don't know whether I'd find it enticing or terrifying. Imagine what she could do to you if you make the wrong move."

"Or break her heart," another added.

Hector sighed dramatically.

"It's official. Oriel is as good as dead. Nice knowing you, friend. Truly. *I'd* rather fight the morgrim."

By now, Oriel had stripped off his armor and was shaking the sand from his cotton underclothes.

"You're all a mess," he sighed. "She asked me out for drinks, not to marry her. So while you're all being dramatic, I'm going to get washed up. Later."

The sun had already slipped below the horizon, casting a warm pink and gold hue across the sky above Xanom, as Oriel stepped into the Crimson Shield Inn and Tavern in the Military District. Already, the building was packed with knights of varying stations, from pages to commanders, all chatting amicably over warm meals and frothing beverages. Across from the door and off to the right, Oriel could see the tavern's owner, Nereus Lex, busying himself behind the L-shaped bar while nodding politely to a pair of young knights who were attempting to engage him in conversation. Sometimes Oriel forgot that Nereus was actually the head of one of the minor noble houses of Xanom. It seemed he always did his best to make others forget the fact; the Crimson Shield felt like a second home even to the soldiers hailing from the Lower Ward.

Quietly, Oriel made a quick scan of the tavern floor. It didn't take long for him to spot Adonia Kallis sitting alone at a table in the corner of the dais-like platform to the far right of the bar. The young man ground to a sudden halt in the doorway when he saw her.

The girl...no, the *woman* before him was not the same soldier who had just bested him in combat a few hours before. Adonia had changed into a sleek silk outfit with a tight bodice and one bare shoulder, covering enough for the imagination but leaving enough of her body visible to make it difficult to look anywhere else.

If Oriel had thought the woman's top was well-fitted, though, he quickly realized that the leggings she wore with the outfit were even more so, following the rise and fall of her long, athletic legs. His eyes trailed down to the tight boots laced up to her knees, and then on down to the long, thin heels that no doubt would make her even taller than he was. The sight made his own feet hurt. Her hair had also been done up nicely. It seemed like she had put a lot of effort into her plans for this impromptu outing.

It took a moment for Oriel to realize every eye in the tavern had turned toward him curiously, and he wondered if the crowd already knew what he had come to the Crimson Shield for. Adonia also spotted him in that moment, and she held a hand in the air, putting the full length of her bare, toned arm on display as she shouted out, "Oriel! Over here!"

If the whole tavern hadn't been paying attention to him before, they certainly were now, and again the young man felt heat rising into his cheeks. Half of him was strongly inclined to turn and run and not look back. But as his gaze circled back to the girl sitting by herself in a corner, blissfully unaware that the others in the tavern were making it a point to sit as far away from her as possible, he couldn't help but find that vivaciousness infectious, and so he stepped forward, ignoring the unwelcome audience as he moved to sit with Adonia.

"Hey, I kinda thought you wouldn't actually show up," the young woman said, beaming over at Oriel as he settled in a seat far enough away as to be polite but close enough for them to have a comfortable conversation.

"Sorry I'm late," Oriel replied. "It took a while to get all the sand off. You've got a mean kick, you know."

Adonia laughed heartily.

"I got lots of practice in with my sister," she said. "So, what would you like to drink?"

"An ale will be fine, thanks," Oriel answered. "To be honest, I'm going to need something for my nerves. You attract a lot of attention."

He fought the urge to look any lower than Adonia's face.

"So I'm told," Adonia shrugged before waving over a waitress and giving the girl their order. When she turned back to Oriel, she leaned in impishly. "But there's just so much of me to love."

Do not answer that. Absolutely do not answer that, Oriel thought, purposely glancing up at the ceiling rather than look down where his instinct directed him.

"Anyway," he said, awkwardly clearing his throat, "do you normally ask people out while you have them pinned to the ground?"

Adonia seemed to pout at the question.

"No, but I clear the tavern when I try in here." Her tone suddenly lightened then. "You couldn't exactly get away."

Oriel glanced back down at her face, and the look of humor he found there seemed to chase away the awkwardness he had felt a moment before. He burst out laughing.

"You're something else," the young man sighed, shaking his head in wonder as two pints of ale were placed in front of him and Adonia. He reached for the closer of the two mugs, picking up his tankard and holding it out toward her. "How about we start properly this time? I'm Oriel Shiloh. Congratulations on your victory this afternoon, Ms. Kallis."

Adonia grinned, striking her tankard against his just enough to cause some of the amber concoction to slosh over the side.

"Adonia Kallis, obviously. And cheers to *your* combat skill," she added. "Honestly, if I hadn't flattened you when I did, I think you would have come out the winner."

Oriel tipped his head in appreciation.

"Maybe someday we'll have to do a rematch."

Adonia's smile broadened.

"I'd like that."

At that, the pair tipped their tankards back, taking in the sharp, aromatic flavor of the ale, and soon they had lapsed into comfortable conversation. Slowly, the hues of red and gold outside the nearby window gave way to the darkness of night, and as time passed, the tavern grew progressively quieter and emptier.

Adonia downed her fourth pint and reeled back, casting her gaze over to Nereus, who still stood at the bar nearby.

"Nerreuss!" the woman called in a sing-song voice. "Another?"

Oriel frowned, watching Adonia's behavior. She wasn't quite beyond reason yet, but definitely she was showing signs of inebriation. Oriel's gaze met Nereus', and the older man raised an eyebrow at him.

"Best you let Oriel take you home now, Ms. Kallis," the man replied. "That's enough for tonight."

Adonia pouted.

"I'm not ready to go home. This is fun!"

At this, Oriel stood, offering the woman a hand.

"Come on," he said gently. "Get any deeper into your cups and you'll break your ankles in those heels of yours."

"I'm fiiinnneee," Adonia protested, taking Oriel's hand in both of hers and all but launching herself onto her feet. The young man had to catch her before she went over on her face, but then she steadied herself. "I'm a master at this. *But*...I'll be happy to have a handsome man to hang on to, if that's what you want."

Oriel and Nereus exchanged another glance, and the younger man could have sworn he saw the tavernkeeper mouth the words, "Good luck," at him. He let out a bemused chuckle, then turned toward the door leading out of the tavern.

"Alright. Where are you staying? I'll escort you."

"At the Kallis mansion, of course," Adonia giggled. "I want *ina* to see me come home with a boy."

"*Ina*?" Oriel questioned, keeping half an eye on his companion as he flagged down a coach.

"Mm-hmm," the young woman nodded. "My mother. My father is a Sinti. *Ina* is Sinti for 'mother.'"

"I see."

Oriel cocked his head, thinking on what Adonia had just said. He remembered that her father was Anthony Kallis, though now it occurred to him that, while he had seen Leona on more than one occasion, he had never seen Anthony Kallis among the ranks of nobility he had crossed paths with. If Anthony was a Sinti, however, it made sense. The Sinti were nomads, hardly more than outcasts in Xanomite society. Even as a noble married to a Crimson Knight, the man likely wasn't welcome in most Xanomite circles.

Still, as Oriel watched the look in Adonia's eyes when she spoke of her family, he could do nothing but smile. Oriel had never known his family, but it seemed Adonia was close with hers. And something about that look of fondness in her eyes made the young man want to know more about this family that made this woman smile with such pride and adoration.

Oriel listened to the clatter of hooves in front of them and, when the coach had finally come to a complete stop, he carefully helped Adonia inside. Afraid she might fall on her face and hurt herself, he settled in beside her and called instructions to the driver. The vehicle lurched, and then they were off, only the clipping cadence of equine feet and rumble of wheels against cobblestone to break the quiet while the carriage swayed like a cradle.

Oriel watched as the lively girl at his side began to become more subdued with the rhythmic rocking of the coach.

"Thank you," she said suddenly, leaning against his shoulder as her eyelids became heavy. "Thank you for not running away and leaving me alone."

The words surprised Oriel, and he turned slightly to get a better look at her. Instead, Adonia buried her face in his chest. Though her voice had become muffled by his shirt, she continued, "I'm going to marry you someday."

Oriel gave a start.

"Um...what?"

There was no reply. The young woman had fallen asleep with her face buried in his chest.

Oriel sighed, staring down at the scene before him.

"I really hope you don't do this with every man you meet," he muttered to no one in particular. "You're lucky I'm a gentleman."

Gently, Oriel took Adonia by the shoulders, turning her so that she wouldn't suffocate with her face pressed against him and wishing he had thought to wear a coat that evening. He steadied the young woman with his arm, then leaned his head back, staring at the ceiling of the coach as it rattled across the bridge that spanned the distance between the Military and Noble Districts. Below, he knew that tiny, thatch-roof cottages were snuggled together in the Lower Ward, the place where society's poorest lived...the place where he had been born. It was hard to imagine that right now, in this moment, a boy from the Lower Ward could be cradling in his arms the descendant of one of the country's greatest heroes.

Bit by bit, his mind replayed the day's events, and the absurdity of it all made him laugh audibly. The possibility of marriage aside, Oriel couldn't help but be amused by this crazy mess of a girl who had fallen asleep next to him. He had never met a woman more beautiful and vivacious than her. No, he had no intention of running. He never would.

12

— · —

THE APPRENTICE

9TH DAY OF MIRIAL, ED 849

The scent of briny ocean air and pungent fish washed over the large port of Calaghorm like the rolling waves in the harbor. Here and there, people of all varieties hurried up and down the streets, all busying themselves with the day's demands.

Most were sailors, sun-tanned faces and hands bearing testament to the tumultuous lives they had lived, but every once in a while, a nobleman or a scholar, a finely dressed merchant or a robe-clad priest passed through the crowds, always on a mission of their own.

Among them, only one small figure, a little elvin girl clad in a plain brown tunic and matching pair of trousers, seemed to move without a destination in mind.

Her name was Aeva.

"Wow! The Broad Docks are as busy as ever!" the girl mused aloud to no one in particular.

Her bright green eyes searched every face in wonder, as if each held a treasure within them.

And to Aeva, they did.

To the little elf girl who wandered the streets of Calaghorm, each person she passed was an untapped trove of stories, and knowledge, and items of ceaseless wonder. Every person was a book, and she wanted to read them all.

It was a fair walk from Aeva's home in the Garden Market District down to the Broad Docks on the southern end of Calaghorm, but the young elvin girl barely noticed it. She had only recently begun exploring this part of the city on her own—much to her parents' chagrin—and there was plenty of activity to keep the girl entertained with all the comings and goings.

In what seemed like mere moments, Aeva found herself wandering along the edge of the piers, eyes wide in wonder as she scanned the ships that had dropped anchor in the harbor. The breeze here, unfettered by the haphazard rows of buildings further up the hill, whipped past the girl in brisk gusts of salt and fish, causing the tendrils of short, black hair she had pulled into a sloppy ponytail to flit about her face as though in a heated dance.

Emerald green eyes skimmed the figures that moved up and down the piers and back and forth along the harbor's edge. Aeva made up stories for all of them.

That man with the eye patch she was sure had been in a fight with a direwolf and had nearly been mauled before killing the creature with his bare hands. Another who passed, this time with burns on his sun-tanned arms—he must have survived a battle with a dragon!

Most were elves, but there were other races here, too; humans of every shape and color, catfolk with fluffy tails that swished as they walked, beings who looked like dragons called drakonites, and dwarves, and the green-skinned orcs, little tiny folk called halflings and gnomes, and big, burly giant-kin. There were occasionally other races, too, some Aeva knew the names for and some she did not.

Which of these, she wondered, were assassins, or thieves, or spies? Possibly even pirates! Which, perhaps, were dragons or gods in disguise? Maybe there were even people here who were secretly from far-off and mysterious places like the Roving Isles. The potential for adventure was endless.

Aeva was just beginning to get lost in a daydream when she noticed a pair of human sailors taking shelter from the wind behind a stack of crates nearby. The pair were hunched together, discussing something over a map spread between them. Even from this distance, Aeva could tell that the map was ornate, maybe even gilded in places.

"I think we should take the Uminel River from Fortis," said the man to the left, sweeping his finger up the map from south to north. "If we can get past Fortis, most of the land along the river is in Erberos and Xidresrir territory."

The speaker had a chiseled appearance, as though carved from stone, and with a head just as bare.

His companion was older, with short-cropped, salt-and-pepper hair coupled with a beard and distinct mustache. He shook his head at the suggestion.

"You're assuming we won't be stopped in Fortis," the older man replied. "Currently the Zinberos and Damarian Alliances share control there, and you've got a good 200 miles of disputed territory between Zinberos and Xidrestrir here."

Again there were motions between south and north.

"It'll be a bit of a risk regardless, but I'd rather pass through Zinberos and Damarian waters and try not to make contact with any of the other factions until we get to Mephel in Herzumin territory."

The older man motioned east to west.

Aeva didn't understand much of what was being discussed. The twelve alliances of Parras were always at each other's throats, though she could never see why, and she cared even less. What she actually cared about was the beautiful map the two human men now bickered over. She tiptoed, waiting for a break in the conversation in which she could speak.

The opportunity came quickly enough as the two men paused to puzzle over their options.

"Excuse me," Aeva said, putting her hands behind her back and leaning over slightly to get the sailors' attention, "what kind of map is that? I've never seen one so pretty before!"

The men glanced up sharply at the girl's voice, regarding her with as much curiosity as she was now regarding the map.

"Just a map o' Parras," replied the one on the left.

The speaker—the man with the chiseled face—eyed the girl warily. He wore a basic set of leather armor, and there was a shortsword strapped at his hip. His eyes were sharp as a hawk's and stormy gray. Aeva wondered if this was the sort of person she ought to be afraid of.

It was only a passing thought.

The older man—clad in studded leather armor, with a heavy, two-handed sword strapped to his back by a thick leather baldric—leaned back on the crate where he sat and gave the small elf girl a hard stare.

"What's a kid like you doing in this part of town?"

"Just exploring," Aeva shrugged nonchalantly. "Mind if I ask where you got that map?"

The two sailors exchanged wondering glances, then the older of the two pointed down a nearby road.

"Just head down that direction and take the first right you come to. It's called Milo's Maps. Careful, though, kid. Place attracts all sorts."

"Thanks!" Aeva smiled, giving the pair a friendly wave as she set off in the direction she had been pointed. "I'll be careful."

The elf girl hummed and skipped as she set out on her quest to find this place called Milo's Maps. What kind of store was it, she wondered. She had been in bookstores before, but never to a place dedicated specifically to maps. She wondered if this Milo person would have a map of the ancient world, too, one that might show her where an ocean kingdom could have vanished into the sea. She loved those stories the best, and she couldn't help but think they might be true.

It was a bit harder to find the cartography shop than Aeva thought it would be, but after a bit of searching up and down the mostly desolate side street, the girl at last happened upon a small, rundown building with a faded, hand-painted sign hanging out front. Milo's Maps. This was it. The place looked more like a home than a shop, and so cautiously, Aeva knocked before pushing the door open.

The inside was just about as dingy as the outside, with maps of all ages and sizes rolled up and stacked in cracked clay pots or on awkwardly balanced shelves around a suffocatingly small room. Even from the doorway, Aeva could see the odd cobweb hung on display, and a fine layer of dust glowed in the dim lamp light that illuminated the shop's interior.

On the far side of the room, in front of a door that led further into the building, sat a roughly hewn desk and, behind it, an old human man. He looked up from the map he was currently drawing when he heard Aeva enter.

The man possessed a worn and haggard face that was riddled with faint scars. His hands were equally as blemished, and it looked like he might be missing a finger, too. For all the unkemptness of his estate, however, the man's snow-white hair was swept back neatly, his full beard nicely trimmed. A ragged piece of cloth had been tied around his head, serving as an eyepatch. The other eye, a sharp, icy blue filled with nothing but emptiness, stared at Aeva from across the room.

"This ain't the toy shop," the man huffed through a graveled voice. "Go play somewhere else, kid."

He then turned his attention back to the map he was working on.

Quietly, Aeva closed the door behind her, moving with reverence through the narrow, cluttered space.

"I've never seen so many maps before," the girl said in awe. "You don't have any of the ocean, do you?"

The old man paused to look up at her, eyebrow cocked.

"The ocean?" he questioned dubiously.

"Mm." Aeva nodded, turning her attention back to the dusty collection. "I've read stories of civilizations that disappeared into the ocean hundreds of years ago because they angered the gods. I've always wanted to find them."

"Those're just stories, kid," the old man grumbled. "And I ain't no bard. Now go home."

Aeva let out a dramatic sigh.

"Home is boring. There's nothing to do there. I've already read all my books at least ten times, and Mother and Father say they can't afford to buy me any more right now."

"Tough luck," came the cartographer's curt reply.

Aeva pursed her lips as she observed the old man in front of her. He seemed to be doing his absolute best to ignore her at this point, but despite his gruff exterior, his aged, wiry hands moved with a deftness the girl had never seen before as he scrawled line after line of ink across the parchment, creating a map with such detail Aeva thought for sure she could see every tree and gully in the landscape.

Aeva's father, Arun, was an artist by trade, so she was no stranger to the craft. Still, this was nothing like the art that her father created. It was mesmerizing.

"You're so good at that," Aeva said in awe, leaning over the table slightly to get a better look while trying not to interfere with the old man's work.

The cartographer let out a frustrated sigh before setting his tools down and turning to the girl with a stern stare.

"What can I do to make you go away?" he asked gruffly.

Aeva cocked her head, thinking for a moment. She didn't mean to be a bother, though it was true she wasn't a paying customer. It wasn't as though she had any money. No, it was mere curiosity that had originally brought her here. Still, though. It would be such a shame to leave now. She had already fallen in love with the dusty old shop full of beautiful maps. It was like a dragon's hoard, and the old man was like a dangerous and majestic dragon. Who knew what sorts of stories could be told here?

That thought wavered in the girl's mind for a moment before her eyes lit up.

"I know!" she exclaimed suddenly. "Can you teach *me* how to draw maps?!"

The cartographer looked taken aback.

"Can I what now?"

"Can you teach me how to draw maps?" Aeva repeated.

The old man frowned.

"Kid, I got no interest in babysittin' you."

"You wouldn't be babysitting me!" the girl replied eagerly. "I could be your apprentice! Maybe someday soon I could even earn the money to buy my own books. And then, when I join the Emerald Tower and become an archaeologist, I can make maps of everywhere I go!"

The cartographer looked appalled for a moment, then shook his head in disbelief.

"You're persistent *and* ambitious," he said. "What makes you think you'll ever become any of that?"

Aeva paused only briefly.

"Mother says I have to wait until I'm at least eighteen before I try for the Emerald Tower Academy, but I've already compiled a list of what it takes to get in. I think that I should be ready in the next six years."

The man frowned.

"You're not a member of one of the houses are you?"

The elf girl shook her head.

"No, my father and mother are both houseless. But that shouldn't matter. You don't have to be a member of a house to join the Emerald Tower."

"You look awfully young for an elf," the old man noted dubiously. "Six years to eighteen...you're not more than twelve then. Can you even use magic?"

"Oh, yes!"

Aeva beamed at the question, pleased to have an opportunity to show off her skills.

Quickly she skipped over to a nearby table covered in dust, making a sharp hand motion and uttering a short encantation. Instantly, a section of the table became clean and smooth, as though it had just been thoroughly scrubbed.

"This is the first spell I learned," the elf girl grinned, motioning to the spot with a showman's flare. "I've been practicing with moving loose soil, too, but there's no use for that in here." She paused, then hurriedly added, "There will be when I become an archaeologist, though!"

The little elf girl trotted proudly back to stand in front of the old man who was, at this point, simply looking bemused.

"Tell me, you said you had run out of books. How many have you read in your life? Do you know?"

Aeva frowned at this, then shrugged.

"I lost count after 300," she sighed, bracing an elbow in one hand and rubbing her chin. "Especially when I started reading them over again."

The cartographer shook his head in disbelief.

"I'm not sure if you're a genius or a lunatic," he said, slowly pushing himself to his feet.

He reached out for a cane that had been leaning against the desk and slowly made his way over to a cabinet in the far corner. He rummaged around in it for a moment before pulling out a small box and a scrap of parchment.

"Here," he said, setting the box and parchment on the edge of his desk and motioning for Aeva to take it, "let's see what kind of student you are."

It had been two weeks since Aeva had first set foot in the cartography shop known as Milo's Maps down in the Broad Docks District of Calaghorm. The old man who owned the place was named Milo Aldrin, though most of the regulars simply called him "Old Milo."

Old Milo was an oddity of a man, skilled in his art but curt with his customers. He had no interest in pleasantries or idle chat, but Aeva was grateful that he did, at the very least, tolerate her presence. The old cartographer wasn't much of a teacher. That didn't bother Aeva overmuch, though. Most of what she had learned in her life was self-taught anyhow.

Whenever she did get frustrated with her own work, and Old Milo was too absorbed in his to give her any pointers, the young elf practiced her magic on the dirty old shop. Her magic had yet to really become strong or reliable, but it was enough to clear up the dust and debris and old cobwebs that had gathered about the room for what had to have been at least a few decades.

The cartography shop was a wealth of information for Aeva. Travelers of every shape and size imaginable came into Old Milo's establishment, a level of variety she rarely saw beyond the Broad Docks. These weren't your ordinary sailors or merchants, either. Nearly all of them appeared to be adventurers looking for unique maps that only Old Milo seemed to have.

Some of the adventurers were put off by the presence of an overly curious young girl, but most seemed to be more than happy to regale Aeva with their tales of far-off places—and even not-so-far-off places, as Aeva herself had never left the protective walls of Calaghorm.

It was a bright, balmy morning as Aeva stepped through the door of Milo's Maps. There across the way sat Old Milo, sketching diligently over an expansive sheet of parchment stretched across the length and breadth of his worktable. He glanced up as she entered, his one pale blue eye regarding her with indifference only a moment before he continued with his work.

"Faithful as ever, I see," he muttered.

"Yes, sir," Aeva replied, bowing slightly before taking a seat at a small desk set off in the corner.

The old cartography tools and a stack of discarded paper shards sat there waiting for her, while a lamp with a half-melted candle rested off to the side, ready to receive the flame that would allow it to brighten the otherwise dreary space.

Aeva traced a small sigil in the air above the misshapen wax stick. Concentric geometric shapes locked into place mid-air, melting into arcane dust that engulfed the blackened wick. In a moment, the candle in the lamp spontaneously flickered to life, dancing with a tiny flame. With that, the elf girl sat down and began to studiously practice the various designs and strokes that Old Milo had taught her.

For several moments, the human man and the elf girl sat in silence, the scratch of their pens serving as the only sound to break the stillness. Then Old Milo's pen quieted, and Aeva glanced up at the sound of the cartographer's cane thumping against the wooden floor. She blinked twice when he set a small pouch down on the desk before her. The contents of the pouch clinked as it landed.

"What is this for?" Aeva inquired, glancing up at the old man with the bright blue eye and the eye patch.

"Thanks. For cleaning the shop," Old Milo responded gruffly, turning to hobble back toward his desk. "Should be enough to get yourself another book."

The elf girl's expression brightened at the thought, and she glanced into the pouch, eyes wide in awe. Inside she could see a handful of gold coins, more money than Aeva had ever personally seen in her life. Before Old Milo could return to his seat, Aeva dashed in front of him, holding the pouch of gold coins tightly to her chest.

"Master Aldrin! Thank you so much! I promise I will use this wisely and buy a really good book!"

"First," the old man said, gently shaking a bent, wrinkled finger in the girl's face, "none of this 'Master Aldrin' business! I ain't no master. Just an old coot. 'Old Milo' is fine just like the rest of 'em call me. Second, it's none of my business what you do with it. Buy the dumbest book for all I care. It'd be better than you spending all your time here. Little girls shouldn't be spending all day with old men."

Aeva felt her heart sink a bit at the cartographer's words, and she clutched the pouch of coins tighter to her chest. She looked up at the old man with pleading eyes.

"Is it because I am annoying?" she questioned. "Or because I am not very good at cartography?"

Old Milo looked taken aback at the girl's questions. Then, for the first time in two weeks, Aeva saw his expression soften ever so slightly.

"Ain't got nothin' to do with you, kid. I'm just a crotchety old man who don't have any business doin' anything but workin'. You don't really wanna spend the rest of your life in this dirty old shop, do you?"

Aeva glanced around at the small room filled to the brim with maps of all shapes, sizes, and ages. To her, the place wasn't a "dirty old shop." It was a treasure trove. She glanced back up at the old human man who was watching her curiously.

"Master...um...Old Milo...I like your shop. And your maps are beautiful. And...I think you're a nice person who doesn't want anyone to think you're nice. I don't really know why, but that's what I think. I want to learn how to draw beautiful maps the way you do. Even though I don't plan to be a cartographer as a profession and I do plan to join the Emerald Tower someday, I want to learn how to do this. I want to become an archaeologist who brings the past to life on my maps the way you bring the present world to life with yours."

Old Milo let out a heavy sigh at this.

"You're nothin' if not stubborn," he grumbled under his breath. "Fine. I guess there's no gettin' rid of you, so I'm gonna put you to work. Got it?"

Aeva's eyes brightened at this.

"Yes, sir! What do you want me to do?"

"First," he motioned to the shop, "your job is to keep this place nice and tidy."

"Okay..."

"When you finish that, you're gonna do small commissions for me. I won't accept anything less than perfect, so you'll practice 'til you get it."

"Understood!"

"Last..." The old man seemed to be thinking for a moment. "Last, whatever new books you get, I expect you to read me a few pages every day."

Aeva cocked her head at this.

"But Old Milo, wouldn't it be easier for you to read the books after me?"

The cartographer waved his free hand slightly in a dismissive gesture as he hobbled back to his seat.

"This one good eye gets tired working on maps all day. Would be much easier just to hear someone else read."

"Oh..." Aeva then smiled brightly and turned to rush toward the front door. "In that case, I'll go buy a book right now so I can read it to you! I'll be right back."

The elf girl hardly noticed the bemused look on the old man's face as she all but flew out the door and back into the alleyway that led to the shop. She wove her way through the spiderweb of roads that led back to the docks. Now, where to look for a good book...

The elf girl retraced her steps, back in the direction of the Garden Market District, before coming to a store with piles of used and battered tomes scattered about, both inside and outside the shop. That ought to do. After spending a good half-hour rummaging through the haphazard piles, the girl came out clutching an aged tome with faded pages but a surprisingly well-kept cover of blue-dyed leather. A gold dragon was emblazoned on the front. From a quick glance over the material, it seemed, unsurprisingly, to be a book on dragons.

"Find something interesting?" the shopkeeper, and older male elf, questioned as Aeva approached the counter.

"Yes, sir," the girl replied, setting the book in front of him.

The shopkeeper flipped the book open curiously, as though he had long forgotten that such a tome existed in his collection, then cast a dubious glance in the girl's direction.

"This is some pretty academic writing. Sure you want this instead of a book for younger readers?"

"It's fine," Aeva smiled, unfazed. "I have already read books that were way harder to understand. Plus, I promised to read this to a friend who is an adult."

The older elf raised an eyebrow at this but inclined his head in acknowledgment.

"Alright then."

The shopkeeper named the price, and Aeva emptied the pouch Old Milo had given her onto the counter. There was just enough in the pouch for the book she had selected.

"All yours," the shopkeeper said, gathering up the coins and waving.

"Thank you!"

Aeva waved back as she hurried out of the store, clutching her new book as close to her chest as she previously had held the coin pouch. Back through the winding streets she went, dodging travelers, carts, animals, crates, barrels, and whatever else happened to be in her way. She was excited and out of breath by the time she at last arrived back at Old Milo's shop.

The cartographer glanced up from his work as the elf girl barrelled through the door.

"Done with your shoppin' already?"

"Isn't this one neat?" Aeva replied, trotting up to the old man and showing him the tome with the blue leather cover and gold dragon imprint. "It's a book on dragons!"

"Uh-huh..." The man looked dubious. "Alright. Pull up a chair. Let's see what you've got there."

Aeva grabbed the chair from the desk she had been working at and dragged it over to sit across from Old Milo. She hadn't even managed to settle in her seat, however, before the door to the shop burst open again. This time, a trio of sailors—a couple of scruffy half-elves and an unkempt full elf—came marching into the shop. Immediately they began rummaging through the maps. Aeva stood watching in horrified silence. At the rate they were going, they were going to damage everything! The full elf regarded the shop with an arrogant indifference before turning his gaze first to Old Milo, then to Aeva.

"You adopting strays now, Old Milo?" the sailor questioned, approaching the desk at the back of the shop with a swagger.

The old human man pushed himself to his feet as the stranger approached.

"It's none of your business who does and doesn't enter my shop, Lortar," the cartographer replied.

Before Aeva knew what was happening, the male elf had taken her by the chin, dragging her forward slightly. He smelled of sweat, and brine, and old booze, and there was something dangerous in his lackluster golden eyes. Aeva visibly stiffened at the look, a reaction that brought a twisted smile to the sailor's lips.

"She's cute, for a kid. How much you want for her?"

Horror had turned to terror by this point, yet for some reason, Aeva couldn't seem to force herself to move out of the man's grasp. Instead, she stared back at him, wild-eyed. The sailor's twisted smile swept into a dark grin, baring sharp white teeth. He was enjoying her terror immensely, of that Aeva was certain.

"Hands off the kid."

Aeva couldn't see Old Milo, but his voice echoed above her like the growl of an angry dog.

"Or what?" the male elf mocked back.

Crack!

Aeva managed to find the strength to wrench herself from her assailant's grasp as Old Milo brought the end of his cane down hard, splintering the wooden floor beneath.

"I may have lost some control of my arm," Old Milo growled, uncowed, as he stared across at the sailor who loomed in front of him. "But I haven't lost my strength. Which means no punches pulled. Don't make me kill you in front of my apprentice."

By this point, the other two sailors had stopped what they were doing to look at their superior. He, too, looked moderately taken aback, though the expression was fleeting. He crossed his arms over his chest, the smug look from before returning to his face.

"Find what we were looking for?" Lortar called back to his companions.

"Got it, boss!" one of the half-elves called back, holding up a worn map he had pulled from one of the piles.

"Good."

The male elf tossed a small coin pouch at Old Milo's face. The human caught the bag mid-air, glaring fiercely at the trio of sailors as they headed back the way they had come.

"Next time, old man," Lortar called mockingly.

"Don't bother," Old Milo growled back.

The sailors shut the door with a laugh and the shop fell back into silence. For a moment, neither Aeva nor Old Milo moved or spoke. Then, at last, the cartographer's voice broke through the gloom.

"You apprentice with me, you gotta learn how to fight back, kid," he said. "The docks ain't some magical land of happy, fun adventures, and that goes double for my shop."

"I'm sorry," Aeva apologized. "I just...got so scared, I didn't know what to do."

Slowly, Old Milo turned and shuffled back to his seat.

"Well, don't make it a habit."

"Yes, sir..."

For a moment, Aeva stood motionless, waiting to see if the old human man would tell her to leave, that she didn't belong there. Instead, however, she heard the creak of his chair as he settled back into it, the light thump of his cane coming into contact with the desk, and then the scratch of cartography tools as he set back to work.

"So," he grunted as he sketched, "what can we learn about dragons?"

IN THE WORKS...

TWILIGHT RAIN - PROLOGUE - THE URCHIN GIRL

There comes a time when pain transcends all feeling or thought, when the body falls into a cold stupor in one last desperate attempt at surviving the feeling of being torn asunder. Aeva had never felt so cold...so tired...so...torn...

Her breath came in shallow, wheezing puffs, her world spinning as she coughed up the metallic taste of blood. She wanted to cry. Or...was she already doing so? It was hard to know what was sweat, what was blood, or what were tears that flowed along with muted sobs muffled only by her ragged breathing and terror of being caught.

Run! a voice screamed inside her head.

I'm trying!

Her mind and body felt detached, untethered, and her legs gave way beneath her. Another muted sob escaped her lips as she curled into a quickly growing pool of her own blood, her last desperate attempt at protecting herself from the agony of the injury tracing its way through her side and from the monsters that were sure to find her soon. And in her mind, one thought raced over and over again.

I don't want to die...I don't want to die...I don't want to die...

How...how had she come to this point?

It had all started...with a ship.

The Arborath was an ancient vessel, a battered old merchant ship with rows of weathered sails and a barnacled hull. Nestled among the newer, more polished carracks, the Arborath appeared downright venerable, and those who made a habit of watching the ships come and go from the Broad Docks of Calaghorm were always quick to recognize its arrival. It was a vessel that made its name through trade with the wider world of Olandris, sailing from the elvin continent of Parras to the elemental Sundering Isles, then on to the rainforests of Tallan and all about the deadly and enchanted Clouded Sea. Rumor had it that the crew of the Arborath had even mapped the coastline of the mysterious island in the center of that foggy expanse: Aurora, Isle of the Gods.

The rumors alone were enough to attract the attention of any curious passers-by. Even more so a curious mind that had spent more than one decade peering across the harbor and the ships that came and went there.

The sky was a baleful shade of gray, roiling clouds threatening an impending storm, as Aeva paused at the edge of the retaining wall overlooking the harbor with its wide, open piers lined with large merchant carracks and sleek-hulled adventuring clippers. The place was called the Broad Docks for a reason.

A stiff breeze kicked across the briny ocean beyond, stirring the waves into a frothing dance and sending ship sails snapping in protest. The wind caught strands of the elf woman's raven-black hair and the corners of the books she was carrying, and she scrambled frantically to keep all in check.

Aeva shifted the stack of books to her other arm before picking a careful path down toward the docks and the crowds of people who came and went there. She had heard that the Arborath was set to drop anchor soon and, at best, the ship would only be in port for a few days. It was for this reason that she had come to Calaghorm today. She couldn't miss any opportunities.

"Farric!"

Her voice only barely cut through the sound of crashing waves and snapping sails as she hurried toward one of the sailors, a particularly tall male elf with pale blond hair who was in the process of rearranging some nearby crates. The man glanced up at Aeva's call, and as he straightened up to his full height, the young woman reminded herself that she was thankful Farric was a gentle and patient fellow. He stood almost a foot taller than her, and his years spent at sea were evidenced by the bare, sinewy arms that now leaned back lazily against the stacks behind him as he watched the girl approach.

Once within proper earshot, Farric quirked a bemused smile at her.

"Aeva," he greeted, gaze flicking briefly at the awkward stack of books in the young woman's arms before shifting back to her face. "Should have known you'd show up."

Aeva shrugged innocently.

"Can you blame me?"

"What about your studies at the Emerald Tower? Or do you always take leave when we're in town?"

"It's fine. I'm ahead of the current curriculum and you know, of course, that we're allowed leaves of absence to visit home."

Farric laughed lightly at the statement.

"And how much have you actually been home, exactly?"

Aeva paused, blinking, then let out a huff.

"Nevermind that. I wanted to ask you about your recent trip."

Farric inclined his head, his two-toned eyes—one a soft hazel, the other a bright jade green—glimmering with amusement. This was not the first year, or even the first decade, that Aeva had cornered him at the docks. And so, turning back to his work, the man began to regale his younger companion with the more interesting tales of his travels: elemental storms around the Sundering Isles, pirates off the dwarven shores of Falgaz, a near-miss with the warring states of Xanaris, even a brush with one of the Roving Isles—an island of giants, no less—on the way back to Parras. All the while, Aeva listened with rapt attention, her keen mind compiling the information gathered and filing it away for later use.

Farric had paused for a breath, stacking another crate into a nearby cart, when a thoughtful expression crossed his face.

"The sea does seem unusually agitated today, though. We encountered some monsters just a few miles out, too." He motioned toward the crashing waves along the horizon, paused, then glanced over at Aeva. "What's the state of the alliances right now?"

Aeva cocked her head, absently glancing back up the hill toward the city center and the glittering silver spire from which a largely invisible dome arched. An anti-magic shield. She wouldn't have known it was there if she hadn't been looking for it, but there it was, faintly glimmering against the stormy sky, promising protection from whatever sort of enemy magic might target the thriving port.

"Well, the Zindark and Espeirian Alliances are pulling their usual stunts," she mused at length. "I don't remember what set them off this time, but it sounds like Paxalim and Erberos have joined them as well. I hear the northern border is pretty badly contested at the moment, though the fighting hasn't made it as far as Glasgalan yet." She turned back to Farric, nodding her head northward. "Thankfully, Xidrestrir is still on our side for now, and Zinberos is remaining neutral for the time being. And since Erberos specializes in defensive magic and Paxalim relies heavily on illusions which can be easily countered by our mages from the Emerald Tower, the conflict with those two alliances seems to be mostly under control. That's all I know of it, though. It's difficult to keep up with who is fighting whom, and I don't have much patience for it anyway. Why do you ask?"

For a time, Farric leaned back against the nearby crates, arms crossed over his chest as he stared out toward the sea again. Then, as though giving up a thought, he shrugged and turned back to his work.

"Not sure. Something just doesn't feel...right."

"How so?"

"Call it a sailor's intuition, I suppose."

Aeva narrowed her eyebrows as she glanced back across the harbor and into the buffetting wind. It was true that the weather seemed especially dreary today, though storms along the coast were no rare occurrence. As far as she was concerned, this was just another stormy day.

The girl shrugged. It was probably fine, and her interests were elsewhere.

"Well, anyway, about that Roving Isle you mentioned..."

Giving no further thought to the gathering storm, Aeva continued to question Farric about his travels, shuffling books about in her arms and awkwardly writing notes in a journal as she followed him back and forth between the ship and the waiting carts. More than one sailor shot the young elf woman a look of annoyance as she darted around and between them to keep up with her long-legged companion, but if Aeva noticed the glances at all, she made no note of it.

She and Farric were just coming to a stop next to one of the carts for probably the tenth time when a shout of alarm rang up from the deck of the Arborath above them.

"What the blazes *is* that?!"

The pair paused and glanced up at the cry, following the direction of the other sailor's outstretched arm. A crowd began to gather along the docks and the railing of the moored ships nearby as others scrambled to see what the fuss was about.

"I don't see anything," another of the sailors called out. "What're you playing at?"

A grumble of disappointment echoed out through the gathered crowd. No one else seemed to see anything alarming, and a good half began to disburse as they made their way back to discarded sacks and crates. Still, the first to make the cry of alarm remained where he stood, eyes fixed on the horizon.

"There *was* something there. I swear it!" he protested.

A few of the number, most likely his friends, patted him on the back and moved to return to their work. Perhaps they thought he had been at sea too long.

Aeva and Farric exchanged wary glances.

"Didn't you say...your ship had run into some sea monsters not far out from port?" Aeva questioned.

Farric nodded solemnly, his gaze cast out toward the ocean.

"There were," he answered.

Aeva glanced about. Well, surely the shield above the city would keep the monsters out, but it could also mean trouble for the ships coming and going from port.

The thought was just crossing her mind when the vaguest hint of a flash flickered across the sky. Had the barrier just...surely not. Aeva shook her head. It had to have been her imagination, or a shimmer of lightning, that for a moment had made it seem as though the protective barrier over the city had flickered out. Still, something in the back of her mind nagged at her. The magic in the air suddenly felt...different. It was only a brief shift, like the passing of a gust of wind, but in all her many decades of life, Aeva had never felt anything quite like it.

Her eyes shifted from the faintly glimmering dome above to the surging waves battering the piers.

"Well," Farric sighed, shrugging, "in any case—"

Aeva's gasp cut him short. Now that she was paying closer attention to the ebb and flow of the angry waves, she could see something there, too. The waves weren't just rocking. They were subtly bubbling, as though the whole harbor had been set to boil. And the water, though naturally dark, was darker than it should have been.

The elf woman could feel her legs begin to tremble, her heart beating a wild rhythm in her chest. She took a couple steps back, hardly even registering a questioning, "Aeva?" from Farric nearby before wheeling around wide-eyed to face her companion. She opened her mouth to shout a word of warning, but the breath left her lungs as something struck her from behind.

It was a strange sensation, Aeva thought. At first, she only registered that it had become much more difficult to breathe. The world spun. Somewhere in the distance, Farric yelled, and chaos erupted on the docks. It wasn't until the object that struck her was yanked back out that the pain registered...and the terror.

Aeva stumbled to the side, turning to see an elongated, piscine face and rows of needle-like teeth. A fishlike humanoid. She wasn't sure what it was exactly, but the sight was horrifying. And it was made all the worse when the elf woman realized it was wielding a jagged, bone-tipped spear covered in blood.

Her...blood...

Her vision spun, and she tottered, tempted to collapse in a heap where she stood. A pained whimper echoed in her ears. It had to have been hers, but it all felt as though she were looking at herself from the outside in, as though her mind and body had been severed with the impact of her attacker's spear. The world, too, seemed disjointed, and for a moment it felt like time was folding in on itself.

Old Milo...her old friend and mentor from her time before the Emerald Tower...he would be livid, Aeva thought, if he could see her standing there staring blankly at her attacker, bleeding from a wound that had pierced her all the way through.

Run or fight, but don't bloody stand there! she could hear him say.

She staggered, attempting to flee, but her legs defied her command. She watched her assailant lift its spear, ready to finish her off, its eyes glowing an unnatural reddish-purple.

Run!

She could hear Old Milo in her mind, screaming at her. She tried again to move. Still her legs refused.

"RUN!"

A scimitar flashed in to intercept the bloodied spear, and suddenly time began to move again. Farric kicked out at Aeva's attacker, knocking it back into the frothing surf, but already there were more of its kind crawling out of the water and up onto the pier.

"Run, damn it!" the sailor was shouting.

He was pushing at her now, trying to move her back toward the retaining wall, and somehow Aeva found her feet again.

Crippled with pain, the girl half dashed, half crawled up the steps toward the warehouses that made up the bulk of the Broad Docks District. The screams of terrified townsfolk mingled with the piercing screeches of the monsters crawling out from the sea. Several times, Aeva felt someone collide with her. A couple times, she fell.

Somehow, between bouts of nausea and dizziness, the girl found her way behind one of the warehouses that bordered the street looking out over the harbor. She coughed, gasping for breath, and the warm, metallic taste of blood hit her tongue. One toe caught against an uneven cobblestone. Her feet might as well have been lead, and the elf collapsed to the grimy street below. Just around the corner, she could hear the screeching of the invading monsters and the discordant patter of their webbed feet.

A muted sob escaped Aeva's lips, and she curled in on herself, fighting the tendrils of cold, aching darkness that threatened to consume her.

I don't want to die...

The scrape of metal echoed in her ears nearby and the girl flinched, tucking into herself just a bit tighter, bracing for whatever was coming at her next.

Please...someone...anyone...help...

For a moment, Aeva heard nothing. Perhaps it was only her imagination that had conjured the sound, the last survival impulse her mind could muster before she bled to death. But then suddenly there were small hands holding her face, the cold bite of a glass vial being pressed to her lips, and the bitter taste of an alchemical healing potion rolling across her tongue.

Again Aeva coughed, gasped, but then sighed in relief as some of the worst of the pain ebbed away. Her eyes blinked open, pausing on the dirt-smudged face of a young human girl. By physical appearance, she could not have seen more than a decade of life, but there was a look in those sharp brown eyes that told Aeva the young girl had already experienced far more life than she herself had ever dreamed of.

The girl looked pleased to see that Aeva was no longer on death's doorstep, but her head snapped up at the sound of a screech just around the corner. There was no time to celebrate. The monsters were advancing, and rapidly. It wouldn't be long before the pair were caught up in the melee again.

The little human girl tugged at Aeva's sleeve, frantically motioning back toward a sewer grate. Despite the wonders of the healing potion, it was still a chore to move, and Aeva clawed at the rough cobblestone beneath her as she pulled herself toward the promise of safety. Once or twice, her hands slipped on the blood-soaked mud and she collapsed, scuffing her elbows. The elf girl whimpered but bit back a full-on cry as the sounds of her pursuers grew ever louder. Perhaps only the dock guards were keeping the monsters at bay now, and she had no way of knowing how much time she had left.

The human girl grabbed one of Aeva's elbows, small hands making a concerted effort to lift and drag the elf toward the sewer grate. She opened the heavy metallic contraption deftly, this time managing to make almost no noise, and a moment later Aeva tumbled shoulder-first into a shallow, narrow tunnel running the length of the alleyway above. Now she did begin to openly cry as pain shot through her injured body. Meanwhile, the child at her side carefully lowered the grate back into place.

It could not have happened sooner. A moment later, a pack of the piscine invaders clattered around the corner of the warehouse, hissing and chirping and snuffling about at the blood trail that ended abruptly a short distance from the sewer grate. This must have been the first time the little human girl had seen the monsters, because she let out a sharp, startled gasp before clasping her hand over her mouth.

The creatures barked, alerted that there was someone nearby. There was no time to lose. The little girl pushed at Aeva, attempting to move further down the tunnel. Up ahead, the elf could see gray daylight streaming through another grate before the tunnel made a sharp turn north. Gasping between quiet sobs, the salty mud beneath her stinging the open wounds on her elbows, Aeva pushed herself forward.

It didn't matter if the whole ordeal seemed hopeless. The little human girl didn't give her a choice. She wasn't exactly strong, and there was no bulk to her, but the child pushed at Aeva with a force that compelled the elf to move.

The fishlike creatures above the grate howled and tore at the metal bars. They had noticed the clamor. Over her shoulder, Aeva could see a narrow piscine snout poke down through the gaps in the grate. She couldn't help it anymore. With a yelp, the elf frantically threw her hands up, almost instinctually casting a spell to move the loose debris that had gathered in the tunnel. Mud and fist-sized stones arched up from the tunnel floor, forming a small barrier between the two girls and their pursuers. It wouldn't be enough to stop them for long, but it might at least slow them down.

On the pair sped.

The fishlike monsters seemed to be tracking them, because they grabbed at the second grate as Aeva and the little human girl passed below it. One jammed its spear through the slats and, had it not been for the metal deflecting the blow and the interference of the creature's companion attempting to lift the grate itself, the spear likely would have impaled Aeva a second time. As it was, she could feel the air rush only a hair's width away from her shoulder as she scrambled stiffly toward the bend in the tunnel, and she and the child at her heels both screamed as they rolled sideways and clamored onward.

Behind her, Aeva could hear the creatures squabbling, no doubt angered by ally interference in the hunt. This was followed by shouts in elvish. The soldiers had found the invaders and intercepted their pursuit.

It was a welcome relief, but still the elf and the little human girl scrambled on ahead until at last the tunnel opened up into a wider hall. It was dark as a tomb here. If not for her sharp elvish eyes, Aeva knew she would never have been able to make out any features of the space at all. The pair tumbled out onto the slime-soaked stone below, for a moment lying limply on the floor as they struggled to catch their breath.

It was several minutes before the human girl slowly and shakily stood to her feet, and a moment later the light of a torch flickered out around them, cutting into the oppressive gloom. The place smelled atrocious, and the air was heavy, but still Aeva lay panting on the floor. She had never appreciated the sewers so much.

A rumbling in her stomach reminded her of the knots that had been there since she had first been impaled, and of the injury that only magic had been able to stave off, and her insides lurched. She rolled to the side and vomited over the edge of the walkway into the opaque water in the channel just beyond.

"You alright?"

The human girl's voice broke the silence and, after a fair amount of coughing and panting, Aeva glanced up to look at her.

"About as well as one can be for having been impaled, I suppose," the elf replied, attempting to sit up as she wiped at her mouth with a torn and grimy sleeve.

She coughed again, again tasting blood on her tongue. Breathing was still a struggle, too. The healing potion could only do so much, and she still felt dizzy.

The child seemed to sense the tenor of the situation, because she nodded solemnly.

"There's a healer in the Garden Market," she said. "This path will take us right there, if you think you can make it. I don't have any other healing potions."

The girl's words sounded more like an apology than an explanation, and Aeva shook her head.

"You saved me back there, you know. Thank you."

The child's smudged face brightened at the elf's words and she nodded.

"You're welcome. It's lucky I had the potion, then." She held out a small hand in Aeva's direction. "We shouldn't stay here too long, though."

Aeva sighed, wishing she could just sit there and rest, but as reason began to return to her, the voice of Old Milo echoed in the back of her mind. The cartographer hadn't just been a cartographer, she realized then. Something in his words...the way he acted...the way he spoke...hinted at a life experience that defied the mundane setting in which Aeva had met him all those years ago. And somehow those words, spoken almost a century before, began to weave their way into the young elf's mind, driving her to stand, to put one trembling foot in front of the other, to keep going even though it hurt to move and breathe.

Thinking she needed something else to focus on, Aeva centered her attention on the little human girl clothed in rags and covered head-to-toe in grime, her tiny form boldly leading the way into the gloom of the deeper parts of the sewers of Calaghorm despite the scare she had experienced only moments before. Her brown hair was a ratty mess, her feet bare, and yet the child carried herself with a level of dignity that would make even a noble envious.

It was rare to find a human in Calaghorm, Aeva thought. Rarer still, a child.

"What's your name?" the elf asked at length.

The human girl smiled over her shoulder.

"Anna," she declared proudly. "You?"

"Aeva," the elf replied. She held one hand out toward the sewer wall, bracing herself against it and away from the channel of fetid water on the other side. She hardly trusted her own feet to carry her forward, and her world still pitched violently from time to time.

"Where are you from, Anna?"

The child considered the question for a moment, then shrugged.

"Here, I guess," she replied.

Aeva wasn't sure if the child meant "here" as in the port city or "here" as in the sewers. Either way, Anna acted right at home on the narrow path that traversed the city's underground.

"Where are *you* from?" the human girl questioned.

Aeva glanced up at the ceiling of arched stone blocks above her.

"Originally, here in Calaghorm." She had to pause to gather her breath before continuing. "I've been in Glasgalan at the Emerald Tower for about ninety years now, though."

Anna's eyes widened at that.

"You elves are so weird," the child giggled. "I would be an old lady by then, but you look like you could be my older sister!"

The comment elicited a slight chuckle from Aeva, despite the pain she currently felt.

"I suppose that's true. Though I have no siblings, so I can't imagine what it would be like to have a little sister."

Anna stuck her tongue out at that.

"Maybe *I'm* the big sister, though, since I saved *you*."

Again Aeva had to laugh, if only slightly.

"Too true."

The banter was refreshing, and before Aeva knew it, she found herself crawling out of a sewer grate into the rising streets of the Garden Market District. It didn't take her long to recognize the cobbled street lined with vibrant potted gardens and half-timbered buildings cloaked in climbing roses and ivy. Her eyes lit up when she spotted one building in particular.

"That's my parents' home!" she gasped, pointing toward a townhouse with a bay window displaying detailed paintings and colorfully woven tapestries. She smiled over at the child standing next to her. "I should be alright from here. Thank you."

Anna almost seemed disappointed, but she nodded with understanding.

"Oh, well, I'll leave you to it then. I'm just glad I could help."

"You did. Truly," Aeva replied. "I owe you."

The child hummed playfully.

"Yeah, I guess that's true."

She smiled impishly, and Aeva could only admire the contrast between that dirt-streaked face and the brilliant smile that defied it.

The elf woman took several steps forward toward the house she had spent her first two decades of life in, but she paused when she considered it might only be fair to invite Anna in. She turned back in the direction the child had been standing, only to find the space empty. There was no sign anyone had been there at all.

Come and gone. Almost like a ghost. Who *was* that child anyway?

The elf turned back toward her family home. Her mother usually kept at least a few healing potions on hand. It ought to be enough to mend what the previous potion hadn't.

But even as she walked through the quiet streets lined with flowers, a world away from the bloodshed she had only narrowly escaped a short time before, she couldn't help but wonder about the little human girl with the grime-streaked face, the one known as Anna. Would they ever meet again?

Well...that was a question for another day.

ALSO BY

Prism World

There are rumors spread across the country, whispers about a secret society of assassins known as the Phantom Legion. Moving only in the deepest shadows and under the darkest nights, the Phantoms are the people's living nightmare, the ghostly right hand of an oppressive government.

Lightning was born and raised a Phantom. Confined to a dark room and released only to do her masters' bidding, it wasn't until she saw daylight for the first time that her mind woke from its dark sleep and she began to realize that there was another world beyond concrete walls and moonless nights.

When a series of events leads the naive Lightning to join an underground rebel force, the young Phantom finds that she must face the demons of her past. With fear, doubt, and angry masters haunting her every step, Lightning sets out on a quest to discover the source behind a strange power dwelling within her, learning to believe in a greater cause as she searches for what it means to be human in a world with many points of view.

Reviews

"I enjoyed this book to the very end. There were very few slow moments. I'm not a huge fan of first person books but the author did this well. I felt that sometimes the emotions running through Lightning's head were a little too detailed and didn't let the read[er] read between the lines. This is just opinion though! I have a tendency to

get bored of books pretty easily, but this story kept me turning pages. For this being one of the first published books by the author, very well done!" – Devin G. (Dec. 2015)

"I heard about Prism World from a friend and just had to give it a read. The story follows the life of a young woman by the name of Lightning. Unlike most young women Lightning is what her society calls a Phantom, which are assassins bred and raised by the government. Her life is spent in complete darkness. She's never allowed any freedom except to kill her next target. However that all changes on one assignment. She meets a rebel named Leif. Her conversation with him sparks a roller coaster ride like you've never read before. Lightning proves to be a remarkable person that has to change her entire perspective on life and death, while at the same time learning to adjust in what is basically a whole new world once she leaves the darkness. I absolutely loved this novel. I found myself enjoying seeing the world thru Lightning's eyes. When she was happy so was I. When she felt sadness and despair I was right along with her. By the end of the book I found myself crying. Throughout all the pain at the loss of loved ones, the new friendships, finding family, and demolishing the hated government I was so sad to see the novel come to an end. I really hope Ms. Gilleland continues to expand upon the Prism World universe, because I would love to find out more about each of the Phantoms, and even hope to see Lightning return as a side character." – Rochelle White (Dec. 2014)

The Four Stars

For years the four friends—Razi, Rayne, Eryn, and Gavin—have lived in relative peace in the little valley they call home, only vaguely aware of the goings-on of the world beyond their sheltered haven. There are whispers, though...rumors that the young friends are more than just mere orphans.

When the Gauls, the age-old enemy of Livania, launch a surprise attack in the mountains, the four friends are unexpectedly called to warn their elvin allies, only to discover that nothing is as it appears to be.

In a matter of days, Razi, Rayne, Eryn, and Gavin find themselves swept up in a whirlwind of change, haunted by the mysteries and legends of the past and driven toward an ancient power that has already lured many to their doom.

Reviews

"This book...tells the story of true bonds of friendship. The types of bonds, that literally draw you into the story. Four very different people that must stop an invasion that threatens their home and work together with powers they didn't know they had. While the story may be aimed at a "younger audience" I think most people of any age can not only appreciate the story but fall in love with the characters and care about what happens to them. The author weaves together a great adventure story in a fantasy world that leaves you not only caught up in the story but laughing at the authors skill with humor." – Amazon Customer (Dec. 2015)

"Wonderful book of the close ties and loyalty of four friends in a fantasy world. They are called upon to help prevent an invasion and discover that they have special powers that allow them to work together to resist the invading army. In the middle of this is their search for what happened to their fathers, who disappeared years before. Great story with lots of humor and action. Probably directed at a younger audience." – Glen Robinson (Sep. 2015)

Made in the USA
Columbia, SC
30 November 2023

26932187R00115